THE SHADOW ON THE GRASSY KNOLL

THE SHADOW
ON THE GRASSY KNOLL

Al Stevens

Mockingbird
Songs & Stories

Mockingbird Songs & Stories, Cocoa, FL

Mockingbird
Songs & Stories

ISBN-13: 978-0-9886623-0-8

This book is dedicated to the 102 members, named and unnamed, who have, by making the supreme sacrifice in service to their country, earned a star on the Memorial Wall in the lobby of the Central Intelligence Agency Headquarters Building.

Acknowledgments

Many thanks to those who helped as I wrote this book: Mary Cain, Bill DeMar, Rosemary Fischer, Don Harach, Betsy Hardinger, Carol Jose, Abe March, Judy Stevens, and Julian Stevens. Others who helped shall remain nameless for various reasons.

Prologue

A breeze whispers through the trees and structures that surround the assassin's position in the plaza. The rain has stopped, and the temperature is unseasonably warm for late November, but the trees shade him from the sun, and his jacket lies folded beside him. He kneels and holds his weapon down and out of sight. He checks his watch. Twenty minutes past noon. People gather on both sides of the street waiting for the motorcade. Cameras appear everywhere. He stays in the shadows, blends in, and hopes no one notices him, takes his picture, or gets in his line of fire.

Minutes pass. His movements are programmed and proficient, his escape well-planned. It seems like forever, but soon the target will be within range. Then, the mission completed, he will exit and escape, while the world stands still, shocked into disbelief, wondering why this tragedy happened and what its consequences will be.

The crowd cheers as the motorcade draws close. The open limousine with its motorcycle escort turns right, then left, and moves toward him. Spectators strain to get a glimpse of their charismatic leader and his lady, who smile and wave at them.

The assassin raises his weapon and rests it in position to fire. With only seconds to go, the limousine passes into his sights, and he looks through the scope and aligns the target in his crosshairs. He releases the safety with his thumb. His forefinger curls gently around the trigger, and he begins to squeeze...

Chapter 1

Nothing in his background suggested he was spy material, that he was what they called a *natural*, someone with *potential*. His origins were without distinction, yet Harold Sands was destined to become the youngest spy ever recruited by the Central Intelligence Agency.

It was late spring in 1950 at an orphanage in central-eastern Virginia, the kids were at the playground for recess, and a fight had broken out on the baseball field.

The fight was one-sided. Nine-year-old Harold Sands was getting the crap beat out of him, and he was not defending himself. Billy, the boy delivering Harold's punishment, was bigger and stronger than most of the other boys. A circle of children surrounded them, shouting encouragement and cheering Billy on, not taking sides, but enjoying the fight and shielding it from the view of the staff.

Today, Billy had Harold on his back in the infield grass on the baseball diamond. Billy bent over him, pummeling him with both fists. Harold's nose was bleeding, and the pain of the beating on his chest and abdomen was worse than usual. He tried to shield himself with his arms, but whenever he did, Billy found another place to hit.

Before today, Harold would not fight back. To do so would have made it worse. This time, however, a kick to his side had produced excruciating pain, worse than before, and he had to stop the beating before Billy seriously hurt him. Through the blood and tears he found a fist-sized rock in the grass within reach. He swung the rock with all his strength toward Billy's chin. It connected like a lucky punch, and the bigger boy fell across him in a heap, blood pouring from his mouth. The circle of children became hushed, and they fell back in awe. Nobody had ever seen Harold do anything like that, and he was as surprised as they were.

He pushed his attacker off and stood, shaking with a rage he'd never felt before. A baseball bat lay nearby next to home plate. He picked it up, raised it over his head, and was about to brain his opponent when one of the teachers came up behind him, grabbed the bat as he began his downward swing, and jerked it out of his grasp.

Both boys went to the hospital. Two of Harold's ribs were cracked, and Billy had lost a tooth and had a broken jaw. Although they occupied adjacent beds, they didn't speak to one another that day or ever again.

An account of the fight went into Harold's file, and Miss Moore, the orphanage administrator, counseled him on how to avoid fights and control his temper.

"Do you know why the other boys pick on you, Harold?" she asked from across her huge oak desk.

"I think, so, ma'am. I'm smarter than them, and they don't like me."

Miss Moore softened at this young boy's insight. Of course he knew why he was unpopular. He was too smart not to know. "Harold, you are indeed brighter than the others. A lot. But that doesn't mean you have to flaunt it. That's what the others don't like."

"Yes, ma'am."

"What started it this time?"

"He was at bat. I struck him out."

"And he didn't like that?"

"No, ma'am."

"And he said something, and you said something, and one thing led to another…"

"Yes, ma'am."

The incident on the ball field was to be the last beating Harold would take at the hands of his schoolmates. He was a loner, usually distant but cheerful and friendly around his young colleagues, but when threatened with bodily harm, he'd remember the beatings and how he'd prevailed over a bigger boy, the rage would ignite, and a serious fight would break out, a fight he usually won.

The rage troubled him, and he pledged to himself every time that it wouldn't happen again. But when it did, he couldn't control it, and he wouldn't stop fighting until his opponent was down and defeated or until someone broke it up. He worked hard to hold his darker side in check, and most of the time he did, usually by retreating into his books and avoiding social contacts and conflicts. But when challenged and pushed, he'd lose control and respond.

The suppressed rage that smoldered inside would become a refined asset in later years and would eventually save his life.

Chapter 2

It was late summer of 1950 in Frankfurt. Mac propped his elbows on the concrete picnic table, put his chin in his hands, and wished he could be somewhere else. In his early fifties, Mac's thin face was lined and dark, revealing a lifetime spent mostly outdoors. His gray hair was uncombed and in need of a cut. He took off his thick glasses and cleaned them with his shirttail.

Snuffy sat across from him, Millie on one side of Snuffy, and Leonard next to Mac. Paulo had called them together and was coming across the lawn to where they waited.

Paulo was in his fifties with a dark mustache and complexion, a wide nose, and full lips. He was management, a handler in the Frankfurt Station, managing field agents and staffing operations. His specialty was difficult missions.

He sat at the end of the table, nodded a greeting to the others, and shuffled his files around. "We're out here because you never know who's listening," Paulo said, gesturing behind him toward the I.G. Farben building. A seven-story structure with six wings, it had been used for chemical research during the war but was now headquarters for the 5th US-Corps and CIA's Frankfurt Station. "This mission is vital, and you folks are the team we've assembled."

Mac looked around at the newly-formed team. He knew, trusted, and respected them all, but even so he would have preferred to work alone. Or maybe just with Snuffy.

Paulo continued. "The bosses have put a sanction on a GRU handler named Andrei Vasilevich. How you deliver it is up to you." GRU was the Foreign Military Intelligence Directorate headquartered in the Russian Embassy in East Berlin.

The team looked from one to the other. "Who's in charge?" Mac asked.

"You are," Paulo said. "Len, your Russian's fluent, right? We'll need it to get next to the target."

"Da. I'm a cunning linguist." He leered at Millie, who looked away. Leonard was a handsome fellow in his late thirties, dressed to the nines, soft-spoken, and articulate. Everybody liked Leonard for his charm and free-wheeling style. They also respected his skills in the field.

Millie was young, a slender girl with a dark complexion and a nature to match. Not your typical assassin, this wisp of a woman didn't talk much and rarely smiled.

"You know," Snuffy said, rubbing his mustache, "no disrespect to the others, but Mac and I can handle this sanction on our own. Hell, Mac can do it alone. Aren't we crowding the field a bit?"

Mac looked with affection at his old friend. Snuffy had come up the hard way, a Marine sniper in the war in the Pacific and now a mercenary, known for his prowess with the equipment and trappings of espionage. He was in his thirties, robust, and with a lot of miles left on him. He was the guy Mac wanted if he needed someone watching his back.

"I know you could handle it," Paulo said. "Anyone at this table could handle it. It's the chief's idea. One of you gets killed or compromised, the others take up the slack. We hand-picked this team with that in mind."

Mac snorted. "Allison doesn't know shit about the field. He hasn't set foot out of that office since he got the job."

Paulo grinned at Mac's assessment of their station chief. Then he continued. "Mac, you'll formulate a plan, make assignments, and oversee the operation."

"We get support from the top?" Mac asked.

"Up front money. After that, the Company doesn't want to hear from you until the target's on a slab. You're all in deep cover. And by the way, the brass prefers this sanction to look like an accident or natural causes."

Mac didn't always understand the motives of management. "Why do they give a shit how he goes?"

Paulo laughed and gazed away from the others into the park. "Allison worries that if the Ruskies know we sanctioned Vasilevich, they'll retaliate with a sanction on him."

Mac frowned and shook his head. "It figures."

Leonard raised his hand like a schoolboy and grinned. "Why Vasilevich?"

"Because he's a pain in the ass," Paulo said. "Every time we plan an op, recruit an asset, whatever, he finds out about it and tosses a monkey wrench in."

"How does he get his information?" Snuffy asked.

"Until yesterday, he had a mole in the station."

"Had?"

"Yeah," Paulo said. "He turned one of our local assets. We took care of that."

"Then why bother with this guy if his source is dried up?" Mac asked.

"He's relentless," Paulo said. "Ambitious. Climbing the ladder. He got one mole, he'll get another. Ruples talk. The locals aren't true to the red, white, and blue. Only to the green."

Two weeks later, the team gathered at their stepping-off site for the op, a small café in West Berlin. Mac ran his hands all around the booth and the surrounding area, looking for bugs.

The café was small like hundreds of others in Berlin, narrow and dimly-lit with oak booths lining the wall. Mac had chosen it because the team could converse in private.

When they were seated and had coffee, Mac said, "Progress reports. Millie?"

"Got the costume and flowers. Len's been coaching me on pronunciation."

"Yeah," Leonard said. "Got rid of that Joisey accent. Now she looks like Olive Oyl and speaks German like a gypsy." He winked at Millie, who returned the gesture with her usual sullen expression.

"Snuffy?" Mac said.

"Borrowed a car and made the rose dispenser. And Len's credentials, too."

"What were you able to use for the rose?" Mac asked.

"Odorless, colorless mist. The target drops with what looks like a heart attack. He's dead meat in a couple minutes."

"Anything Millie and Len need to know about it?"

"Don't breathe it," Snuffy said. "We got a venue?"

Mac nodded. "A café down the street from the embassy. Small and quiet like here, but wider, an open floor with tables. Right here on the map." He unfolded a street map of Berlin and shoved it across the table to Snuffy. It had the locations of the Russian embassy and the café circled in red and the escape route highlighted.

Snuffy pored over the map and showed it to Millie. "How's it look to you, Millie?"

"Perfecto," was all she said. Millie didn't often offer much in the way of opinions or suggestions. Whatever the bosses wanted, she'd do. Unless they got something wrong. Then they'd hear from her.

"I sat in that café every day for a week," Mac said. "Here's floor plans." He handed sketches to Leonard and Millie. "The target should be sitting here." He pointed to a table icon drawn on the sketch. "Gives us direct access to the door afterward. Len, is your cover solid?"

Snuffy spoke up. "Len is a newly-appointed GRU officer visiting from Moscow to meet staff. Nobody here knows him, so the impersonation is sound."

Mac made more notes and studied the street map. "Len, you think you'll have any problem luring Vasilevich out?"

"I outrank him. I'll invite him to lunch. He won't refuse."

"Okay," Mac said. "Looks like we're ready. If there's any reason we can't go in today, speak up now." He looked around the table. Everyone sat still.

"Good. Let's go." He folded the map and gave it to Snuffy.

They went out, climbed in the car, and drove to the eastern sector, going through one of the checkpoints reserved for German citizens. As usual, Snuffy's forged papers and Leonard's fluent German got them through.

Between the border and their destination, Leonard changed into his Russian officer's uniform. "Don't watch, Millie," he said. "You might get excited."

Millie ignored him and looked out the window.

When they arrived at the café, Leonard left for GRU headquarters on foot, and Snuffy waited in the car.

Millie and Mac went inside, sat at a table, and ordered coffee. Millie took a few sips and went into the toilet. She came out with her brown hair down and bare feet. She wore a white flowing dress that fell off her shoulders, a red sash around her waist, and a necklace and bracelets of beads and bangles that rattled when she moved.

"How do I look?" she asked Mac, spinning around for him so her dress flared up.

"Pass the tealeaves," he said.

She went out to the car to wait with Snuffy. Mac stood and paced the floor. He looked at his watch and fidgeted, sitting at the table, then getting up to pace again. If everything was going according to the plan, Leonard was in the embassy, establishing his bona fides, and getting to know Vasilevich. But this was taking too long. They should've been here by now. Mac wanted the target taken down before the dinner crowd started pouring in. He looked at his watch again. If Leonard wasn't back soon with the target, the op would have to shut down.

Mac was seated when Leonard and their prey finally came in at about five. Vasilevich led the way and chose a table. Leonard shook his head and pointed to the one Mac had chosen. Vasilevich hurried to the other table, and held Leonard's chair for him.

Vasilevich was a short man in his fifties with a pot gut. He was dressed in civilian clothes that didn't fit and that were heavy for this time of year. His face maintained a wide grin and sparkling eyes as he hovered over Leonard, getting him seated and comfortable. He summoned the server with an officious urgency and sat across the table from Leonard.

They engaged in quiet small talk, smiling and laughing, drinking dark beer, and nibbling pretzels while they waited for their meals.

When the server brought food for the two, Mac stood and walked to the window. Two Russian privates with rifles stood guard outside the door. Those would be Vasilevich's bodyguards, and they would be a problem. He signaled to Millie, and she opened the car door. He returned to his table. Now it would happen.

Leonard looked up when the gypsy girl came in the door with a basket of flowers suspended from her neck on a strap. Vasilevich followed her with his eyes as she eased over to Mac's table.

"Hey, good-looking," Millie said in a quiet voice no one else could hear. "There's comrades out there with guns. Want a rosebud to nibble on?"

"*Nein. Fortgehen*," Mac said loudly, and she tossed her head and walked to the table where Leonard and Vasilevich sat talking.

Millie made one of her rare smiles, said to Vasilevich, "*Kaufen eine Blume für Ihre Frau?*" and held out a long-stemmed rose.

"*Nein, nein, Sie danken*," Vasilevich said in a thick Russian accent, waving at her to go away.

Mac rested his hand on the pistol concealed in his jacket pocket. Leonard covered his face with a handkerchief and Millie held a silk veil over her mouth and nose. She shoved the rose under Vasilevich's nose. As the Russian pulled back, she squeezed the stem, and a clear mist sprayed out of the blossom. Vasilevich clutched his chest and fell forward onto the table, gasping for air and convulsing. She turned and walked toward the door followed by Leonard and Mac. The two privates snapped to attention and saluted when Leonard came out.

The getaway car waited at the curb, its engine running, its doors open, and Snuffy at the wheel. A commotion arose from inside the café when the staff discovered Vasilevich face down in the weiner schnitzel. One of the guards looked in and rushed to tend to his charge. The other guard loudly commanded the team to halt. Mac tried to pull his pistol, but the hammer got hung up in his pocket lining.

"Shit!" he said as he tugged on the piece.

The private chambered a round and lowered the rifle's barrel, pointing it directly at Mac. Snuffy came out of the driver's side door with a Luger, put one round in the private's heart and another into the brick wall alongside the other private, who was rushing outside with his rifle raised. Millie pulled a .32 semi-automatic pistol from the flower basket and put a round into the soldier's head.

They jumped in the car, and Snuffy screeched tires getting away. He headed for the western sector at about eighty kilometers an hour through the narrow streets.

"So much for death by natural causes," Snuffy said over the sound of the motor.

Millie threw the flower basket out the window. "Could have avoided all this trouble and just shot the sonofabitch."

Mac smiled as he thought about Bert Allison keeping a low profile until the heat was off.

They barreled through the city, squealing around corners, chasing pedestrians to the curb, and taking shortcuts through alleys and down an occasional sidewalk to bypass the traffic.

"What took so long to get to the café?" Mac asked as buildings, signs, and lampposts flew past them in a blur while the car hit every bump and rut in the street.

"I was a visiting dignitary," Leonard said, hanging onto the back of the front seat. "I had to meet every fucking comrade in the place. They all talked endlessly about their heroic adventures on the Eastern Front. I thought I was going to have to shoot my way out."

"Still might," Mac said, his pistol drawn and ready.

The speeding car bounced over another bump in the street, a big one this time. Leonard held on more tightly. "Jesus, Snuffy, go back. You missed one."

When they got to the checkpoint, Snuffy slowed down, and Mac hoped word hadn't made it to the guard shack. The conspirators were prepared for a firefight at the checkpoint if necessary, but Leonard stuck his head out the window and barked a command in Russian to the sentry, who saluted and waved them through.

They drove the five hundred plus kilometers straight through to Frankfurt, stopping only for fuel, and arriving just after midnight. Once there, Snuffy ditched the borrowed car, and they split up and went their separate ways. The three men wouldn't see one another for about two years. It would be much longer before any of them saw Millie.

Chapter 3

On the twelfth of June in 1952, summer vacation had begun, and the children had the whole day every day to play outdoors. A noisy group of boys gathered at the edge of the playing field and formed into teams, chosen one boy at a time for a baseball game. The boys yelled and cheered at each choice.

Harold sat alone on an embankment next to the ball field, reading a book and trying to remain oblivious to the sandlot game forming up a few yards away. The June heat in eastern Virginia beat down, and beads of perspiration dotted his forehead and upper lip. Every now and then he'd pull out a red bandanna and wipe the sweat off. He sat facing away from the sun to let his shadow reduce the glare on the book's pages.

"Come on, Harold, we need you to pitch." He looked up from his book. The captain of one of the rag tag teams stood next to him.

"I have to finish this book."

"What book is more important than a ball game?"

Harold held up a copy of Joseph Conrad's *The Secret Agent*.

The kid made a face, said, "Aah," and ran onto the field. Harold smiled. The other kids had never appreciated his tastes in reading.

He pushed back his thick brown hair, wet his palm with his tongue and tried to flatten his stubborn cowlick, which popped up again like it always did.

"Chickenshit," someone said. Harold looked up. A larger boy stood over him, frowning, fists clenched. He was a new boy, and Harold knew him only as Wallace.

"What'd you say?" Harold asked.

"I said, 'Chickenshit.' You're supposed to be this hot shot pitcher, but you're too good to play with us."

"Go away, I'm busy."

"Chickenshit." Wallace moved nearer braced for a fight.

Harold felt the rage coming on. His pulse quickened, and he could feel the thumping in his chest, almost hear it. His temples throbbed in time with the pulsating tunnel vision that saw only Wallace leaning over him. Pressure in the pit of his stomach pushed up.

Apparently no one had warned Wallace about provoking Harold. Or if they had, Wallace had decided to meet the challenge.

No longer in control, Harold set his book aside and jumped up, his feet apart, his chin jutted out. He looked Wallace up and down. Wallace was bigger, but that wasn't a concern. Harold was past being intimidated by size. If Wallace wanted to fight, Harold would fight.

"You don't want to do this," he said, but it sounded to him like someone else said it.

"Fuck you, you little faggot," Wallace said and kicked Harold's book to one side.

The other kids came running to see the fight. Harold and Wallace circled, facing each other, their fists raised, not taking their eyes off one another, each one waiting for the other to make a move, provide an opening. Then Wallace moved in and took a healthy swing, but Harold pulled away, and the punch missed by a wide margin. With Wallace off balance, Harold kicked him in the groin, and as Wallace bent over in pain, Harold clubbed him in the jaw with a haymaker. Wallace hurtled sideways and lost his footing. He went down, and his head struck the edge of a large jagged rock poking out of the red clay embankment. He rolled over and lay on the ground motionless, his head bleeding profusely and his eyes closed. Harold stood waiting, but Wallace didn't stir.

With his opponent down and not getting up, Harold's burning rage subsided, and he was in control again. He looked at what he'd done, and the rage was gradually overtaken by regrets and shame. But, he told himself, Wallace had taken the first swing. Harold had only defended himself.

He moved to another part of the playground, sat on the merry-go-round, and opened his book, still trembling and breathing hard. The other kids ran into the building, and the nurse came running out. Soon an ambulance pulled up, and they took Wallace away on a stretcher. Harold couldn't see whether Wallace was conscious, and he worried that this time he might have gone too far. He wanted to cry, but he wouldn't let himself do that. The other kids might see it. Tomorrow he'd be twelve, and big boys don't cry. He returned to his book.

Someone called his name. "Harold!" He lowered the book and looked across the playground, shading his eyes from the sun with a cupped hand.

A little girl came running from the main building. She bounced up and down with each step, and her curls jumped in the air with each bounce. Harold cocked his head to one side and watched her run toward him.

"Harold!" she called to him. "Harold! You're wanted in the office."

He closed his book and walked toward the building. He went inside and to the counter. The secretary said, "Go on in, Harold. Miss Moore wants to see you."

He flattened the cowlick again, went in the office, and sat in a chair across the desk from Miss Moore, the orphanage administrator. He waited for what he was sure was coming.

"Harold, I called the county, and they agree. This fighting is getting out of hand."

"How's Wallace?"

"He has a concussion, but he'll be fine. He was lucky and so are you. You might've killed him."

"He started it, ma'am."

"Harold, you've put two boys in the hospital and sent others to the infirmary, and you're now regarded as a threat to the other children. We aren't set up to handle that. I'm sorry but we're going to have to send you away."

Harold looked at the floor. He'd been expecting this and dreading it. But he had no choice.

"We're sending you to Staunton," she said, referring to a state facility for juvenile delinquents and teenage orphans. The other boys had said he'd go to Staunton someday, calling it "a bad place for bad boys."

"Get your things ready. Use a suitcase from the supply room. Say all your goodbyes, and be on the front steps tomorrow morning at seven. A bus will pick you up."

"Yes, ma'am. Can I take this book? I haven't finished it yet."

"Sure. You might as well take the others too. They're way over the other kids' heads. If you can carry them, you can take them."

She smiled at him, came around her desk, and gave him a hug. The gesture made him uncomfortable. He wasn't accustomed to affection. "Good luck, Harold. We'll miss you, but I predict great things for you. Keep that temper under control, and you'll be fine. And happy birthday."

Harold left the office and went to his dormitory room to pack. He wondered what she had meant about "great things." What could be great about the future of an orphaned boy nobody wanted and who blew up under pressure? And now he'd be one of the smaller kids again but this time in a "bad place for bad boys."

Chapter 4

Five a.m., Central European Time. June 13, 1952. Mac stood alone in Frankfurt's red light district. An extended search throughout Western Europe had led him here. He hadn't slept in two days.

Leonard was close. Mac could feel him. After a trek across Europe, the search had brought him back to where he'd started.

Mac removed his thick glasses and wiped the mist away with the webbed cuff of his leather jacket. This mission was deep cover and solo, his preferred *modus operandi*.

It was too quiet, too still. Something wasn't right.

Paulo had told him when he gave him the assignment, "It's a sanction, Mac, not a burn. No exceptions. No forgiving."

Sanction meant only one thing. Find Leonard, terminate him, and try not to get caught.

First he'd have to find Leonard before Leonard found him.

Mac wanted a cigarette, but he couldn't risk a flame calling attention to him. He began his prowl.

He crept through the district, staying close to the buildings and in the shadows, examining every doorway, peering around every corner, looking over his shoulder, watching, listening. A foggy mist shrouded the street, a morning chill filled the air, and the sun hadn't yet risen to burn off the fog and dry the pavement. He slipped into an entranceway out of sight and zipped up his jacket. Leonard might be inside somewhere.

Street lights shone down, diffused by the mist, casting a yellow glow along the fronts of buildings and painting crescent-shaped reflections on the cobblestones, shined to a high gloss by centuries of foot and wheeled traffic. The strains of a blues saxophone from an old record player sang through an open window somewhere above him.

He could feel Leonard nearby, waiting, maybe watching. But from where? He was weary and hungry, and his old wounds ached from the cool damp air. The thought returned as it always did when tensions built and danger was at hand.

I'm getting too old for this shit.

But it needed to be done. Too much depended on it. Leonard was on the Company's elimination list, and Mac had the sanction.

Paulo had said, "When he went rogue, he stole the asset ledger. If it winds up in the wrong hands, people die, covers get blown, safe houses exposed, missions aborted, and we're set back years. You're the only guy I can give this to, Mac. You won't let friendship stand in the way."

Leonard was good, and he wouldn't fall without a fight. If Mac failed, all the names in that ledger would line up, eager to take the sanction. But Mac rarely failed. It might take a while, but he wouldn't fail.

Mac looked up and down the street.

If he's here, he won't see the fog lift.

The search had sent Mac all over Europe. Leonard was slippery and stayed a step ahead of Mac at every turn. Leonard was shopping the ledger around, looking for his price. A tip from an asset in Zweibrücken had led Mac to Frankfurt, this street, this brothel.

Mac had driven all night, ditched the borrowed car, and gone on foot into the red light district in search of a blind, a place sheltered from street lights and hidden from other eyes but with an unobstructed view of the street, sidewalks, doors, and windows.

His source had told him someone else was looking for Leonard. Would Mac and the other operatives get in each other's way, and would he have to eliminate the interference? He would if that's what it took to take Leonard down. He figured his opposition, if such they were, would likewise try to eliminate him if they had to. Another complication.

Mac stepped onto the sidewalk. No traffic in sight. The street, always busy in the early evening hours, sprawled still and quiet in both directions. Everyone had settled in. Johns not staying the night had gone home. Hookers, hangers-on, and the city slept.

A black Mercedes sedan stood against the curb, the only car in sight. Mac walked to the car and looked inside. The driver had left the keys in the ignition. He pressed the palm of his hand on the hood. Warm to the touch. A lamp burned in a second-story window. Was Leonard in there? In the open window a woman's bare arm raised up and pulled down the shade. The lamp went out. The record player reached the innermost groove and turned with a scratchy, ticking sound, seventy-eight ticks per minute.

Maybe Leonard was the john with the Mercedes. According to the Zweibrücken asset, he lived in this district when he was in Frankfurt, usually in this brothel. Better than a hotel. Brothels don't have registers to sign, and they don't collect passports. Leonard would come out soon if he was in there. For breakfast. Brothels don't have restaurants, either.

Mac patted his weapon inside his jacket pocket, a war-surplus Luger P08 semi-automatic pistol, the magazine loaded and one in the chamber. Where could he wait? Maybe over there in that alley. Maybe the entranceway across the street. Maybe leaning against a lamppost, waiting for Leonard to come out. Plug him and go to breakfast. Getaway? No problem. The Mercedes was warmed up and available to be borrowed.

The whine of an automobile engine from behind him broke the silence. He turned away from the Mercedes and looked up the street in the direction of the sound. A Volkswagen came bouncing around the corner, a rifle barrel stuck out the driver's side window.

Had Leonard spotted him and was bearing down? Mac scanned the block for a place to shield himself. The VW plummeted down the street toward him, and before Mac could take cover, the driver fired from the window. Mac ducked, but the driver wasn't shooting at him; his shots were aimed toward the Mercedes.

Mac spun around in time to see Leonard slump to the street next to the Mercedes, his weapon dropping in front of him. Mac turned toward the VW, which slid to a stop beside him. The door opened and the driver jumped out, still holding his rifle, his face in shadows. Mac tried to pull his pistol out of his jacket pocket, but it was caught up in the lining.

"Goddammit, again!" he said.

Then he took a good look at the shooter. It was Snuffy.

"Hey, Mac. What brings you here? Looking for some nookie?"

"Snuffy! Where the hell'd you come from?"

"Around the corner. Been watching you." Snuffy walked to where Leonard lay, still breathing. "He might make it."

"No he won't," Mac said and pointed the Luger at Leonard's head.

"Wait. Why are you after him?"

"A sanction. Took the asset ledger when he bolted. Been trying to peddle it on the street."

Mac ordinarily wouldn't tell such details to anyone, but this was Snuffy.

"He doesn't live to see the fog lift," Mac said. "Why are you after him?"

Snuffy looked up and down the street. "For a banker in Switzerland."

"What? Did he rob the bank?"

"Kind of. Went to the bank to open an account, hid out in a bathroom, came out at night, broke into the banker's office, and stole a ledger with account information."

"Why'd he want that?"

"It lists all the numbered accounts."

Mac kept an eye on the street. "No shit. He could've cleaned out the bank."

"They froze everything. He was holding it for ransom. Took a bunch of cash too. I guess he closed out his account, you might say."

"I knew he had balls, but that big? How'd he get out?"

"Went out the front door and walked right past a street cop like he belonged there."

"I don't get it, Snuffy. Len used to be one of the good guys."

"There's no accounting," Snuffy said and pushed at Leonard with his boot. Leonard moved his arm slightly and moaned.

"Still breathing," Snuffy said.

"So we were both after the asshole. He didn't stand a chance." Mac grinned.

"And both looking for ledgers. Small world. Anyway, don't shoot him yet. I want to ask him about my ledger."

Mac looked at where the bullet had entered Leonard's body through his jacket. A clean shot below the rib cage had taken him down. "How come you shot him if you need to grill him?"

"Well shit, Mac, he came out from under the car and was going to shoot you. How come you didn't look under the car?"

"Didn't occur to me. Losing it in my old age. Anyway, that's another one I owe you. Let's search him."

They went through Leonard's pockets. Nothing. No hotel receipt, safe deposit box key, nothing at all. Leonard's eyes were glassed over and stared upward, and he groaned. Blood seeped from the corners of his mouth and the front of his jacket.

"He's gut shot," Snuffy said. "He won't be answering questions."

"The car," Mac said. He went to the Mercedes, took the keys from the ignition, and opened the trunk. "Here they are," he said and came up with two worn green and gray cloth-bound ledgers. He flipped through the pages. "It's them. I can't believe he had them in the trunk. Under the spare tire."

Mac walked over to the Mercedes, pointed the Luger at Leonard's head, and pulled the trigger. The shot echoed up and down the street. Leonard went limp, dead. The fog began to lift.

"What day is it?" Mac asked.

"Friday the thirteenth."

"Thought so. Unlucky day."

Mac took out a pocket knife and cut a notch in the Luger's grip. Then he wiped it down and tossed it into a nearby alley.

The sanction delivered and the ledgers recovered, Mac considered it not a bad day's work for a couple of old spies. And they hadn't even had breakfast.

"Let's get out of here," he said." We've been kind of noisy." He pulled the crumpled pack of Camels out of his jacket pocket, shook a cigarette from the pack, and lit it with his Zippo. He snapped the Zippo shut, took a drag and headed for the car. They drove away from the red light district, and cruised around until they found a small café. While they sat and drank coffee and ate hard rolls, Mac flipped pages in the asset ledger. "We're all in here. You, me, Paulo, Millie, Sam, Bert, everybody."

Snuffy chewed his roll, swallowed, and said, "I was supposed to meet him here and swap money for the book. Only I didn't bring any money. Anyway, I'm on the next train to Zurich." He paused and downed the last of his coffee. "Weren't you and Len kind of close?"

"Not close, really. I first met him back in the thirties in the states. Knew his ex-old lady better." Mac's face took on a wistful look. "Guess I'll have to look her up and tell her she's an ex-widow."

"Well, It's a goddamn shame. We were a good team at one time," Snuffy said.

"Us and Millie. Unstoppable."

Snuffy smiled. "Yeah. If they'd given her the sanction, we could've stayed home. Well, I better go catch that train. Drop you somewhere?"

"I have to report in to Paulo. And Allison."

"Bert still here? I would have thought he'd be running the Agency by now."

"Still here. He should know you saved my ass again."

Snuffy smiled at his old friend. "Getting to be a habit."

"No shit. Maybe he'll have something for you."

"I need to go to the states. I miss the family. Barb sends pictures. Danny's growing like a weed. But then, you wouldn't know about that kind of shit, would you?"

Mac looked across the table and down the street. Traffic picked up as the city came to life. "Not for not trying. I've had a tomato or two in my time. Never any good at hanging on to them. Most women aren't like Barb. They won't put up with all this shit. You're lucky."

Snuffy didn't answer, but stared into his coffee cup.

Then Mac said, "I'll go with you to Zurich. I want to meet your banker. Might be what I'll need when I drop out of this rat race."

Chapter 5

Early morning on Friday the thirteenth of June, 1952, and today was Harold's twelfth birthday. He stood on the front steps of the orphanage and waited for the bus to take him to his new home. He craned his neck and shielded his eyes from the morning sun to get a glimpse of the bus when it came around the bend a half mile away. As he looked over his shoulder for one last look at what had been home for as long as he could remember, he clung to the battered suitcase that contained everything he owned, and he waited.

The dingy yellow bus appeared at the bend in the road. He watched it grow in his view until it pulled up in front of the orphanage promptly at seven. The suitcase bumped down the steps behind him, and he dragged it across the sidewalk and to the curb. He boarded the bus, lifting the suitcase one step at a time. When the bus pulled away, he didn't look back at the orphanage. He didn't know what was in store, but the past was no longer a concern. He did know one thing for certain. For the first time in a long time, he'd be one of the little ones again, and he'd have to prove himself all over. He hoped he could keep his temper in check.

He tried to read to pass the time, but reading in a moving vehicle made his stomach queasy, so he put the book away and watched the trees, hills, pastures, and the occasional farmhouse pass by along the rural route.

When they approached the center, Harold was overwhelmed by the spectacle of its profile against the horizon, a combination of a prison and medieval castles in history books. The bus dropped him off at the entrance and drove away. He dragged his suitcase up the concrete stairs and through large double doors into the lobby and approached a receptionist behind a counter.

"Name, please."

"Harold Sands, ma'am. They brought me here from—"

"I know where you're from. Wait over there."

He sat in a chair and waited. After a while, a man in a white jacket approached him. "Sands? I'm Gary. Follow me." When Harold struggled with the heavy suitcase, Gary took it and grunted.

"What's in here?"

"Books," Harold said.

Gary led him into a wing in the residential section to a room with three beds, two of them made.

"Your bed," he said, and pointed to the one with no sheet or pillowcase. He put the suitcase next to the bed. "Sheets, blankets, and pillowcases are in that bureau. Make your bed every morning and change it once a week. That chest is for your stuff." He pointed to a small unpainted, scratched and faded chest of drawers next to the bed. "Put the suitcase out in the hall when you've unpacked. Follow me."

He led Harold out of the room and through a maze of corridors, pointing out places Harold would need to know about. "The bathroom's down the hall...The laundry is here...Cafeteria is down that corridor...This is sick bay...When you outgrow your clothes, you swap them for others in that room there...That room is timeout. You don't want to go in there."

They went through a large common area where boys, most of them older than Harold, sat at tables in small groups talking among themselves. They looked up and watched Harold go by. Past the common area, Harold followed Gary into a suite of offices where another receptionist sat at a desk.

Gary said to the receptionist, "This is Harold Sands, a new resident. Sit over there, Harold." He pointed to a row of straight-backed chairs against the wall. The receptionist left her desk and went into an adjacent room. When she returned, she gestured for Harold to come in. Harold went into an office where a stern-faced, middle-aged man sat at a desk. The receptionist left them alone and closed the door behind her. A nameplate on the desk said:

Mr. Pruitt: Center Director

"Mr. Sands," Pruitt said, "sit down."

Harold sat in a chair across the big desk and faced Pruitt, who looked first at Harold, then at the papers on his desk, then at Harold. Each time he looked up, he said, "Hmmph!"

Harold fidgeted in his chair, uncomfortable being examined by this stern man with his gruff manner.

"This is your entrance interview, Sands. So you know how things work here."

Harold sat without speaking and paid attention.

"For starters, we don't take a lot of crap. You go to school and do whatever work we assign you. Obey the attendants. Their word is law. If you want to make an issue of something they tell you, bring it to me. My word is final."

Harold squirmed around in his chair. He wished the lecture would be over.

"Don't start trouble, and don't get into fights." He shuffled the papers on his desk. "According to your file, you have a tendency to get into fights."

"Yes, sir. I'm trying to—"

Pruitt ignored him and kept talking. "All that will do is get you a few days in timeout." Harold didn't know what that meant. "One thing we know here is how to deal with boys. Unless somebody comes along and adopts you, which is unlikely, you'll be here until your eighteenth birthday. Until then, try to stay out of trouble. You'll find the rules posted in your room. Read them, remember them, obey them, and we'll get along fine."

"Yes, sir."

"You can go to your room now and unpack."

He walked alone through the common area where the boys stared at him again, and he negotiated the labyrinth of corridors to his new room. His suitcase had been opened and his clothes and books scattered on the bed. Nothing was missing, probably because he owned nothing of value, but it angered him that someone had searched his possessions. He re-folded his rumpled clothes and put them in the chest of drawers. He stacked his books on top of the chest and put the suitcase out in the hall.

He opened a drawer in the bureau and found sheets and pillowcases. Another drawer had blankets. He took what he needed and made his bed. Then he went to the common area and sat alone at a table. None of the boys said anything to him. They had seen him twice, and now they ignored him.

A bell rang and they all filed out.

One boy yelled at Harold, "Come on, dummy, if you're late, you won't eat."

He followed them to a large cafeteria, went through the line, filled his plate, found a seat at the end of a table, and ate alone.

After lunch, he returned to his room. His new roommates were there, each sitting on his own bed. They watched him for a while, apparently sizing him up.

"I'm Philly, this is Barry," one of them said after a while. "Who are you?"

Harold looked the two boys over. "Harold. What's there to do around here?"

"Not much in the summer," Philly said. "Baseball sometimes."

"Did you guys go through my stuff?"

Barry looked at Philly who looked at Barry. "No. That would be one of the gorillas," Barry said.

Harold didn't understand. "Gorillas?"

"White jackets. Looking for cigarettes, drugs, knives, dirty pictures. But anything valuable, they'd have taken that too."

Harold sat on his bed and faced the two boys. "You guys been here long?"

"I got here a year ago, Barry a couple weeks later."

"Where from?" Harold asked.

"Orphanage upstate. We were bunkmates there so they put us together here."

"Why'd you have to come here." Maybe his new roommates had social problems too.

"Overcrowding is what they said. Who knows?"

Barry nodded. "Yeah, overcrowding."

"What's timeout?"

Philly said, "Break the rules big time, they put you in timeout, a small padded room with a toilet and no windows, no furniture. They lock you in for as long as they want. I've been there once. Believe me, you don't want to do anything to draw timeout."

Harold remembered what the kids at his orphanage had told him. "Is this really a bad place for bad boys?"

"Some of the boys are juvies from the cities. You'll spot them right off. Walk around like they own the place, looking for trouble."

"What keeps them from running away?"

"They lock them in at night in a dormitory on the other side."

"Are we locked in?"

"No. We're not convicts. We got no record. Just no parents. The main difference between the juvies and us is when their sentence is up, they get to go home."

Harold had no sentence to serve and no home to go to. As far as he knew, he'd be there until he was an adult. He looked at the bleak two-tone green cinder block walls and sparse furnishings, despaired of a future confined here, and wondered whether anyone had ever escaped.

The doors to the rooms had no locks. A boy had no secure place where he could protect his possessions from theft or vandalism. He had to earn the respect of the other boys such that they wouldn't mess with his property.

That respect came to Harold one day when he walked into his room and found one of the older boys rifling his chest of drawers. The boy's name was Hollins, one of the juvies, and he was supposed to be a real badass. Philly and Barry sat across the room on their beds, obviously afraid of Hollins.

"What the hell are you doing?" demanded Harold. "That's my stuff."

Hollins turned his head and looked at Harold, sizing up the smaller boy. "Only what I don't want." And he turned back to the chest.

The rage kicked in, and Harold rushed Hollins, swung his clenched fists in a wide arc, and nailed the bigger boy in the back of the head with everything he had. Hollins's face flew forward and hit the lamp, knocking it over and bloodying his nose. Philly and Barry drew back on their beds, hugging their knees, watching to see what would happen next.

Hollins turned, clearly planning an immediate dispatch of this runt who dared to hit him. But Harold didn't wait; he drove headfirst into Hollins's midsection and threw him off balance. Hollins fell backward and hit the floor on his butt. Harold picked up a dictionary from the top of his chest and slammed Hollins upside his head. Hollins fell sideways, stunned. When he wobbled to his hands and knees to pull himself up, Harold kicked him in the head and jumped on him, punching him in the face. Gary and another attendant came rushing in, grabbed Harold and pulled him off. The other attendant made a quick examination of Hollins's scrapes and bruises. Then he helped Hollins up and led him out of the room.

Harold was breathing hard, but he didn't struggle.

Gary said, "Sands, you're in trouble. And not only with us. Hollins is going to be laying for your ass."

"Why am I in trouble? He was stealing my stuff."

"Fighting. You know the rules. We're going to let this one go. Next time, you go to timeout. You don't want that."

He walked out and left Harold, Philly, and Barry alone.

"Why'd they let me off," Harold asked.

Barry spread his hands. "Paperwork. They don't like to do it."

The fight with Hollins had ignited the uncontrolled rage smoldering inside Harold. He didn't want to hurt anyone, but once he started, he couldn't stop. Something inside told him if he stopped before his opponent was disabled, the other guy would hurt him bad.

Because of fights, he drew timeout once for two days and the second time for a week. He sat in the padded room, read his schoolbooks, and waited for his meals. Timeout wasn't as bad as they had said, but after the one-week session, he'd had enough.

The other boys kept their distance after that. Everyone knew picking a fight with Harold would invite a major ass-kicking. Harold wasn't proud of his reputation. It was only a question of time before he hurt somebody, and he wanted to avoid that trouble as long as he could.

Chapter 6

One day after Harold had been at Staunton for several months, Gary stopped Harold and Philly in the corridor and looked at his watch.

"What you two doing out here?"

"Going to the bathroom." Philly held up the hall pass.

Gary stood in Harold's way. "You got a hall pass too?"

"No. Mrs. Simms told me to just go. She only had the one."

Gary leaned over and put his face close to Harold's. "That's 'no, sir,' boy."

"No, sir," Harold said, but his words dripped with sarcasm.

"You boys are going in there to smoke, ain't you? Give me the cigarettes."

"We don't have any," Harold said, backing away from him.

Gary grabbed Harold by his shirtfront and ran a hand into his pocket, and when Harold pulled away, Gary backhanded him with enough force that Harold stumbled against the wall.

"Show respect, boy." Gary turned and walked away.

Harold put his palm on his burning cheek, felt the rage welling up, and jumped forward to go after Gary. Philly grabbed him from behind, wrapped his arms around him, and said in a harsh whisper, "No, man. That's a month in timeout."

Harold struggled, but Philly held on. "They'll gang up on you. Take you to the cellar. They know how to hurt us without leaving a mark."

Harold started to settle down.

"Not only that, but they'll put you in with the juvies. You don't want that."

By then Gary had turned down another hall and was out of sight. Harold calmed down and said, "Thanks, man."

That night after everything was shut down, Harold shoved his clothes into a pillowcase, slung it over his shoulder, and slipped out into the corridor. He'd never seen anyone patrolling the halls at night when he'd go to the bathroom, but he kept his eyes open and alert as he made his way to the front entrance.

Escaping from the minimum-security facility turned out to be easy. He simply walked out. The exits were locked from the inside to keep intruders out, not boys in, and the highway was a half-mile away. This wouldn't be an escape. It would be a departure. He was glad he wasn't locked in with the juvies. He didn't know how he'd have found his way out.

He walked along the highway with his thumb held out. He didn't have a destination in mind but wanted to get away from the center. He didn't know what he'd eat, where he'd sleep, or how he'd live, but he didn't worry about those things. They'd take care of themselves.

He walked all night. The few cars that went by ignored his thumb. Finally, a car stopped.

"Need a ride, boy?" The driver was an older fellow, dressed in a business suit. "Get in."

Harold climbed into the car and put his bindle on the floorboard. The car pulled onto the highway.

"Where you going, boy?"

"Down the road a ways. Into town."

"We'll get you there. My name's Joe. I sell brushes and other household items."

As they drove, Joe kept looking at Harold and kept a line of chatter going.

"Kind of late for a boy to be out here...Where you from...Where's your folks..." He never waited for an answer, but kept the comments flowing.

Every now and then, Joe punctuated his banter by patting Harold on the leg. Harold felt uncomfortable being alone in the car with this man and being touched, but he didn't know why.

They pulled into a truck stop.

"Why are we stopping here?" Harold said.

"Got to take a leak. Don't you?"

"No, sir," Harold worried something bad was about to happen.

"Well come on in with me anyway. Keep me company while I take one."

"No thanks. I'll wait here." Harold had already decided that as soon as Joe was out of sight, he'd leave and hide until Joe was gone.

Joe reached across and touched Harold between the legs. Harold shrunk back, but there was nowhere he could go. Then Joe opened his door, grabbed Harold by the arm, and said, "Come on, boy. You're coming with me."

Harold didn't know what Joe had in mind, but he knew it wouldn't be good. Being touched and grabbed was a threat unlike any he'd known. He was more scared of this man than he'd been of either of the bullies at the orphanage or the attendants at the center. His heart pounding and the rage rising, he fell back on the seat, drew his legs up against his chest, and kicked forward with all his strength, hitting the man in the face and chest. Joe tumbled out of the car onto the pavement, and Harold opened his door, grabbed his bindle, and ran toward two parked tractor-trailers. He looked over his shoulder. Joe was on his feet brushing himself off. Then he pulled himself into his car and drove away. Harold breathed a huge sigh of relief. Now what?

The sun was coming up, and his fear had subsided. Harold realized he was starved. For a moment, he actually missed the slop they called breakfast at Staunton. Well, almost.

The diner at the truck stop was open, and he went in. Two truckers at the counter looked up and then turned back to their food. The aroma of their breakfasts made him hungrier. A lady behind the counter looked him over and said, "What can I do for you, sonny?"

"I'd like breakfast, ma'am, but I don't have any money. I can work to pay you."

"Well, we need a dishwasher. There ain't no dirty dishes yet. But they'll be piling up soon enough. Sit over there, and I'll bring you something."

One of the truckers called out, "Give the boy whatever he wants. Put it on my bill."

"Sure. What do you want, sonny?"

"It doesn't matter," he said. "Whatever you think."

She put in an order, and the cook whipped up a meal of bacon, eggs, and hash browns. She looked at his bindle when she put the plate in front of him. Staunton's stencil on the pillowcase was in clear view, so he turned it over. She brought him a glass of milk to wash the food down. While he wolfed down his meal, she went to the pay phone and made a call.

Harold was finishing his breakfast when two policemen came into the diner. They looked at Harold, and one of them said, "This the boy you called about?"

"Yeah, let him finish eating. Then you can have him."

They walked over and sat across from him. Harold looked from one to the other. Their faces were kind, and they weren't frowning at him. He didn't know whether to be scared or relieved. He'd had no experience with the police, but he was sure that as long as they were around, nobody would try to hurt him.

"You from Staunton, son?" one of them asked.

Harold looked down. "Yes, sir."

"When did you leave?"

"Last night."

"Ready to go back?"

"They'll punish me, sir. Maybe whip me. Put me in timeout. Isn't there someplace else I can go?"

The other cop grinned. "Well, I guess we can lock you up. We got a vacancy downtown in the drunk tank."

That didn't sound too inviting. "No, sir. I guess I'd rather go back."

As he left with the cops, he called back, "Thank you for the breakfast."

They drove him to the front door of Staunton and let him out.

"Do we need to go in with you?"

"No, sir. I'll be okay. Thank you."

"You're not going to run away again, are you?"

Harold remembered Joe trying to drag him out of the car and into the men's room. "No, sir. I'm not."

"Okay, son. You need any help, you call us."

They drove away, and Harold went to the front door and pulled it open. He'd left it unlocked the night before. The big clock on the wall said it was almost time for the bell to ring. He went to his room. Barry and Philly were still sleeping, so he unpacked his things as quietly as he could and climbed into bed.

Next thing he knew Philly was shaking him. "Harold. Get up. Time to go to breakfast."

He yawned and said in a groggy voice, "You guys go on. I'm not hungry."

Chapter 7

In June of 1954, when Harold was near his fourteenth birthday, word came down that Director Pruitt wanted to see him. He hurried to the director's office.

"Sands, this is Mr. and Mrs. Bentley. They're looking for a boy about your age to live with them and help around their airport. They read your file and asked to talk to you."

Harold looked the couple over. Both in their fifties, slender, both short with gray hair, hers wavy and pinned back, his close-cropped and curly, they had the faces and hands of working people. She wore a simple blue house dress. He wore slacks and a blue work shirt open at the collar.

"We read in your file you've been in a few fights," Mr. Bentley said. "Do you like to fight?"

"No, sir. I hate it. I never started a fight."

"But you finished them?"

Harold looked at the floor. His reputation would follow him the rest of his life, he feared. "Yes, sir," he said. "Usually."

"Harold," Mr. Bentley said after a moment, "would you like to live at an airport?"

Harold's face brightened. "And ride in airplanes?"

"Yes. And if you stay with us, you can learn to fly one too, when you're old enough. If you go with us today, we'll fly home in one."

Harold was excited now. The Bentleys could be his ticket out of this place. "What would I have to do?"

"Go to school, get good grades, help Mrs. Bentley with chores around the house and me with jobs around the airport, pumping gas, sweeping the hangar, washing airplanes, all kinds of odd jobs."

"Are there other kids there?" Harold had never lived anywhere without other children around.

"No. There would be just you," Mr. Bentley said.

"Do I get my own room?"

"Yes. There's a spare room that will become yours."

Harold tilted his head and looked at them, first one, then the other. "When do I go?"

"Today as soon as you can be ready. We have the paperwork filled out."

Harold turned to leave and pack his things. Then he stopped, turned around and faced the couple. "Uh, what do I call you?"

The Bentleys looked at each other. Then she nodded and he said, "How about Mom and Pop?"

Harold grinned.

"Sands," Pruitt said, "Mr. and Mrs. Bentley aren't adopting you. You will still be a ward of the state in the foster care program. The state pays foster parents to take care of children like you. If you mess up, they'll bring you back and get another boy, simple as that."

Harold looked askance at Pruitt and didn't answer. Then he turned to Mr. Bentley. "I can be ready soon, sir. I don't have much to pack. Wait for me."

Mrs. Bentley's eyes welled up and she bit her lower lip as Harold rushed out to pack his belongings and say goodbye to Philly and Barry.

The flight from Staunton took about an hour and a half. Harold rode in the co-pilot's seat. He'd never been in an airplane, and the clouds, mountains, and tiny farms, towns, and houses delighted and amazed him as if they were miniatures on a model train layout. He studied the instrument panel, trying to figure out what each switch, dial, and gauge was for. He held the aeronautical chart for Pop to navigate by. Pop showed him where they were located by pointing first at symbols on the chart and then at landmarks on the ground.

As they approached their destination, Pop pointed to the little airport. Harold strained to find it in the forest and fields ahead. Then there it was ahead of them. Pop flew parallel to the runway, turned left, then left again, and lined up with the grass strip runway. He pulled on the throttle, the engine idled, and they glided down. The little aircraft floated above the ground and touched the runway with a bump, rolling out to about half-way down the landing strip.

The airport was small with a two-thousand foot grass strip and a gravel taxiway up to the pumps, office, and service hangar. The Bentleys' small house sat to the east of the runway at the south end next to the road. Pop taxied the Stinson up the taxiway between rows of tied-down airplanes. He stopped at the pumps in front of the hangar and shut down the engine. Harold climbed out and gave Mom a hand. Then he took his suitcase from the baggage compartment and followed them. He looked over his shoulder at the airplane while he walked to the house.

A new chapter in Harold's life unfolded. Summer had begun, and he didn't have school yet, so he dove into the work at the airport. Soon he had a regular schedule of chores to keep him busy most of each day. He pumped fuel, mowed the lawn and the runway, washed airplanes, helped Sid the mechanic, and did anything else they could come up with. He didn't mind the work at all. He loved it.

Chapter 8

It was well into the summer of 1954 in Frankfurt. Temperatures were mild, and humidity was low. Mac parked his car on the street and headed toward the I.G. Farben building.

He walked across the expansive front courtyard and went in the entrance and through the lobby. He stepped into an ascending compartment of the *paternoster* lift and rode it up, stepped out, and strolled down the corridor to the end where station chief Bert Allison had a modest window office overlooking *Grüneburgplatz*.

"Good morning, boss," Mac said. "You sent for me?"

"Yes, Mac. Sit down."

Mac took a seat in the hard, straight-backed guest chair in front of the desk. He crossed his arms, and tilted the chair onto its rear legs. He rocked back and forth.

"I thought station chiefs had nicer furniture," he said.

Allison turned his head away and gestured at the window behind him. "Hell, I can't complain. At least I got a view. Took me seven years to get that."

"You get any time to enjoy it?"

"No." He waved his arms over his cluttered desk. "Up to my ass in paperwork."

"Then what good is it?"

Bert folded his arms and looked upward. "To impress field agents."

Mac laughed. No way he'd want an office job. "So what brings me here to where the upper echelon hangs out?"

Bert leaned forward and hesitated as if he had bad news and didn't know how to deliver it. Finally, he said, "We're pulling you in, Mac."

"In where?"

"Off the street. You're going stateside."

"What the hell for? We got nothing going there I can do."

Bert picked up a pasteboard-bound document with a Top Secret cover sheet stapled to it. He slid it over to Mac. Then he said, "You know about the Farm, Mac?"

Mac picked up the document and paged through it, keeping the chair balanced on its rear legs. "I heard something about it. What's that got to do with me?" He put the document on the desk.

"You're getting a little long in the tooth for the field, don't you think?"

Mac lowered his chair and slid back about a foot. "Bert, I can do any job in this station, including yours. Nobody in this station, including you, can do what I do."

Allison laughed. "You want my job?"

"I wouldn't have your job up my ass if I had room for a sawmill. So why don't you forget this stateside bullshit and let me do what I'm best at?"

"No can do, Mac. A lot's going to waste."

"A lot of what?"

"Knowledge. Experience. You know shit. We can't let that knowledge die with you. It's time for you to get off the street and into the classroom. Kids are coming along who need to learn what you know."

Mac pulled out a fresh pack of Camels and his Zippo. He pulled the red cellophane strip off the pack with his teeth, unfolded the foil liner, shook a cigarette out, and lit it. He took a deep pull, exhaled it, and a plume of smoke floated up toward the ceiling.

"Hell, Bert, I ain't no teacher. I'm a field agent. It's all I know."

"But you're slowing down. You're a valuable asset, but you're due to get shot at once too often. We'd rather put you out to pasture where you can nurture the young bucks."

"Christ, you make me sound like a goddamn piece of livestock."

"Well, it's not negotiable. You're headed to the states. You'll work at Headquarters as a handler for domestic operatives. And maybe some shit in Cuba and South America. You'll do frequent stints at the Farm training recruits. Paulo says you got nothing going now, so be ready to travel in a couple days. And don't give me that hangdog look. I'm probably saving your worthless hide."

By the end of the week, Mac was in the states and had moved into an apartment a floor above where Snuffy and Barb lived. Snuffy wasn't around much—he traveled a lot in his work—and he'd asked Mac to keep an eye on Barbara and his son Danny, so when Mac found a place in the same small apartment building, he took it. Barb was a night nurse at a local hospital, so Mac watched Danny while she worked. He enjoyed having the boy around, and Danny was helpful with errands and such.

One evening he was visiting with Barb and Danny when he asked, "Is Val still around?"

"She moved to Fredericksburg," Barb said. "She's still grieving for Len after all this time. We talk every now and then."

"Maybe I'll go see her." Mac remembered how taken he'd been with the beautiful young woman Leonard had abandoned so many years ago.

"That would be nice," Barb said. "Snuffy said you were there when Len was killed. But that's all he knew."

All he knew, my ass.

Mac intended to make that visit but never did. He was uncomfortable knowing Val was still grieving for the man he'd sanctioned several years before, and he didn't know how he could face her. The next time he asked about Val, Barb said she'd moved, but Barb didn't know where.

Chapter 9

Harold had never had a father or even a father figure, so Pop Bentley took him under his wing and taught him things a boy doesn't learn in an orphanage, outdoor things, such as how to camp, hunt, and fish.

On one such hunting trip, Pop left him alone on a plot of dense woods in the mountains of Virginia along the eastern ridges of the Shenandoah Valley. He had several acres to himself, posted land. Pop knew the owner.

He stood next to a pine tree in a forest of tall pines. Pop's Winchester 94 rested on his shoulder.

A six-point buck strolled out of a thicket into a clearing upwind of his stand. It stopped and sniffed the air. Harold, little more than a teenage tenderfoot, lowered the Winchester and drew down on the buck. He viewed it from down the barrel and across the sights and cocked the hammer.

The animal was majestic, a creature of grace and strength. He was about to kill it.

He froze.

Pop had told him this would probably happen, that most new hunters felt the same reluctance to kill a deer. Harold had shot rabbits and squirrels and had never given it a thought. He'd beheaded chickens for dinner and shot crows to keep them out of the cornfield. And snakes. Plenty of snakes.

He had killed.

But this buck was something else. It wasn't a rodent, a serpent, or a pillaging, screeching bird. It wasn't something to be reviled. He admired it. He didn't want it to die. It should be alive and free to run through the mountains and valleys. A part of nature, free as the wind, with a right to live.

Pop had said, "If you don't kill the buck, he won't last the day. The woods are full of hunters. They outnumber the bucks. Don't envision a beautiful creature of nature. See a freezer full of steaks, cut and wrapped and able to feed you through the winter. Know that by your act of death, you contribute to the greater good by filling your freezer and helping to control the deer population.

"Understand that intelligence and equipment have put our species at the top of the food chain in a natural world where many predators are larger and faster, and some are better equipped to kill."

He recalled Pop's words that day in the woods. But he hesitated and admired the majesty of the creature he couldn't quite bring himself to slay.

Something startled the buck, and it bolted and ran into a thicket. Harold lowered his gun. The buck rustled the brush as it made its way down the foothill away from his stand.

A gunshot sounded out, and the buck's movements stopped. Someone else would fill a freezer, would eat venison steaks this winter, and would hang a six-point rack on the wall.

He didn't kill the animal he admired, but the buck was dead, and that couldn't be changed.

Even though he didn't kill a buck that day, he learned the first lesson of the hunter. Nature is cruel without bias. To survive, you kill.

Pop took Harold to Senators and Redskins games, and Mom took him to the Smithsonian and to visit the sights and monuments in town.

She seemed to enjoy her role as surrogate mother. She encouraged him to read and listen to music. She took him to the library at least once a week where he scoured the shelves for spy novels. He checked out Ian Fleming's *Casino Royale* and imagined someday he would become an international spy like James Bond, with assignments of mystery, intrigue, and action, and, of course, a way with the ladies.

He wouldn't have to worry about that last part. Older women liked him and he knew it. His looks had a lot to do with it, but so did his beguiling manner.

"That boy's going to break a lot of hearts someday," they'd say.

The women customers at the airport, his teachers, librarians, the ladies in church, and women in the community, all wanted to mother him.

"Poor lad, to have to grow up never knowing his mother."

He made one friend in high school, Jamey Barrett, a boy Harold's age who looked a lot like Harold. Jamey wasn't a bright kid, but they formed a lasting bond, the only one Harold had outside his new family. Jamey's father ran a gas station, and Harold learned to work on cars there.

One day Harold brought a book about radio repair home from the library. He sat in the living room that night and read it cover to cover. The next morning, a Saturday, he was at the workbench in the hangar taking apart a radio from one of the older airplanes. A trip to the Allied store in town resulted in a small pile of electronic parts. It took several days of trial and error, making mistakes and correcting them, and constantly going to the books to figure something out. But before long, the radio was in the airplane, working not perfectly but well enough to be useful.

With practice he got better at fixing things. Neighbors would bring him TV sets, radios, record players, anything electronic, and if they were fixable, he'd have them working in short order.

Pop would tell the neighbors, "Now you give the boy some money for this. Think what it would cost to have a repairman come out."

When he wasn't at work or in school, he'd go to the library and read everything he could find about cars, locks, firearms, anything mechanical. He was, on his own, gaining a practical and well-rounded education through his appetite for understanding how things work.

He believed somehow he would forge his uncertain future based on these skills and aptitudes, but he didn't know how.

Chapter 10

Approaching sixteen, Harold was almost full-grown. His frame filled out, and the work around the airport and Barrett's gas station kept him fit and trim.

Harold and Jamey hung out evenings in Jamey's room and drank beer filched from Mr. Barrett's refrigerator. They talked about girls, sports, cars, and whatever else interested them. Typical of teenage boys, their conversations often went way out into left field.

"Harold, do you think if you danced with a nun long enough you'd get a hard-on?" Jamey was leafing through a Playboy magazine he kept hidden under his mattress.

Harold was studying the Operating and Maintenance manual for the M-1 Carbine. "Can't say. Never tried it. But I'll put it on my list."

Jamey laughed at that. "How about an old maid teacher?" he said. "Mousey Messick. Could you get a boner dancing with her?"

"I think a nun's more likely. You think the Redskins'll do as good this year?"

"Better if they had cheerleaders."

"Fat chance," Harold said. "But if they did, I'd dance with one."

Jamey started laughing. "And you'd get a hard-on, and she'd run screaming from the field."

True to his promise, Pop taught Harold to fly, insisting he learn in a basic tandem two-seater Piper J3 Cub. "If you can fly a rag-wing tail-dragger, you can fly anything," Pop said. The little J3 had no electrical system, no radios, no running lights, no gyros, or any of the conveniences student pilots were spoiled with. Compass, altimeter, tachometer, and needle, ball, and airspeed were it.

On Harold's sixteenth birthday after his tenth hour of flight instruction, he landed the J3 and taxied toward the ramp. As usual, Pop was in the front seat with Harold in the back.

At the turnoff from the runway, Pop said, "Pull over here. Keep the engine running."

Harold stepped on the heel brakes and closed the throttle.

"Give me your logbook." Pop scribbled something in the logbook and climbed out of the airplane. "Take her up and do three takeoffs and landings, Harold. You're on your own."

Harold was excited. He had been waiting for this ever since his first lesson a few weeks earlier. He taxied to the end of the runway, turned into the wind, took a deep breath, and pushed the throttle forward. Without Pop in the front seat, the little J3 was lighter, and it lifted off after a much shorter takeoff run. He climbed to four hundred feet above ground level, turned left, and then left again onto the downwind leg parallel to the runway.

He took a few seconds and looked around. He was soloing an airplane for the first time, all by himself, with no one to correct his mistakes, keep him safe, and guide him to earth.

Opposite the numbers on the landing end of the runway, he pulled out the carburetor heat control and backed off on the throttle to about eleven hundred revolutions per minute. Using trim and elevator to hold the airspeed at about fifty-five miles per hour with a five hundred feet per minute descent, he turned left onto the base leg and left again onto the final approach. The little craft descended, and just above the numbers, Harold closed the throttle and pulled gently on the stick, putting the J3 in a three-point touchdown position. The little yellow bird floated downward until the main gear and tail-wheel touched the grass strip runway. The airplane bounced up, but then it settled down with a gentle bump. He pulled the stick all the way back into his gut and rolled out, steering with the rudder pedals, braking gently with his heels on the brake pedals until he reached the cutoff to the taxiway. Harold let out a loud whoop. He had done it. Not perfect, but as Pop had said, "Any landing you can walk away from is a good landing." Now he had to do it two more times.

He taxied the J3 into takeoff position and repeated the take-off and landing procedure twice, getting better each time. A full-fledged solo pilot, he proudly taxied the airplane up the ramp and to the gas pump.

Pop was waiting for him with a pair of scissors for the traditional cutting off of the new pilot's shirttail. When Harold stepped out, Pop spun him around and cut the back out of his shirt. Then they walked together into the office where Mom waited with a ballpoint pen.

"Why'd you wear one of your best shirts today?" she asked with a grin.

She wrote his name and the date on the shirttail, and they ceremoniously tacked the inscribed piece of cloth to the bulletin board along with several others from other students who had recently soloed. They both gave Harold a huge congratulatory hug. He couldn't keep from grinning.

Harold was proud. He had soloed an airplane. He lay awake well into the night, thinking of the events of the day. He could hardly wait to be airborne again.

In the days that followed, Pop gave Harold basic instruction in navigation with two cross-country flights to other airports.

After that, Pop let him take the little J3 up anytime the weather was good and his chores were done.

On one such flight he flew northwest for a while and was enjoying the scenery from fifteen hundred feet when he looked around and didn't recognize any landmarks. Nothing was familiar. He compared what his chart showed to what he saw on the ground and was completely befuddled. Being lost aloft gave him a sense of urgency. His mind raced at breakneck speed as he looked first left, then right, then forward, and nothing made sense. Just trees, farms, and roads as far as he could see. A rural setting like countless others. But which one?

What if he ran out of fuel before he found an airport? Where would he put it down? How much time did he have? Was he in a restricted area?

Could he be run over by an airliner? His heart was in his throat.

A small town nestled in a shallow valley straight ahead, and he flew toward it. A water tower reached up from the middle of town, and he descended to take a look. He read the name of the town on the tower, and it surprised him. He knew the town. It was where they went to church. He was only twenty miles northwest of the airport, and he'd flown over this town several times. Now everything looked right. He turned and tracked the river to home, glad no one was around to witness his blunder.

In the fall, Harold flew into the Blue Ridge Mountains to see the changing colors of the trees. He flew with the side doors open and latched to the wing and fuselage and bathed in the view from five hundred feet above the peaks. The colors defined the ridges, peaks, crevices, and slopes of the mountains, something earthbound tourists never saw. The sculpture of the mountains controlled how much sunlight hit each facing and for how long as the sun passed over. Each exposure was awash with its own combination of colors, a spectacular view.

In solo flight, Harold sharpened his appreciation for a world of color, shapes, and beauty, a world a fellow could absorb and understand alone, and not need the reinforcement of like-minded souls or the camaraderie of kindred spirits. He was more comfortable with solo activities, but he wondered how a person could forge a lifetime of single purpose and single accomplishment without dependencies on others. He wasn't sure he could do that.

Chapter 11

The weather was favorable for flying this weekend, and business was brisk. Harold was in the hangar waxing an airplane. Pop was on the ramp talking to a large, imposing fellow who had been taking flying lessons. The discussion escalated into an argument, and the customer yelled and cursed. Harold stopped his work and looked on. Pop tried to calm the customer down, but the man continued to yell and make threatening gestures. The next thing Harold knew, Pop was on the ground and the customer stood over him, kicking at him. Mom called out from the office door, "Stop, don't hit my husband!"

Harold grabbed a metal tow bar, ran up to the customer, and swung the tow bar with full force. It hit the man in the side of his head, and the guy went down, bleeding from his ear. Harold hit him in the head, shoulders, and body with the tow bar and kicked him. The man cringed on the tarmac and tried to shield his body from the beating with his arms. When he moved his arms to cover where Harold was kicking, Harold kicked him somewhere else or hit him with the tow bar. When the customer scrambled to escape, Harold was right there, pounding and kicking.

Mom yelled, "Harold, stop!" but his rage blocked out her pleas. He raised the tow bar for a final, lethal swing at the customer's head when Mom's arms clamped around him and pulled him away.

"Stop, Harold, please!"

Another customer grabbed the tow bar. Mom, the other customer, and Sid, who had come running when he heard the ruckus, held Harold away from the big guy, who lay on the tarmac, groaning and holding his sides. Pop was on his feet, dusting himself off.

Pop went to the downed man and said, "Now you get off my property. Do it now, or we'll turn the boy loose again."

The guy pulled himself to his feet, hobbled to his car, and drove away.

Pop came over to Harold, who was breathing hard through clenched teeth. Mom held onto him tightly. He didn't resist her.

"Jesus, boy," Pop said. "Calm down. It wasn't that bad."

Mom said, "Come on in the house, Harold," and she led him away from the scene.

Pop whispered to Mom as she led Harold to the house. He couldn't hear what they said, but that night, supper included all his favorites. At the supper table Pop told Harold they'd probably hear from the police but he shouldn't worry.

"People saw what happened. Your actions were justified. But don't ever do that again. You'd wind up back at Staunton, and we could lose the airport."

A knock came at the door, and Mom went to answer it. She came into the kitchen.

"There's a Detective Ambrose here from the county police." She had a worried look on her face.

They went into the living room and sat on the sofa across from the detective. "What's this about?" Pop asked.

"Fellow named Carter came in this evening and said he was assaulted here this afternoon. He had cuts and bruises all over. Looked like he'd been beat up pretty bad. Said a teenager did it."

"It was me," Harold said.

"Detective Ambrose," Pop said, "my son was defending me."

Harold looked at Pop. Neither of them had ever referred to him as their son.

Pop continued. "Carter was a customer. He'd been drinking. When I wouldn't let him rent an airplane, he knocked me down and started kicking me. Harold stepped in and maybe saved my life. Plenty people saw what happened."

"Do you have their names?"

"Well, you can start with Sid Bellows. He's my mechanic. He's gone home for the day. I'll get you his address."

"Any others?"

"I saw the whole thing," Mom said. "It happened just the way my husband said it did." She took Harold's hand and held it.

"A couple other customers were there," Pop said. "I'll get you their names."

"That will be helpful. Carter wishes to prefer charges. If I determine a crime has been committed, I'll have to take your son in."

"Tell Mr. Carter if he does that, I'll swear out a warrant on him for assault and battery and attempted murder. I have bruises too." He stood and raised his shirt. His side and belly sported several large bruises.

"Carter does have a record of domestic violence," Ambrose said. "Harold, once you'd put a stop to the assault, why'd you keep beating on him. He said you hit him with a metal bar."

"Yes, sir, a tow bar. He was kind of big. I wanted him to stop kicking Pop and stay down. I thought if he got up, he'd hurt Pop more and maybe Mom and me too. I just meant to keep that from happening. Are you going to lock me up?"

"No, not tonight. I'll talk to the other witnesses and decide what to do. I'll also inform Mr. Carter about the counter charges if he proceeds with his action. Just stay available."

"He'll be here, Detective," Mom said and squeezed Harold's hand. "Thank you."

That night Harold sat on the edge of his bed and recalled the events of the day, not only the fight but that he might have gone to jail. He had been ready to kill that man. It troubled him. A lot. He didn't want to be a murderer, he didn't want to end anyone's life and go to prison for it, but he'd almost done just that. He worried that someday no one would be there to stop him as Mom had done, and he'd go too far. And there'd be no turning back. He wanted to control his anger, but even so, no one was going to hurt his family, not if he was there to stop it.

They never heard anything more about the incident.

Chapter 12

In 1958, Harold was fully grown and, like most seventeen-year-old boys, he was eager to take on the world, impatient to find his place, and ready for whatever life had to offer. He was lean and trim, a quiet, good-looking young man. He stayed to himself more than not except when he was with his foster parents or Jamey Barrett.

He had a car now. Pop had bought him an eight-year-old Ford on his seventeenth birthday. It was a two-door sedan with a faded pea-green paint job, and a shabby interior. Harold loved the little car. The radio didn't work at first, but he had it fixed within a day or two. Pop had paid up the insurance and tags for a year and put the title in Harold's name.

In the springtime, about two months before Harold graduated, tragedy struck. His folks had flown to Tazewell County in western Virginia to visit relatives, but Harold hadn't gone with them this time. School was still in session, so he'd spent a few days with Jamey and his Dad at their home. Sid usually watched the office while the folks were away.

The day after Mom and Pop were due back, Harold came home from school and found two men sitting on the living room sofa drinking coffee. One of the men was Pop's brother Ralph from Tazewell. Harold didn't know the other man.

"I guess you're Harold," the man said. He was middle-aged, wore a dark suit and tie, and held a briefcase in his lap.

"Yes, sir," Harold said.

"I'm Mr. Daggert. I have bad news, Harold. Your foster parents were in an airplane crash yesterday morning. They're both dead."

The news stunned him. He sat in Pop's easy chair and took a while before he said anything.

"How?" he asked in a quiet voice.

"We don't know the details," Ralph said. "The plane went down in the mountains. They found them late yesterday."

Daggert said, "Harold, I was Mr. and Mrs. Bentley's attorney. They didn't have a will. We kept talking about it, but they never got around to it. I understand you're their foster child."

Harold felt numb. "That stops when I turn eighteen in June." He stopped to reflect. "Or would have."

"You don't plan on staying here, do you?" Ralph said, a challenge in his voice.

Harold tilted his head and frowned at Ralph. "Mom and Pop said I could stay here until I graduated. They were going to send me to college." His voice almost broke as he fought back the tears. He couldn't let them see him cry.

Daggert said, "I guess you can forget about that. And you'll have to move out as soon as you can. Mr. Bentley here plans to sell the property. I already have buyers lined up."

Harold was in control now. "I'll be out tomorrow."

"Make sure you only take what's yours," Ralph said.

Harold shot him another look but didn't respond.

After the two men left, Harold went outside and into the hangar where Sid was loading his tools into the back of his van.

"You heard?" Sid said.

"Just now. I have to move out tomorrow."

"I didn't get that much time. I thought the brother was going to try to stop me from taking my own tools. Asshole."

Harold looked at the blue and white Piper Tri-Pacer parked in the hangar. He was supposed to wash and wax the airplane the weekend coming up. It would have looked nice with the grime scrubbed away and a fresh coat of wax. He walked out to the tarmac and down the line of small airplanes parked on the grass between the hangar and the runway. He'd flown a few of them, and he stopped at each one, looked it over, patted it on the cowling, and said goodbye to it. He made sure the planes were tied down, one of his evening chores at the airport, now being done for the last time. He almost broke down when he reached the empty tie-down space reserved for Pop's cherished old Stinson, now just a tangle of burned, twisted metal tubes and cables somewhere in the Blue Ridge. He stood there holding one of its tie-down ropes in his hand and looked west through the trees to the horizon. He choked back the tears and went in the house.

That night he slept in Mom and Pop's bed. He cried well into the night, ashamed of the tears, and tried without success to stop the sobs that racked his body. He vowed no one would ever see him like that.

The following morning he rose early, packed his clothes, toilet articles, and books, loaded them in his old Ford, and left for school.

He found Jamey in home room.

"I need a place to live for a while until I get a job. Is your couch available?"

"Sure, Harold. I don't think Dad will mind. He knew your folks. They were good people. He always said so."

Harold attended the funeral alone. He'd gone with Mom and Pop to funerals of people in the community, but he'd never known any of the people who died. This one was different. This one was close to home. This one was home. Was home. No more.

There were customers from the airport, Mr. Barrett, Jamey, Sid, and the examiner who gave flight tests. Virtually all the neighbors were there. Harold had met Mom and Pop's relatives when they took him on visits to Tazewell. He avoided Ralph Bentley but spoke with most of the others. He listened to the usual funeral chatter.

"Such a loss."

"They will be missed."

"So young to die like that,"

And one Harold couldn't stand. "Well, at least they died doing what they loved most."

Bullshit! Nobody loves crashing an airplane.

They kept the caskets closed to conceal the charred, grisly remains of the only two people he'd ever loved. At least he wouldn't have to hear the one he hated the most.

"Don't they look like themselves?"

Harold had no experience with grief and didn't know how to display or share it. So he hid it. Everyone would think him a cold potato. He didn't care. Let them think it.

The family had a funeral reception at the airport in the hangar with a buffet luncheon, flowers from the funeral, and pictures of Mom and Pop on display. They had invited everyone, but Harold didn't go.

He'd never known a loss like this, and he pushed it away rather than think about it. When reality set in, the experience left him with a cynical outlook about the promises of life and the future.

Harold would often look back on these times as the best in his life, the happiest. There would be other days to come, and some would be better than others, but not much could compare with his years as a teenager at the airport with Mom and Pop Bentley.

But he concluded that whenever you think you've found happiness, something comes along and snatches it away. He promised himself he would never again be close enough to anyone to be that deeply affected if he lost them.

Chapter 13

Harold was out of the welfare system. The social worker agreed it wasn't worth finding him another foster home for only two months, particularly since he had a place to stay. He was on his own. For the two months before he graduated, he lived with Jamey and pumped gas and did small repairs at the gas station to pay for his room and board.

"Glad to have you here," Mr. Barrett said. "You're a good influence on Jamey."

Jamey and Harold looked alike, and people often mistook them for brothers. With Mom and Pop gone and the crew at the airport scattered, Jamey was Harold's only friend, his only family.

With no plans and no money, Harold wasn't sure what he'd do after he graduated. Miss Messick, his high school counselor, called him into her office.

Miss Messick was a slim, dark-complexioned lady in her early thirties with dark brown hair pulled back into a bun, horn-rimmed glasses and a grim expression. The guys in school often laughed at her behind her back. They'd speculate about whether "Mousey Messick" could ever get laid.

Miss Messick had counseled Harold after the Bentleys died. He didn't put much stock in grief counseling, but he went because the school nurse said he should. Now he sat in her office to talk about the future. She had a small interior office with a desk and two chairs.

"Harold, have you given any thought about what you'll do after graduation?" She had a soft voice and rarely smiled. Harold liked her, but he didn't know much about her.

"Yes, ma'am, I have, but I don't have any firm ideas. I guess I'll keep working at the gas station and see what comes up. Maybe find a job fixing TVs or something. But you need tools for that. I can't afford it."

She had a file folder in front of her. She flipped through the loose leaf pages in the folder.

"College?"

"Like I said, I don't have any savings. My plans got kind of derailed when my folks died."

"The military?"

Harold wasn't interested in a uniformed, disciplined way of life. He didn't want to close any doors, but saluting and marching were not his style. He squirmed in his chair, uncomfortable with this conversation. "I don't know a lot about the service. It doesn't appeal to me."

"You know, the school has a career night coming up for seniors who aren't going to college."

"I saw that on the bulletin board."

"Try it, Harold. Military and civilian government recruiters will be there. They might have something for you you'll like. Something that pays better than pumping gas. Maybe you can save enough money to go to college later." She looked at the files again and turned a page. "Which ought to be in your plans."

As he left her office, she picked up the telephone.

On career night, Harold talked with recruiters from all three branches of the military. Nothing they offered interested him. Then he talked to a man from the Central Intelligence Agency.

"We're looking for chauffeurs and couriers, Harold. You'd drive government cars around town. Do you have a driver's license?"

"Yes, sir."

"Good. You'll need to pass a background check to get a security clearance, which the Agency will provide."

"What do I have to do to get that?"

"Nothing. We take care of it. What do you think?"

He looked around the large room with tables set up for recruiters from various potential employers. It all looked bleak and uninteresting. He could become a bag boy at a grocery store, a dishwasher or waiter at any of several restaurants in town, an enlistee in the armed forces. He'd rather pump gas. But the courier job with CIA was close to his boyhood dream of becoming James Bond.

"I don't know," he said, shifting from foot to foot. "Driving cars around town doesn't sound like it has much of a future."

"That would only be a start," the recruiter said. "There's no telling what you might be doing after you've been with us a while."

"Beats anything else I've seen tonight."

"If you're interested, read this literature, fill out these forms, and mail them in this envelope. We'll get back to you."

The salary would be more than he'd make pumping gas, so Harold applied for the job and was accepted, thus beginning a career that promised to forge substantial changes in his life and in the world too.

In August, Harold reported to work at the Pool, an eight-story office building three blocks from the White House. CIA recruits worked at the Pool while they waited for security clearances.

To be closer to work, Harold moved out of the Barrett house and into a rooming house in D.C. He reported to the Pool each morning, took tests, attended lectures, and did whatever work they assigned him, usually mindless clerical tasks.

One morning, Harold's supervisor handed him a card tucked in an envelope.

"This is for your fingerprints. Take it to any police station. It's part of getting a security clearance."

Harold took the envelope to his desk and removed the card, careful to handle it only by the edges. The card had his information typed in with a place for his signature. He signed the card and returned it to the envelope. Nothing in his background concerned him—at eighteen he'd never had brushes with the law, much less been fingerprinted—but, being the suspicious, cautious guy he was, he didn't like the idea of his fingerprints in a government file forever. That afternoon he drove to Mr. Barrett's gas station. Jamey was there.

"Hi, Harold. You need gas?"

"No. Take a ride with me."

As they drove, Harold explained what he wanted. "Have you ever been fingerprinted?"

"Never have."

"You're about to. Did you ever do anything illegal you didn't get caught doing, but left fingerprints?"

"I don't think so."

They drove to a state police station several miles south.

"Take this card in and ask them to fingerprint you," Harold said. "It's for a government job. Here's my driver's license for ID. Tell them you're me."

"What's this about, Harold?"

"It's a joke."

When Jamey returned, he handed the envelope to Harold, who held it by its edges so he wouldn't leave any of his own prints on it. The next day at the Pool, Harold dropped it on the supervisor's desk.

About a week later the pool supervisor called Harold into her office.

"I need you to deliver this pouch to E Street," she said. "You can catch the shuttle out front."

As Harold rode the bus between the Pool and Headquarters, he looked at the pouch, a closed manila envelope with official classifications stamped on its outside, "confidential" and "eyes only." A red string attached to the flap was wrapped around a circular tab on the envelope to hold the pouch closed. His instincts told him the pouch was booby trapped. If he opened it, even for a peek, the recipient would know, and Harold would not be returning to the Pool. He laughed that they thought their recruits were that stupid.

When he delivered the pouch, the lady asked him to wait. She opened the envelope and removed a document. She put another document in the envelope, closed it, wrapped the string around the tab, and stamped the outside of the envelope, "Top secret."

"Return this to your supervisor," she said.

When he returned and handed her the envelope, he said, "I figured out the trap."

"What trap, Harold?"

"The way you can tell whether I opened the pouch."

"Really? And how's that."

"Simple. I'm right-handed. So are you. So was the lady that got the pouch. But you both wound the string around the tab counter-clockwise as if you were left-handed. If I had opened it, I would have instinctively rewound it clockwise. That's how you'd know."

"You think you're pretty damn smart, don't you?" she said, making a note on the file in front of her and smiling.

He turned to return to his workstation.

She called after him, "Don't be spreading it around, Harold."

Getting a CIA security clearance included a polygraph test. Pool recruits knew about it and feared it. They called it, "sitting with Polly."

When Harold's day came to sit with Polly, he reported to an office where the machine was set up. The examiner explained the procedure.

"Harold, you'll be connected to these wires. They register changes in your body on this graph paper."

Fascinated, Harold examined the machine. The circuitry and mechanical parts interested him.

The examiner continued. "The questions need 'yes' or 'no' answers. Sit quietly and relax. I'll ask control questions. You are to intentionally lie on some of them. After that, we'll proceed with the real test."

The examiner taped several sensors on Harold's body and started the graph paper rolling. The needles moved up and down slightly. Then came the control questions.

"Is your name Harold Sands?"

"Yes."

"Are you eighteen years old?"

"Yes."

"Do you live in Virginia?"

"Yes." A lie. Harold had recently moved into D.C.

"Is your birthday in January?"

"No." True.

"Do you live in Virginia?"

"No." The examiner stopped for a moment and studied the graph paper.

When the real test began, Harold was to answer all questions truthfully. The test included questions about his personal life and history. Then the examiner asked about whether Harold had ever stolen anything, had a homosexual relationship even as a child, taken illegal drugs, or drunk to excess.

He asked about brushes with the law. Harold told him about the man who'd tried to molest him when he ran away from Staunton and the two cops who took him home and about the incident with the customer at the airport. The examiner framed yes/no questions about those events.

The last section addressed Harold's loyalty to his country and anything about him a blackmailer could use to gain secrets.

The test took two hours. Harold was exhausted when he left.

No one ever told him how he did on the test. For a week, they gave him a battery of tests to measure his intelligence, interests, and personality. Then he settled in to mindless clerical duties.

One day his supervisor called him in and said, "Congratulations, Harold. Your Top Secret clearance is in. We have your first assignment."

"What'll I be doing?"

"You'll be a computer programmer after you take classes. At least for now."

A computer programmer for now. Harold didn't even know what a computer programmer was. He hoped it was something a guy could do alone.

Chapter 14

It was a typical late summer morning in Washington D.C., muggy and hot with no air moving and the threat of afternoon thunderstorms. When Mac arrived at his office at CIA Headquarters, the first thing he did was crank up the undersized window air conditioner and start the huge floor fan moving the heavy air around the room. Next, the obligatory jacket and tie came off. Then he sat at his desk where a package waited for him. The Top Secret cover sheet said it had been routed to him from Bert Allison. A note clipped to the cover sheet said:

Mac, I got the attached memo from Emma at the Pool. The kid's file is enclosed. FYI.

Mac opened the package. It contained a typed memo addressed to Allison and the personnel file of a recent agency recruit. Mac read the memo:

We have a new employee about to join the Agency. His name is Harold Sands. He's only 18, but we believe him to be a person with potential for a Company assignment in three years.

Attached are his test scores. Pay particular attention to the test question results during the polygraph examination.

Mac leafed through Harold Sands's documents and was astonished at what he found. The kid had far and away more skills than the typical eighteen-year-old recruit fresh out of high school. His potential reminded Mac of Snuffy when they were younger, same eclectic interest in his environment and similar proficiencies and aptitudes.

The boy's psych profile interested Mac as much as his other attributes. It defined a loner who preferred solo activities without close attachments to other people. Just like Mac.

The small head shot of Harold grabbed Mac's attention. A handsome young man with a dark and penetrating stare and thick wavy hair, Harold's young face looked out at Mac from a long time ago.

He checked the file to see how Harold had been recruited and was pleasantly surprised to see Millie's name on the form. She was listed in the agency directory so he dialed her number.

"Hello," said the voice from years before. Apparently she wasn't onsite. She didn't answer with her extension number.

"Millie, this is Mac."

"Mac! I'll be goddamned. Hold on."

He heard the phone hit the desk, shuffling around, and a door close.

"Where are you?" she said.

"Headquarters. Riding a desk." He hated admitting that, but what else could he say?

"Out of the cold?"

"Warm and toasty." He settled back in his chair and stared at the wall. It was good talking to Millie after all this time.

"Me too," she said. "The field got too exciting for me."

The bushy eyebrows went up. "I doubt that. Tell me about Harold Sands."

"Harold? Great kid. Smart. Has a dark side."

"Like what?"

"A bit of a temper. Do you have his file?"

Mac shuffled through the papers in the folder. "Yeah, right here."

"Did you see the part about fighting?"

Mac leafed through the pages. "Yeah, so what? Boys get into fights."

"What it doesn't say is he had what ought to have been a couple schoolyard scraps and damn near killed the other boys."

That caught Mac's attention. Add fighting skills to a willingness to fight, and you have an assassin in the making.

"Do you know anything about his birth parents?"

"No. That was all sealed by the state. His mother gave him up when he was a small boy is all I know, and there's no record of a father, but I did notice the last name. Is that why you're asking?"

"Partly. Mainly because of his potential."

"You could probably find out all about him if you tried. I don't have those resources."

Mac closed the folder and gazed at the dingy ceiling tiles. "You been well, Millie? Happy in your work?"

"Ecstatic. Call again, Mac. I'd like to see you and get caught up. Maybe for a drink."

"Yeah. We had good times in—where was it—Paris?"

"Close enough. See you."

Mac put a note in the file saying the Company should keep a watchful eye on Harold Sands for the next three years and perhaps recruit him to the covert side when he came of age.

Chapter 15

When he completed the programming classes, Harold reported to a computer lab in a row of temporary frame buildings east of the Lincoln Memorial along the south edge of the Reflecting Pool.

When he wasn't at work, he spent time in the library. When he had a few spare bucks, he'd go to the airport and take a flying lesson. He missed having Mom and Pop there. It didn't feel right with strangers running the airport.

Then his life changed. The day Harold met Dottie Mills, she was sitting across from him at a conference table during a department indoctrination lecture. He ignored the lecturer and gazed instead at this pretty young woman with the brown hair whose name he didn't know. He could see her from the waist up only. The table blocked his view of the rest of her, but he liked what he saw. He tried to take a look at her left hand to see if she was engaged or married, but she kept her hands folded in her lap under the table. She avoided eye contact too and seemed to be engrossed in the boring lecture. That didn't stop him from looking at her, though.

When they took a break, she stood to go for coffee. She was about five-foot-three and had a nice walk. He still couldn't see her left hand.

But the view from behind was terrific.

He followed her into the coffee room, and her hands were in view. She wore no rings on her left hand.

"Buy you a cup of coffee?"

"The coffee is free." Her voice was reserved and cautious.

"Give you a cup of coffee?" That made her laugh.

When they returned to the lecture, he sat next to her. She slipped her shoes off under the table. Even her feet were pretty.

When the lecture was over, he walked with her to her office.

"Would you like to go out with me sometime?"

She seemed reluctant. "We've only just met. I don't know anything about you."

"How much safer could you be?" he asked in mock surprise. "This is CIA. We don't hire child molesters, purse snatchers, and second-story men. Just spooks. And this spook has just met the prettiest girl in seven states and wants to take her out."

"Seven states? How many states have you been in?"

"Six." That made her giggle.

They went out the following Friday to a movie. Afterward, he bought burgers at the Mighty Mo drive-in, then took her to Pete's, a small pub in Foggy Bottom where Agency personnel hung out. She talked and he listened.

"Well, for starters, I come from a small town. My parents wanted me to go to college, but I wanted to come out on my own and make enough that I could attend school without having to work at a job at the same time. How about you?"

"No family," he said. "I'm an orphan."

"Oh, that's sad. Where'd you grow up?"

"Nearby. Orphanages. Foster care. It's not all that sad when it's all you know. So, did you leave a string of broken hearts when you left home?"

"Only about two dozen." She sipped her beer and watched him across the rim of her glass.

Harold smiled and said, "Anybody special?"

"They were all special. Just none special enough. Do you play chess?"

"I know the moves, but that's about it."

"We'll have to have a game sometime. I was in the chess club. I bet I can beat you. Are you a Democrat or a Republican?"

"I don't know." He didn't know because he'd never given it any thought. Mom and Pop had been Republicans, but they'd never tried to influence him one way or the other.

"I'm a Democrat," Dottie said. "I love Senator Kennedy. He's smart and handsome. And such a beautiful wife. I bet he's president someday. Do you plan to go to college?"

"I hope to."

She talked and talked. She asked questions about him, and he kept his answers brief and sometimes just smiled and didn't answer. When they left the bar, he knew all about her, her family, her home town, her friends, and her interests, hopes, and plans. But he hadn't talked much about himself.

As they drove to her boarding house, she said, "I've been doing all the talking. You know all about me. But you haven't said anything about yourself."

"I'm a good listener," he said.

They spent time together at work when they could and sometimes in the evenings. They often had lunch together, and he drove her home when he didn't have plans. Sometimes she'd ask him up, but he couldn't stay past ten. Boarding house rules. Other times they'd drive to his rooming house and hang out in the common area to watch TV or play chess. She had been right. She won every game.

"You're letting me win," she said after a three-move checkmate.

"No. I told you I don't play very well."

"Well, maybe I can give you lessons. You can't go through life being that bad at chess."

He enjoyed Dottie's companionship. She put up with his quiet nature and could draw him out when she needed him. They went out every week or two, usually to a movie. They'd stop afterward for something to eat, then often to a dark, smoky basement lounge with checkered tablecloths, candles in wine bottles, and a honky-tonk piano player. Other times they'd go to Benny's and listen to rock and roll.

Dottie gradually wore down his resolve to never be close enough to anyone to care about them. But only her. He was still careful to avoid making or accepting casual attachments with other people.

Women found Harold attractive, so when they walked together, Dottie held his hand or clung to his arm as if to let the world know, "He's mine; hands off." He didn't mind. He liked having her close.

They often went to the "submarine races," local slang for lovers' parking along the banks of the Potomac. They couldn't take their new love affair to the proverbial next level, however, because both rooming houses had strict rules about visitors.

Dottie had said emphatically, "My first time will not be in a car," an attitude Harold reluctantly respected. "And we're not going to a motel, either," she added.

With a permanent job and a steady paycheck, he found an apartment in Virginia across the river from work, which eliminated Dottie's objections. She was as happy about it as he was.

Dottie had insisted that when and if they made love, they would have to use condoms. Harold had never bought condoms. They had called them "rubbers" in high school. The only other name they used was "prophylactics."

He went to a small drug store and milled around until no customers were nearby. Then he moved up to the counter and nervously said in a low voice to the clerk, "Pack of prophylactics, please."

The clerk, an older fellow, was discreet. He leaned over and said, almost in a whisper, "Any particular brand?"

Harold said just as quietly, "Trojans," which was the only brand he'd ever heard of.

He looked around the store. The other customers paid no attention to the nervous, self-conscious young man.

"Pack of two, or pack of five?" whispered the clerk.

Harold wasn't sure. "Five, I guess."

"Yes, sir, just a minute," said the clerk in the same soft, private tone.

Then he raised his head and yelled loud enough to be heard throughout the store, "Hey, Doc! Where do we keep the rubbers?" Muffled laughter sounded from all around.

Harold, red-faced, completed the purchase and left.

Their first evening together had the usual problems new lovers have. Eventually, however, it all came together, and by their second and third times, they were veteran lovers.

Afterward he said, "Now can we do it in the car?" which made her laugh.

According to Dottie, they were a couple in a committed relationship. One night she asked him, "Are we a couple?"

"I don't know. A couple is two. There's two of us. Unless you're pregnant."

"No, silly, not that. You know what I mean."

He just smiled and let it drop, and she didn't push it any further.

Chapter 16

The next two-plus years saw changes in the lives of Harold and Dottie as they moved along with their careers and their relationship. Harold's job as a programmer was interesting and fulfilling, and Dottie became the administrative assistant to a deputy division chief.

They didn't discuss work. "Need to know" was the Agency's internal motto, and neither of them had a need to know about the work of the other.

It was mid-January, 1961, and Harold and Dottie had lunch together in the cafeteria as they often did. "You going to the inauguration?" she asked.

"Are you?"

"Wouldn't miss it. Come with me. Did you hear what Eisenhower said?"

"What?"

"There's a 'military-industrial complex,' and we ought to be worried about it. Defense contractors taking over the government."

He scoffed at the idea. "Don't worry, Dottie, they aren't taking the Agency over. I'd worry less about what our friends do and more about our enemies. Cuba, for example."

"Well, that too, but you ought to be mindful of what's going on here as well."

The day before the inauguration, a huge snowstorm dumped eight inches of snow on the D.C. area. The next day, the snowfall had stopped, but the side streets weren't cleared yet. Harold and Dottie trudged down snow-covered sidewalks to the Capitol Building to watch the inauguration.

After the swearing-in ceremony, they found a spot among the spectators lining Pennsylvania Avenue to watch the processional from the Capitol to the White House. Harold was impressed with the level of security the president had. Secret Service agents were posted all over the place. They were easy to spot. Dark suits and topcoats, sunglasses, and walkie-talkies.

As the motorcade passed where they stood, Dottie joined in with other proud spectators who whistled and cheered as the new president rode by, waving at everyone.

The inauguration would mark the first of four times Harold would see the president in person.

Dottie seemed proud of their new president, young and vital and with a young wife and beautiful children. Kennedy's "New Frontier" was of and for the younger generation. Harold silently reserved his approval until after he could see the president in action.

Later that evening Harold and Dottie roamed the streets, sloshing through the snow, stopping in bars, joining in the festivities, and enjoying the celebrations. She was caught up in the youthful fervor that embraced the town, and her enthusiasm was contagious. It was truly the dawn of a new era.

They sat at a bar in Georgetown, drinking beer and watching TV coverage of the inaugural balls.

"You know what's exciting about today?" Dottie asked.

"What?"

She took a sip of beer. "Old guys aren't running the country anymore."

"There's still plenty of them around. Congress, that military-industrial complex, the bosses at the Agency..."

"I mean in the White House, honey. We'll be seeing more people our age in the news after this."

They drank up and left to continue bar-hopping. As they plodded through the snow down Wisconsin Avenue, a motorcade of limousines with a motorcycle police escort drove by, inching its way through the snow.

Dottie strained to see who was in the limo.

"Look," she said. "It's President Kennedy and Jackie. Wow!"

She jumped up and down and waved at the new president, who rolled down the window and waved to his pedestrian admirers.

"Look, Harold, he's waving at us. Hi, Mr. President!"

"He shouldn't travel out in the open like that," Harold said. "There's a lot of nuts out here, and some of them have guns."

That was the second time Harold would see President Kennedy in person.

Chapter 17

Snuffy Wheeler led the squad of South Vietnamese soldiers down an overgrown jungle path thirty kilometers south of Saigon. A murky swamp stretched out to his left, and thick brush and trees clustered together on the right. The aroma of red hibiscus blooms and the squawks and chirps of various species of jungle birds marked this region and were familiar to Snuffy. It was hot, which was typical for South Vietnam in the winter. A mist rising off the swamp made it sticky too. Altogether an uncomfortable day in the jungle.

He wished he could go home and be with Barb. Danny was fourteen now and needed a father around. At least he had Mac, but Snuffy wasn't sure whether Mac was the right role model for a teenage boy. Couldn't be helped. Snuffy's work was important, and he didn't know another way to earn a living. The pay as a CIA consultant wasn't great, but it was steady. His skills had taken him around the globe doing odd jobs in the intelligence business in strange and exotic places. He freelanced for private clients occasionally, but most of his work was for CIA. Whenever they needed a special solution, Snuffy was their man.

CIA had sent him to Vietnam to train ARVN snipers for jungle duty, and today he was pushing a reluctant squad of young soldiers through the steamy hot swamps and plush green overgrowth.

Snuffy was known among his contemporaries as a number one operative who got the job done no matter what it entailed. The younger guys always deferred to him and told him he was a legend in intelligence circles. Today he was mostly just hot, sweaty, and swatting mosquitoes.

He barked orders at the troops, but they ignored him. His khaki shirt with no insignia, blue jeans, and field boots identified him as a civilian with no authority. He was training the reluctant squad for their war against the Viet Cong, and today was the camouflage field test.

"Come on, goddammit, keep moving!" he shouted as he double-timed alongside the column. His translator Hien echoed his instructions in Vietnamese, and the soldiers ignored him too. Hien was sixteen and the lowest rank in the South Vietnamese Army, so most of the soldiers outranked him. Hien was dedicated to his job, however, and he stayed close to *Lahn tu* Snuffy so he wouldn't miss anything Snuffy said.

The soldiers plodded along at their own pace, weighed down by their packs and M14 rifles. Snuffy could tell they didn't want to be there any more than he did. Didn't matter. Another day, another few bucks in his account.

Snuffy halted the troop movement at the edge of a long, wide field of waist-high grass.

"Okay, guys, form up into two-man teams. You'll take turns being sniper and spotter." He paused for Hien to translate and for the soldiers to pair off. "Head into those woods, get enough branches and foliage to cover your sorry asses, and then come back here. Move! Now!"

The group dropped their packs and rifles on the ground, dispersed, and disappeared into a nearby patch of woods. When they returned with what they'd gathered, Snuffy showed them how to paint their faces with brown and green camouflage makeup.

"The idea is to disappear into your environment. Your face shouldn't look like a face, and it should blend with the leaves and shadows."

Hien struggled to keep up with Snuffy's fast-paced directions. "Slow down, *Lahn tu* Snuffy. Cannot listen and interpret at same time."

"Sorry, Hien." Snuffy liked his loyal interpreter who was also his unofficial aide. Hien was never far from Snuffy's side.

Snuffy showed the soldiers how to apply the makeup, and they smeared the base color on their faces and hands and painted themselves with dabs of secondary colors.

When they were all painted, Snuffy showed them how to wrap themselves in branches and leaves to further disappear into the trees and bushes.

"Now," he said. "Everybody out into the field. Take your rifles, walkie-talkies, and binoculars and crouch out there in firing position facing this way. Don't move a muscle. If all you can find is grass, become a bush. In ten minutes, I'm coming to find you. Anyone I can't find, beer is on me tonight in the canteen."

Snuffy checked his watch and shouted, "Go!" He turned his back and listened to the trainees hustle through the brush. Tomorrow he'd teach them to move without making a sound. He walked away to the edge of the woods to claim a starting point for his search.

The field covered several acres. If they did a proper job of concealment, Snuffy would be buying a lot of beer tonight. He hoped so.

When he reached the edge of the woods, he turned and stopped. He shifted his weight and stepped on a hard place that felt like a tree root. It gave as his weight pressed it down.

He didn't hear the explosion. He heard only Hien screaming, "*Lahn tu* Snuffy!*" and running toward him. He felt the warmth of his own blood on the lower part of his body and saw the bright red discoloration of his blue jeans as his legs flew out from under him, and he fell to the ground. He could smell the discharged explosive, but he felt no pain. Then everything went blank.

Headquarters had moved to Langley. Mac sat at his new office in the shiny new facility and plowed through the endless pile of paperwork associated with being a handler. He didn't care for this part of the business: the office, red tape, bureaucracy, and politics.

He did, however, like the extended trips to the Farm where he trained teams of recruits on the finer points of espionage. He got a kick out of watching young people as they learned and grew. He considered it his sacred duty to turn out fledgling operatives who had the skill and determination to complete missions and stay alive. When Mac kicked them out of the nest, he wanted them ready to fly.

But today he was at Headquarters. riding a desk, moving paper around, and oiling the gears of a huge bureaucracy. Just when he was near the bottom of the pile, another pile came in through the door. It never ended.

Bert Allison surprised Mac when he strolled into Mac's office and closed the door. Bert had been transferred stateside shortly after Mac, and now they were both posted at Langley. This was an unprecedented visit. Usually, when Bert wanted to talk, he summoned Mac to the ivory towers. Something was up.

Bert pulled up a chair and sat across from Mac. "Bad news, Mac." He took his time, and Mac waited. No point in hurrying bad news. Then Bert continued. "Snuffy got hit in 'Nam."

"Hit? How?"

"Stepped on a mine. He survived the blast, but it's touch and go for a while. They don't think he'll walk again."

Mac rolled his chair back. "Holy shit! What's the Company doing for him?"

"He's in an Army hospital in Saigon. If he makes it, they'll bring him home. After that, he's on his own."

"Jesus, Bert, the guy took one for the Company. Isn't there some kind of fund?"

"We paid him for his services, Mac, and he knew the risks."

Mac had heard this line before when operatives bought it in the line of duty. The Company always weaseled out of any responsibility. Mac was glad he didn't have family. "Snuffy never once went rogue," he said. "Goddamn, Bert. He's got a wife and kid. Can't you do anything?"

"No. Sorry." Bert stood to leave. Then he turned to Mac. "I was wondering. Since he wasn't on the books, we have to keep arm's length distance. Someone should let his wife know. Can you do that?"

"Sure, Bert, I'll do your fucking dirty laundry. Maybe you can dedicate the next football pool to his benefit."

Bert didn't seem to take offense. "Can't even do that. As far as the Company's concerned, he doesn't exist."

Bert left the office, and Mac shoved the paperwork aside, sat quietly, and prepared himself for the unpleasant task ahead.

He drove from Langley to his apartment building. Instead of going up the stairs, he knocked on Barb's door, number three. She'd be home. Her night shift didn't start until later. She opened the door and looked at Mac standing there.

His face gave it away. "Mac, what is it? It's Snuffy, isn't it? What's happened? Where is he?"

Mac put his hands on her shoulders. "He got hurt, Barb. He'll be home as soon as he can travel."

"Hurt? How bad?"

"They don't know if he'll walk again."

"Oh, no! No!"

She started sobbing, and the two of them stood together in the doorway, Mac holding her tightly while she pressed her face to his shoulder.

She pulled her head back. Her face and Mac's shirt were wet with her tears, but she was under control now. They went into the living room and sat on the sofa.

"What do I tell Danny, Mac? What do I tell people? I don't even know where he is."

"Accident on the job, Barb. Not much else you can say."

"Say? It's all I know."

She started crying again. Mac sat and held her for a long while.

They brought Snuffy home a week later. His legs were bandaged, and he rode in a government-issue wheelchair. Mac helped him from the car into his apartment. They lugged him onto the couch, feet propped up.

"He wasn't ready to travel," Barb said to Mac as she examined his bandages. "Why'd they send him home in this shape?"

"I'm not active duty," Snuffy said, "so they didn't think they had to treat me."

"We'll get you to a VA doctor right away," Barb said.

"Oh, great. Those guys are all thumbs." He looked around at the humble surroundings. "Jesus, Mac. How am I going to make a living?"

"We'll figure something out, Snuffy. First get yourself well. Then, who knows? You haven't lost all your skills. There's clients out there. I can find them until you get on your..."

Snuffy laughed. Then he said, "I don't have the equipment, Mac. The Company always provided all that. That shit's expensive."

"Make a list," Mac said. "Whatever you need, I'll get."

"You got that kind of money?"

"Money? Who said anything about money? The Company's going to provide whatever you need."

"No shit, Mac. Midnight requisition?"

If anybody could find equipment laying around unguarded at night, Mac could.

"Some."

"How'll you get it out?"

"The headquarters mail room. I'll ship it to you parcel post."

Snuffy bent over laughing and almost fell off the couch.

"Plus my next mission will definitely have a bloated budget for informants, assets, whatever. They won't miss a couple K one way or the other. Fuck 'em. If they won't help you directly, they can do it indirectly. Piss me off..."

"Think you can requisition me some morphine too?"

Barb frowned at Snuffy, but Mac laughed. "Whatever you need, pal. Say the word."

"Where am I going to set up this equipment?" Snuffy asked.

Barb adjusted his pillows. "Don't worry, sweetie. You can have Danny's room. He can have the sofa. At least until we can afford something bigger. Whatever won't fit in his room can spill out here. We'll make it work."

Mac looked at Barb and saw the affection in her eyes for her wounded, broken husband. She was one in a million, and Snuffy was lucky to have her.

He wondered what would become of him if he was ever disabled on a mission. He hoped he wouldn't have to find out.

Chapter 18

Two weeks after the inauguration, Harold's supervisor sent him to an office at Langley. Harold drove across Memorial Bridge, up the parkway to the entrance ramp of the new headquarters, his first time there. He parked, entered the building and went to the office they'd told him to visit. A middle-aged man at the desk in the office greeted him.

"Sit down, Mr. Sands. I'm Bert Allison. Thank you for coming. I want to discuss a new assignment."

"What kind of assignment?"

"You'll transfer into the Company and enter training to be a field agent."

"A spy?"

"You would become one of our operatives."

Harold enjoyed computer programming, but the idea of being a spy fascinated him.

"What made you ask for me?"

"Your potential."

Harold didn't know exactly what that meant, but he wasn't going to argue with it.

"What do I have to do?"

"Come here Monday for a briefing and to fill out some paperwork. Then you'll go to the Farm. You'll be the youngest trainee there, but don't let that intimidate you. You'll do fine. Here's a document that describes your cover. Sit over there, memorize it, and put it in a burn bag."

Harold was excited. He'd have a cover. That was the real thing. He read the document. To the outside world he would still be a computer programmer with a small firm in Washington. He memorized the details and tossed the document into a burn bag next to his chair.

Monday morning found Harold sitting in a conference room with a long table and an easel at the back with briefing charts. Several other people sat around the table, all of them a bit older than Harold. Most of them drank coffee and smoked cigarettes. Harold poured himself a cup and took a seat.

No one seemed to know anyone else, so there wasn't much conversation. After about five minutes, Allison came in and stood next to the easel.

"I'm Bert Allison. Many of you know me. Most of you come from within the Agency." He looked around the table. "I see a few former military and one former FBI who made the wise decision to cross over to where the real intelligence work is done."

Everyone laughed at Allison's comment.

He flipped to the first page of the briefing charts and recited a detailed history of US intelligence operations.

They broke for lunch, and when they returned, a new chart explained CIA's covert operations organizational structure. Alison briefed them on that.

One of the women raised her hand. "Mr. Allison, what are sanctions?"

"When an individual is creating trouble, getting in the way, and compromising our mission, we put a sanction on him and eliminate the problem one way or another."

Harold raised his hand. "It says 'Foreign Intervention.' What's that?"

"When we influence or interfere with the operation of other governments. We've got one of them—a big one—in the works now, and some of you will probably be involved."

"Is there anything we can do to prepare now for such an assignment?" Harold asked.

Allison smiled. "Sure. Brush up on your Spanish and stock up on suntan lotion."

The group laughed.

Allison flipped the page. The next page had only two words. It said, "Deep cover." This got Harold's attention.

Allison continued. "Deep cover means only you, your handler, and those working on the same mission know what you're doing. To the rest of the Company, you don't exist. This is sometimes called being 'out in the cold.'"

The next page said only, "Rogue agent."

"A rogue agent is a former CIA operative who works freelance but not for us. He's a potential threat. You don't want to go rogue on us. If you want to resign, do so, but find a different line of work. Most rogue agents are rogues because they were—"

Then he turned to the final page, which said, "Burned."

"Burned is what we do if we no longer wish to retain your services for any reason. You're out, and we don't know you."

They sat in silence and considered what Allison had just said.

"Okay, gang, come back tomorrow morning and we'll discuss our past missions and some others still in planning. Do not discuss any of what you learn here anywhere on the outside."

Two days after the briefing at headquarters, Harold drove to the Farm, situated on a nine thousand acre military base in Virginia. He drove to the gate, slowed to a stop, and showed his pass to the guard.

He found his barracks, went in, chose a bunk, and dropped off his things, after which he went to an indoctrination in another building.

At the session, Harold met again his fellow trainees from Langley along with several others he hadn't met. At twenty, he was younger than the other trainees, and Allison had been right. It was kind of intimidating being the kid in a room of older and possibly more experienced trainees. Everyone sat in folding chairs in a long room with a podium at one end. A middle-aged fellow took the podium and addressed the group.

"Ladies and gentlemen, you are here for your initial training to work as operatives in the field. Think 'boot camp.'"

He leaned forward on the podium and lowered his voice.

"You will learn here the basics of covert operations. These classes are introductory. You won't become experts. You'll learn enough to get started and maybe keep from getting yourselves killed."

He paused for what seemed to be dramatic effect.

"Everyone here winds up scattered to the corners of the world under cover, deep or shallow. You might never see one another again. If you do, do not openly acknowledge any former relationship."

He took another pause and looked directly at each of them, one at a time.

"Take the rest of the day and explore. Learn how to find your way around. Make sure you can find your barracks and the mess hall and where to take a piss. If you master those three skills, you might just graduate. Get to bed early. The hard part starts tomorrow."

Everyone at the Farm had a nickname. You didn't choose your nickname. Your colleagues did. They named Harold *Sandman* because his last name was Sands and because he went to bed early.

Training at the Farm involved long hours, intense classes, total immersion study, and physical conditioning. In a short time, Harold learned electronic surveillance, special weapons, wiretapping, and hand-to-hand combat. He already knew the basics for much of it, but the Farm classes took everything to a new level.

Harold worried that forced combat simulations would ignite his inner rage, but it didn't. Facing off with an opponent on a wrestling mat didn't bother him.

The martial arts instructors taught a hand-to-hand technique named *Defendo*, with which you use an opponent's weight, center of gravity, leverage, and body pressure points against him. It disabled an opponent without injuring him.

The science behind Defendo interested Harold as much as its application did. He checked out anatomy and martial arts books and studied them in his spare time. Then he designed a more lethal application of Defendo principles.

He pitched the idea to his Defendo instructors and demonstrated on one of the other students.

"Get your opponent on the floor, flip him face down, put your knee in his back, and use your hand and opposite forearm to twist his head and break his neck."

His maneuver impressed the instructors, and they named it the *Sandman Snap* after Harold's nickname.

All except Spider, one of the instructors, an older guy with extensive field experience. Spider was a legend, good at all the bad stuff, hand to hand, weapons, explosives, poisons, and such. He had tattoos on both arms, and close-cropped hair. He had a field-worn tanned face and cold blue eyes.

Spider said, "That Sandman Snap bullshit won't work. A skilled opponent could use countermeasures to disable anyone trying to use it."

"Only if he knows it's coming," Harold said.

"A skilled combatant is ready for anything," Spider said.

Because of Spider's opposition, the instructors didn't teach the snap. Harold suppressed his disappointment, believing others could benefit from his invention, but at least he had it in his own arsenal.

One evening after classes, Spider approached Harold.

"Let's go in town for a beer, Sandman."

Harold was proud that Spider, the legendary black ops agent, wanted to spend time with him.

"I'll probably close the joint," Spider said. "You have to rise and shine. Separate cars."

They met at a small roadhouse in a town just north of the Farm and sat at the bar. A large burly fellow dressed like a biker came in and took a seat next to Harold. A few minutes later, the fellow jostled Harold. Then he said, "Watch what you're doing, asshole."

"Sorry. Didn't mean to get in the way."

"Well, you are in the way, runt. All you pricks from that Farm are in the way."

"Sure," Harold said, and turned away.

"Hey! Don't turn your back on me!"

"Mister, leave us alone." Harold's rage was coming on, and he tried to beat it down. "We're not bothering anybody,"

"You're bothering me!"

The bartender came over. "Sir, you'll have to leave. Go somewhere else to start trouble."

"Fuck you."

The bartender lifted his hands above the bar. He held a sawed-off shotgun, which he leveled directly at the guy. "Leave now, or I call the cops."

The guy chug-a-lugged his beer and stomped out of the place.

"A local?" Harold asked.

"Never saw him before."

Harold turned to Spider. "Weren't you going to help?"

"You're supposed to be able to take care of yourself."

"Think we've seen the last of him?"

"He'll be out there."

They downed their beers and went outside. Sure enough, the biker was in the parking lot. "We're not finished," he said. He pulled a hunting knife and lunged at Harold. They had just practiced throws and holds for when an opponent pulls a knife. Harold flipped him over. Spider leaned against his beat-up old Chrysler, lit a cigarette, and watched. The two men tussled on the ground, and the biker almost stabbed Harold. The rage kicked in, and when Harold had the biker down, he put a knee in his back and did the Sandman Snap. A loud cracking sound echoed across the parking lot, and the biker went limp.

"Shit!" Harold said as his control returned. The sound of the snap brought him out of it. He stood and looked down at the biker. "What do I do now?"

"You get the fuck out of here. I'll take care of this." Spider had a smirk on his face.

Harold left immediately. His hands trembled as he gripped the steering wheel and drove straight to the barracks. His bunk mates were asleep, which was good. They wouldn't see his distress, and he wouldn't have to answer questions about it.

He sat on his cot and played the incident over and over in his mind. He had killed a man. That would always be with him, would never go away, would follow him the rest of his life. Never mind that he was in a camp that trained assassins, never mind that he had defended himself against a knife-wielding redneck, the fact remained. He had killed a man.

He'd held the rage under wraps for a time, but the incident in the parking lot proved otherwise. The rage was still in there, waiting to erupt.

It took several hours for him to fall asleep.

The next day he looked in the newspapers and saw no reports of a body being found. Spider had probably disposed of it, but Spider wasn't at the Farm after that, and Harold couldn't ask him. Whatever Spider had done to quash the incident had worked because Harold never heard anything more about it.

From that fight, he learned that even when the rage was ignited, his technical skills were not impaired. He could still function in the most threatening and dangerous of situations. That should have eased his regrets about the incident, but it didn't.

Chapter 19

Not long after the fight, Harold started a new class on facility penetration and escape. On the first day, he entered the classroom and took a seat near the back. Several other recruits came in and took seats scattered around the room.

A man who looked to be in his early sixties came in and took his place at the front of the classroom.

"Hi, kids, I'm Mac," he said. He lit a cigarette and sat on the edge of the teacher's desk. "I'm retired from the field, and the bosses are letting me ride it out by baby-sitting."

Mac didn't look anything like the spies Harold had seen in the movies.

Mac continued. "So pay attention, boys and girls. This is where an operative learns to stay alive to carry out the mission, whatever that is."

He wrote on the chalkboard, "In and out."

"From time to time, you'll be required to go into a facility where you're not supposed to be. While you're in there, you'll have to penetrate locked rooms, cabinets, desks, safes, and like that. After that you'll have to get out. Let's start simple."

He opened the desk drawer, took several items out, and placed them on the desk. Then he pulled a pistol out of his hip pocket, put it in the drawer, took a key from among the items on the desk, and closed and locked the drawer.

He put the key in his pocket and said, "Anybody here think they can get that pistol out of there?"

Harold raised his hand. Mac looked at him.

"Anybody but you, kid."

Harold didn't understand why Mac wanted someone else to go first. No one else volunteered.

Mac pointed to Harold and said, "Okay, kid. Come on up."

Harold walked up to the desk.

"What's your name, kid?"

"Sandman."

"Okay Sandman. You think you can do it? Show me. Use anything you want from what's here on the desk. Let's see how long it takes you." He looked at his watch and said, "Go."

Harold selected a paper clip, a screwdriver, and pliers. He made a couple bends in the paper clip, shoved it and the screwdriver into the lock, jiggled them, and the lock turned. He opened the drawer and pulled out the pistol. The rest of the class applauded, and Harold grinned.

"Not bad, Sandman, But it took you half a minute to get that piece. How do you think you could go faster?"

"I'm not sure," Harold said. "I guess with practice..."

"And with preparation. Most of your time was spent bending that paperclip. But if you had one in your pocket already bent, you'd have had that piece in less than five seconds. It's all in the preparation. Let me demonstrate. Here's the key. Lock the pistol in there again."

Harold did, and Mac stood at the desk and said, "Look at your watch and say when I should start."

Harold looked at his watch and said, "Go."

Almost immediately, Mac said, "Bang." He had the pistol in his hand. The recruits applauded again.

"How'd you do that so fast?" Harold asked.

"Preparation, kid." He held up a second key. "Like a boy scout, be prepared."

When the laughter died down, Mac said. "Now, gang, I want you to learn how Harold picked that lock. Harold, you're the teacher. Show them how, and everybody practice. The piece is loaded. Try not to shoot each other. I'll be back later this afternoon."

The Farm was a secure facility, fenced in with barbed and electric wire and patrolled by armed guards and dogs. The gates stood as impenetrable barriers, in or out, well-guarded checkpoints.

Mac addressed the class. "Who knows the first rule of facility penetration?"

No one responded.

"Here it is. Getting out is more important than getting in. Keep that in mind at all times."

Several trainees wrote Mac's first rule in their notepads.

"Okay, people, here's the drill. You got to escape from this place. I'm turning you loose right after this. Your assignment is to bust out of here, go all the way into D.C., and call me to come get you. If I'm not here, call back. You have until tomorrow morning. You can go in teams or solo. Take whatever you need. Except for one thing. Leave your gate passes here on the desk. That's the hard part. Getting off this facility without being caught by the guards. Okay, get the hell out of here."

Rumor held that no one had ever succeeded with the exercise, and Harold was determined to be the first. While the others messed with disguises, counterfeit passes, bolt cutters, and tunnels, Harold waited for nightfall, went to the Farm's airstrip, stole an airplane, and flew toward Washington D.C., intending to land at National Airport.

Now came the hard part. Harold had never flown into a controlled airport alone. Control tower operators had their own language, and they expected pilots to follow procedures to the letter. Harold had ridden with Pop when he flew into National, but he'd never done it himself solo. He didn't even know the tower frequency, and there were no charts in the airplane. He circled over a suburb and wrestled with his newest self-inflicted problem. If he just landed without a clearance, there'd be hell to pay, and he might spend the night in the lockup.

He could hear his one allowed phone call. "Hey, Mac. I'm in D.C. In jail. Come get me."

Why hadn't he brought a sectional chart? His own charts were in his car back at the Farm. He'd been so proud of how clever he was. Now he'd screwed up everything.

He looked past the airport across the lights of the city and saw what might be his salvation, the flashing beacon at a small general aviation airport near the Maryland line. Harold remembered the airport from when he was taking lessons from Pop. It had no control tower, so he would not have to call in. He headed for the beacon, flew into the pattern, and landed.

He taxied to the ramp, tied down the airplane, took a cab into downtown, and called Mac from a phone booth.

"Hey, Mac, it's Sandman."

"Sandman? Where the hell are you?"

"Benny's."

"How'd you get there?"

"Flew."

"Way to go, kid. It'll take a couple hours."

"I'll be here listening to the rock and roll. I'll buy you a beer."

Later they sat together at a table, drank beer, and talked over the loud sounds of guitars and drums.

"What if one of the other recruits calls while you're out?" Harold asked.

"Don't know. Never happened."

Mac excused himself to make a phone call. When he returned, he said, "The Company pilot is pissed."

"How come?"

"He has to get somebody to drive him all the way up here so he can get the fucking airplane."

"Why didn't he ride up with you?"

Mac grinned. "I left before anyone noticed the plane was gone."

"Call him," Harold said. "Tell him I'll bring it back."

Mac laughed. "I don't think so. You made them look foolish. I doubt they'd let you lay hand one on that bird again."

They sat a while. Mac chain-smoked Camels, and they finished off a couple more beers each and listened to the band. After a while, Mac said, "That was some stunt, kid, some stunt. They'll be talking about this for years. When you graduate, you're on my team."

Chapter 20

Even before the escape incident, Mac had taken a close, personal interest in Harold's development as an operative. When Harold graduated, Mac recruited him for his team and became his handler.

Mac assigned Harold duties as an intelligence analyst, and he pored over documents from various sources: the agency, other intelligence organizations, financial reports, newspapers, anything that was on paper and current. His ability to take mental snapshots of charts, graphs, and facts and correlate them and draw conclusions made Harold a perfect intelligence analyst. The work held his interest, but Harold itched to be assigned to the field and see some action.

In April, after Harold had pestered him endlessly for a field assignment, Mac said to him, "Okay, kid. Pack your bags. You're going to Florida. Operation Zapata. Here's the battle plan." Mac handed him a document with a Top Secret cover sheet. "Read up on it before you go and leave it here." He handed him an envelope. "These are your orders. Open them when you arrive at the Miami Station."

According to the plan, the Company was engaged in a covert operation to invade Cuba and overthrow Castro by using expatriated Cuban exiles as its invasion force. Harold would be a part of that plan. He didn't know what his assignment would be, but he was excited.

He took a commercial flight from Washington to Miami. He retrieved his suitcase and walked out to the arrival ramp. A young man approached him.

"Señor Harold. I am to drive you to the South Campus."

He led Harold to a blue unmarked sedan in the parking lot, and they drove south from Miami. When they arrived, he dropped Harold off at the curb in front of a two-story frame building.

"What now?" Harold asked as he stepped out of the car.

The driver shrugged and drove off. Harold sat on a park bench and opened his orders. The envelope contained a pass with Harold's picture on it and a sheet of paper, which said:

Sam Montague, South Campus, Bldg 25.

The building in front of him had a shingle on the front that said "25." He went in the front entrance where an Air Force MP was standing guard. Harold showed his pass and said, "Mr. Montague, please."

"Second corridor on your left, third door on your right."

Harold followed the guard's directions. Room 14B had a sign in a framed slot beside the door:

Station Chief. Authorized Personnel Only

He tapped on the door, went in, and introduced himself to an Air Force private who sat at a desk just inside.

"I'm Harold Sands, reporting to Mr. Montague."

Before the private could answer, a man in civilian clothes stuck his head out of an office. "Harold," he said, "I'm Sam. Mac TWXed that you'd be coming down. My guys will get you set up." He turned to the private sitting at the desk. "Private, take Harold to the radio lab."

Harold still didn't know what his job would be. The private led him to a large room with workbenches, tool cases, and electronic test equipment, pointed out a desk, and said, "That's yours. Mr. Hunt, your supervisor, will be here later today. If you have any questions, ask him."

"Just out of curiosity, what's my job?"

"Shit, Harold, I don't know. Most days I don't know what my job is. Whatever they tell me to do, I do. Ask the supervisor." He grinned and made his exit.

Harold sat at his desk and with nothing else to do, he took a walkie-talkie maintenance manual from a bookcase and studied it.

After about an hour, a civilian in his forties came into the lab. "Harold," he said, "I'm Everette. I'm your supervisor."

"Good to meet you," Harold said and extended his hand. "What's my job?"

"You know about the operation?"

"Yes. But I don't know the Company's role in it."

"Your role is all you need to know. The invaders need radios. We provide the equipment, and most of it comes from military surplus. Your job is to get it tested and working. Some of it is over there against the wall. The rest will start pouring in soon. Except for meals, sleep, and to relieve yourself, you stay at that bench and work. With luck, we'll all be out of here in a few days."

Everette turned and left the lab, and Harold never saw him again.

Harold was disappointed. He'd wanted to see action, but instead he was stuck here in a windowless lab surrounded by junk that didn't work.

One by one he tested and repaired radios. As quick as the Air Force guys took them out, they'd bring in more. Harold worked eighteen-hour days and sometimes longer depending on the workload.

At least once a day, Montague stuck his head in the door and railed at Harold. "Come on, goddammit! We need those fucking radios. Step it up." The pressure was on, and Harold did his best to support the effort. He understood the op, and he empathized with the small number of exiles who themselves were in training to do the impossible. The least Harold could do was bust his ass so no man went into combat without the radio gear and support he needed.

When the invasion began, Harold monitored its progress on radios he'd fixed but that hadn't been deployed.

CIA had assumed the Cuban citizenry would rise up against Castro and overthrow the government. That didn't happen. Apparently the citizens weren't as anti-Castro as the exiles.

Harold heard it all go down. He listened with frustration while the invaders pleaded in Spanish for backup, reinforcements, air support, or any kind of help. One by one their transmissions went silent when the Cuban military captured and shot them. Every time he heard that, his heart sank.

After a few days, what would come to be known as the Bay of Pigs Invasion was over, an abysmal failure, hundreds of men on both sides dead or wounded, a major embarrassment for CIA and the president.

At the exit briefing, Sam Montague stood at the front of the room and addressed a group of disappointed Company operatives.

"We blew it, people. We'll probably be blamed. But it wasn't our fault. The invasion needed air support, and that chikenshit asshole we call a president bailed on us. God knows why. You'll all return to whatever you were doing before this. I hope I still have a job."

He stomped out of the room and slammed the door.

Harold's first field assignment had been a miserable failure, botched from higher up. He came away believing that what they were calling Camelot and the New Frontier didn't live up to their promise. Kennedy had let them down.

Harold had cautiously withheld his approval of Camelot and waited to see how Kennedy would perform when the chips were down. Now it seemed he had been right to wait.

Harold saw President Kennedy again in November in the dedication ceremony of the new Langley Headquarters building. In his address, Kennedy said:

How grateful we are in the government and in the country for the services that the personnel of this Agency render to the country. It is not always easy. Your successes are unheralded, your failures are trumpeted. I sometimes have that feeling myself. But I am sure you realize how important your work, how essential it is, and how, in the long sweep of history, how significant your efforts will be judged.

After the ceremony, Harold sat with Mac in the cafeteria.

"What did you think of the speech?" Harold asked.

Mac stirred his coffee. "About what I expected. Hollow words. He's already said he wants to dismantle the Agency. Egg on his face about operation Zapata, and nobody to blame but us. All that talk about what a great job we did is bullshit."

"If we did such a great job, why'd he fire Dulles?"

"Yeah, that pisses me off. Dulles was a spook in the trenches when Kennedy was making ca-ca in his silk diapers."

"How do you think the new DCI will do?"

"McCone? Loose lips and no experience. He couldn't carry Dulles's snuff box."

They sat and looked at their coffee for a while.

"You know, Mac, if you were president, who's the last people you'd want to piss off?"

"CIA."

"Just what I was thinking."

The dedication ceremony would be the third of four times Harold would see President Kennedy in person.

Mac had become not only Harold's handler but his friend and mentor too, and Harold was disappointed when Mac announced his retirement in August, 1962. But Mac had put in his time, done a lot for the Company, and needed a rest. He deserved it.

They threw a party for Mac at Pete's in Foggy Bottom. Management closed the bar to the public, and only CIA personnel were allowed in.

Mac got falling-down drunk. He danced with all the ladies, told jokes, and fed the jukebox. Everyone wanted him to make a farewell speech, and when they urged him to say something, anything at all, he climbed on a table, weaved around, held his drink high, and said as loud as he could, "Goddamn! This is fun! I'm going to retire again next week!" Then he fell off the table, breaking a chair on the way down. He sprawled on the floor and laughed, unable to get up, still holding his drink high, not a drop spilled.

Harold was surprised to see Miss Messick, his high school counselor, sitting at the bar, and he pulled up next to her.

"Remember me?" he said.

"Sure do. I guess it worked out for you."

He waved at the bartender for another beer and asked, "What do you know about me coming to the agency?"

"Nothing."

"Bullshit. All along I thought you were this compassionate angel of mercy looking out for the futures of helpless and hapless teenagers. But all the time you were a spook."

She laughed. "Mousey Messick," she said.

Later, Mac wobbled as he gripped the bar to stand next to her without falling. He whispered in her ear, and she shook her head and laughed.

When the party was over, Harold offered to drive Mac home.

"No, kid, just walk me outside."

A van waited at the curb. When Harold and Mac came out, a teenage boy came up to them and took Mac's keys. The boy turned, ran over to Mac's car, and drove away.

"How old is that kid," Harold asked, worrying about Mac's car.

"Thirty-seven," Mac said with difficulty and with a bubble forming at the corner of his lips.

With Harold propping him up, Mac staggered to the van and pulled himself into the passenger's side. A woman waited in the driver's seat. Harold couldn't see her in the dark.

He closed the door behind Mac. "This your family, Mac?"

"Yeah," Mac yelled out the window as the van pulled away. "She's my great-grandmother."

Harold went in the bar and looked for Miss Messick, but she had left too.

In October, Bert walked into the computer room where Harold was busily poring over listings of intelligence message traffic.

"Harold, we need you in the photo lab. Pronto."

"Must be important if they sent you," Harold said, meaning it as a joke. Allison didn't smile.

They went into the photo lab where multiple aerial photos of what looked like military installations were spread out on a large table. Several lab technicians and an analyst stood by. Harold looked closely at the photos.

"This what you want me to see?"

"Yes," Allison said, "what do you make of it?"

"High-altitude images. How'd we get these?"

"We have this airplane..." Bert said, referring to the U-2.

"Where were these taken?" Harold said.

"Never mind that just yet. I want an objective readout. What does it look like?"

Harold picked up a magnifying glass and went from photo to photo examining the images.

"This is Cuba," he said.

"How'd you know?"

"See right here? That's a missile launch site. Under construction. There's been reports of Russian cargo vessels going in and out of Havana the last month or two. No way they'd need that many shipments of potatoes and vodka."

"What reports?"

"Intelligence messages. From local assets in Cuba. It's been in my daily briefing notes. Look over here. More missile sites. So, is it Cuba?"

"It is. Thanks, Harold. Keep what you saw here close to your chest."

Things became busy at Langley. Everybody went on standby for the duration of what they called the Cuban Missile Crisis. There were no field assignments, though. Harold just stood by like everybody else and moved the rush of paperwork through his analysis processes.

Eight days after the discovery of the sites, the president addressed the nation and told them about the crisis. The country went nuts reacting to what everyone assumed would be all-out nuclear war.

Five days later, when Kennedy and Khrushchev had negotiated a settlement and the crisis was over, Harold walked into Bert's office and got right to the point.

"Have you given any thought to putting me in the field?"

"I have, but we still don't have an assignment that fits."

"How about if I just return to the Agency and write computer code?"

"That can't happen, Harold. We have too much invested in you. And they don't have any openings. Besides, we need you here doing what you're doing. This is where you belong. Just keep it up until we can find something that fits."

"That's not the way I see it." Harold had his resignation typed, signed, and dated. Now or never. It would be a field assignment, a transfer, or a timely departure. He handed the resignation to Bert. It had the usual two-week's notice. Bert read it and placed it on his desk without saying anything. As Harold left Bert's office, Bert was picking up the telephone. When Harold arrived at his desk, a man from Security was waiting for him.

"Come with me," the security guy said.

He escorted Harold to a conference room where a team of men debriefed him, which is to say they told him what he could and could not do on the outside with respect to what he knew about Company operations.

The security guy escorted Harold to his office and said, "Get all your personal effects, please."

Harold gathered his things: car keys, a pen, a handkerchief, a picture of Dottie, sunglasses, and a couple of books, and put them in his briefcase. The security guy watched him as if to make sure he didn't take anything that wasn't his. Getting the boot like this reminded Harold of Pop's brother at the airport, and he resented it.

"Let's go," the guy said and escorted him out of the building and to his car in the parking lot.

"I'll need your badge and parking permit."

Harold handed the credentials over, and, without a word, the guy turned and walked away.

I never even learned the name of the guy that burned me.

Chapter 21

A chilly March day in 1963, spring wouldn't poke her head in for at least a month, and patches of grimy crusted snow decorated lawns, streets, and parking lots. Harold worked as a computer programmer, a young man in a young occupation. The technical work appealed to him because it involved him, the computer, and nobody else.

On this morning, after a less-than-successful test session in the computer room, he took the stairs down to the second floor, walked to his office, and plopped down. A telephone message sat on his desk, prominently positioned where he couldn't miss it. His eyes opened wide when he read the message:

Mac called at 0900. He'll call again at 1030.

He looked at the office clock, took the printouts from his briefcase, and laid them out on his desk. But the telephone message pulled him away. What would Mac want?

Harold hadn't seen or heard from Mac since the retirement party. He looked at the clock again. Five minutes after ten. He passed the time poring over listings as he looked for reasons why his program had crashed. But he couldn't concentrate. He gave up and sat, watching the clock.

The phone rang at ten-thirty on the dot. The secretary in the next room answered it and called out, "Harold, line one." He picked up the receiver.

"Hey kid, what's up?" Harold would know that raspy voice anywhere.

"What's up with you, Mac? What brings you out of hiding?"

"I want to talk. You up for lunch?"

"Sure. There's a cafeteria here."

"I'll bring lunch. I'll pick you up. Walk up to that little shopping center a block north of you. I'll meet you in front of the movie theater. Is noon okay?"

Harold made it to the shopping center a few minutes before noon. He stood in front of the theater and looked around, waiting, eager to learn what Mac wanted. Mac pulled up in front of the theater at exactly noon. Harold climbed into the car, and they shook hands. Both men smiled. Harold was happy to see Mac, and Mac seemed glad to see him.

"I was parked around the corner watching," Mac said. "Making sure you weren't followed."

"You haven't changed."

"You got older."

Mac pulled his car out, made his way to the parkway, and headed north.

"We going to Langley?"

"No, just a quiet place to talk. I retired, remember?"

"One never knows."

Mac pulled into a small scenic-view parking area by the Potomac River. He reached in the back, retrieved a paper bag, took two deli sandwiches out, and handed one to Harold.

"What's up?" Harold said.

"Eat, kid. Take your time. When do you have to be back?"

"Whenever I get there."

They ate in silence. When Mac was finished, he took a Camel from a pack and offered one to Harold, who declined the smoke. Mac broke the silence.

"Why'd you quit the Company, kid?"

"It's a long story."

"I got all day."

Harold paused to look out the open window through a stand of tall pines and at the river flowing from the mountains to the west down to the Chesapeake Bay. The water spilled over rocks and half-submerged tree branches and formed whitecaps. A beer can floated by, hit a rock, and spun around to continue its journey to the bay. Harold wondered how far upstream it had joined the flow and who drank the beer.

"I got all that training," he said. "Then they stuck me at headquarters to shuffle paper. That's not what I signed up for. So I quit."

Harold rolled down the passenger-side window to let Mac's smoke out. Mac opened his window too. Mac paused to inhale a lung full of smoke. He blew it out the open window into the fresh air.

"You went to Florida in '61."

"And sat in a lab and fixed radios." Harold took the opportunity to vent his frustration with life at the Company, and he intended to say it all. "Why wasn't I sent in?"

"You were too young. Besides, that operation wasn't our pissing match."

"Well. I turned twenty-one. And still never got into the field. I sat at a desk with my thumb up my ass. Nobody could tell me why."

"I can. Maybe Allison should have, but that's not policy. So, here's why. Guys with your potential are a rare commodity. They couldn't put you at risk on small shit."

Harold laughed. "I thought this was supposed to be a risky business."

Mac's cigarette was down to his fingertips. He snuffed it out into the ashtray, which was already overflowing with butts. The car was chilly with both windows open, so Harold closed his. Mac lit another cigarette. Harold opened his window again.

"So, anyway, Mac, what brings you out of retirement?"

Mac looked outside the car and around the small parking lot. "Let's go sit on that bench."

They got out of the car and walked to a small concrete bench facing the river. The March air was cool, and a breeze blew down from upstream. Harold pulled his jacket around himself and sat.

Mac said, "Sorry about the cold. I never know when my car's been bugged. Don't take this wrong, kid. I got to frisk you."

"I'm not carrying."

"I know, but I need to be able to talk knowing only you can hear me."

Harold stood. He knew better than to argue with Mac. "Have at it."

Mac patted him down both sides, front and back.

"Better safe than sorry. Have a seat."

They sat on the bench and Mac started.

"Kid, I run a service organization. I broker security, espionage, and intelligence assets outside the government. I solve problems for folks who need special solutions and who can't do their own fixing."

Harold was interested. He sat on the edge of the bench and stared at Mac. "What kind of solutions?"

Mac watched the river flowing downstream. He tossed his cigarette butt to the ground, crushed it with his shoe, and lit another one.

"You name it. Industrial, trade secrets, breaking and entering, all that. Dirty tricks, discrediting someone, setting targets up for blackmail or extortion. And hits."

"And what does this mean to me?"

Mac looked at Harold and put his hand on Harold's forearm. "Kid, you're one of a half-dozen people I've known that I'd trust to do what we do."

"Who are they?" Harold asked.

Mac counted on his fingers. "One's a cripple. Can't do the field anymore. You'll meet him. The second one's a competitor, you might say. Ex-Company like us and a cold sumbitch. I hope you don't have to meet him. You're sitting next to old number three, and you're number four."

"You said a half-dozen. Who are the other two?"

"One's still with the company. We won't talk about her. The other got killed during a mission eight, nine years ago. Anyway, I want you to join my team. Just like before. What do you think?"

"Who do I have to kill?" Harold smiled at his own joke.

"It ain't funny, kid. If it ever comes to that, you won't be laughing."

Harold turned on the bench. "Sorry."

Mac went silent for a few seconds. Then he said, "You think you might want to come in with me?"

"I'd like to. But what do I have to do to get on board?"

"Quit your job. Can't have anybody noticing that every time something goes down you were on leave."

"What else?"

"Your girlfriend. I seem to recall that you were sweet on a little bird when we were at Langley."

Harold softened at the mention of Dottie. "Yes. That's Dottie. She works at the Agency."

Mac winced. "Can you ditch her without getting all weepy about it?"

"Why would I do that?"

"It's a necessary sacrifice, kid. Operatives have to live, work, and move around solo. Not many can do that and maintain a relationship. You know how dames are once they get their hooks in you. They cling like jellyfish, and you can't concentrate on the important shit. Plus if you piss them off, they'll blow your cover all over town just to get even. Hell hath no fury and all that shit."

"But you just said one of your most trusted colleagues is a female."

"I did? I guess I did. She's different. Not many like her. Believe me, kid, this is from experience. If you want into this line of work, you'll deep-six the girlfriend."

Harold hesitated. He didn't like the way this was going. But he could guess what Mac wanted to hear. He shifted around on the bench before he answered. "I suppose. Would I start work right away?"

"You start when I get you an assignment. That'll be whenever something comes up that suits your skills."

"How much do I get paid?"

"More money than you've ever seen as a card walloper. Are you interested?"

"Definitely. But one more question. Are we rogue agents?"

"No, although there are those who might disagree."

"Anything else I have to do?"

Mac sat back on the bench. He lit another Camel. "You need a new identity. New name, where you live, a different car. There's only one problem."

"What's that?"

"Your prints. When you joined the agency they took your finger-prints. The FBI keeps them on file."

Harold smiled. He knew what was coming, and he was ready.

"What have you done about that with your other assets?"

"So far nothing. I did all the high-profile stuff myself, the kind of shit you'll be doing."

"Just took the chance you wouldn't get caught and printed?"

"Not quite. A buddy of mine at the Bureau removed my fingerprint file." Mac looked from side to side the way people do when they are about to let you in on something. He lowered his voice. "He likes teenage girls, and I arranged one for him. Bought him a hooker. She was twenty-nine, but that chippie could look like a high school cheerleader when she wanted to. I told him she was my niece. She must have had the car bouncing at the drive-in. The old fart thought he was sixteen again."

They both laughed. Mac coughed, tossed his cigarette, and lit an-other one.

"He kept his end of the bargain. He stole my card from the Bureau's files and gave it to me. He kept asking about seeing her again. I told him she went into a convent. Then he wanted to know if she had a sister." Mac took a drag on his Camel and laughed until he coughed again. "But my prints aren't on file anywhere, now. Best fifty bucks I ever spent."

They both laughed at Mac's story. Harold didn't know whether to believe it. You never knew with Mac.

"But I don't go in the field anymore," Mac explained. "Work's pick-ing up, and I need to stay home and mind the store. Plus my age. My re-flexes aren't what they used to be. So, anyway, now we have to think about your prints."

"We got nothing to worry about."

Up went Mac's bushy eyebrows. "How's that?"

Harold explained how he'd persuaded Jamey to stand in for him at the fingerprint session.

"Well. let's hope Jamey-boy never does anything bad," Mac said. "His prints are on file next to your name."

Mac rummaged around in his jacket pocket and pulled out a bulging envelope. "Get started on the identity. In the meantime, take this money to live on. It's ten grand."

Harold stared at him. "Ten grand? I don't make that much in a year."

"I know. It's an advance, a loan. It'll hold you until the first assignment. Here's one more thing."

He handed Harold a slip of paper. "These are names, addresses, and phone numbers for my cover identities. Use them for references. Previous landlord, employers, and all that. Let's head back."

They returned to the car, and Mac drove to the shopping center. They didn't speak during the drive, and Harold watched the trees and houses go by.

Mac pulled up in front of the movie theater. Harold stepped out of the car, and Mac got out too, put his hands on Harold's shoulders, and said, "Change that identity and get new digs right away. Stay portable, able to pull out on short notice. If it doesn't fit in your car, get rid of it. Don't call attention to yourself. And don't become a regular at restaurants and bars. Or whorehouses. And don't go anywhere you used to go."

Mac grinned and climbed in the car. "Big things, kid, we're going to do big things." He waved and drove off.

Harold watched Mac drive away. Then he walked back to work, the envelope full of money bulging in his jacket pocket. His mind was filled with the events of the past hour and a half. And he wondered what the future held.

Chapter 22

Harold drove to the coal region of central-eastern Pennsylvania, situated about a five hour drive north, taking him through D.C. and Maryland and into Pennsylvania where he drove through the mountains to a scattering of small towns. He was impressed by the stark scarring of strip mines, some still in operation, others abandoned and left ugly and black where trees had been felled, the ground opened, and the coal hauled away.

He visited cemeteries and searched for tombstones of infants born in 1940, his own birth year. He scanned newspaper archives of editions published in the months surrounding his birth, reading obituaries and articles, looking for accounts of infants' deaths.

After visits to countless cemeteries and two area newspapers, Harold drove to a small town named Shenandoah and visited the offices of the Evening Herald.

A receptionist sat at a desk just inside the door. She was about twenty, with a bleached-blonde beehive hairdo that doubled the height of her head. She was busily filing her nails.

"Excuse me, miss. The morgue?" He used newspaper jargon for the archives of past editions. He had done this twice before and was learningthe lingo.

The receptionist looked up and smiled. "Down the hall, the morgue is," she said in a nasally Pennsylvania Dutch dialect. She cocked the beehive toward the hallway and returned to her nails.

The morgue was just like the others, a large room with a library table and chairs and a counter that ran the width of the room. Rows of shelves stood behind the counter. Stacks of yellowed newspapers populated the shelves. A woman of about sixty stood at the counter and looked like she'd been there forever.

"Can I help you?" she said.

"Yes, please. I'd like to see all the newspaper editions for 1940."

"Yes, sir. January, 1940 coming up. Have a seat at the table. It'll only take a minute."

She disappeared into the rows of shelves and returned with a stack of newspapers.

"Here you go," she said and dropped the stack on the table.

"These on microfilm?"

She laughed. "No, sonny, just what you see here. We ain't got the budget for microfilm."

She returned to her post behind the counter.

Harold set out a notebook and pencil and sorted through the newspapers. He scanned the front pages, the local news pages, and the obituaries. Each time he finished a stack, he called to the librarian, and she relieved him of the current stack and brought him another one.

The fifth of August had a promising obituary. An infant named James Raymond Dodson Jr. had died with his parents in an automobile accident on the second of August. The only surviving relative was the infant's paternal grandmother, Martha Ellen Dodson. The remains of all three victims had been cremated.

The librarian went into the back of the room behind the shelves. When she was out of sight, Harold removed the pages about the Dodson family from the two editions, folded them, and put them in his briefcase along with his notes. He returned the newspapers to the counter. The librarian sat in the back smoking a cigarette. He waved at her, and left, his mission accomplished. No one else would learn about the death of James Dodson Jr. in these archives.

Harold spent the next day at newspaper archives in neighboring towns, removing accounts of the death of James Raymond Dodson Jr.

The day after that, Harold drove to Harrisburg, Pennsylvania to the Bureau of Vital Statistics. He found the Birth Records office, and submitted a request for five copies of the birth certificate for James Raymond Dodson Jr., born the twelfth of July in 1940. They'd be ready later that day.

He walked down the hall to a door marked "Death Records," went in, and stood at the counter. A woman in her middle forties sat at a desk reading a magazine.

"Good morning, ma'am," he said. He'd worked out a ruse to access the death certificate files. Now he hoped it would work. "My grandmother lived in Shenandoah in the forties. She probably died a long time ago, but we didn't have much family and nobody knows for sure. I was raised in an orphanage and am trying to reconnect with whatever family I might have. If there's a way I can learn whether she has died, I can stop looking for her. Could we search the death records to see if she died? All I have is her name and last known address."

The clerk put her magazine on the desk and came to the counter. "Those records are filed by county and date of death. People wanting a death certificate usually know the exact date and location. For insurance and inheritance purposes, not just to find out if somebody's dead. They usually already know if somebody's dead. That's not something you don't usually already know."

Harold wanted to laugh, but he only smiled.

"I don't want to create extra work. I'm willing to look through the files myself."

"Well, no one is allowed back here." Harold made the sad face that usually melted older women. "But perhaps I could make an exception this time. You being an orphan and needing to find your family and all and maybe getting to meet your grandmother after all these years. If she's not dead, that is. Wouldn't that be nice?"

She led him through rows of filing cabinets. The aisles were narrow, and she pressed against him when she could.

"Are there copies of these records on microfilm?" he asked.

"No. They keep talking about doing that, but it's never in the budget. I hope they wait until after I retire. It'll be a mess. What you see here is all we have."

They came to a cabinet marked "Feb 1940 - Nov 1940."

"When you're done with this one, come get me, and I'll show you the next cabinet." She smiled at him and returned to her desk.

Harold opened a drawer filled with rows of death certificates. He thumbed his way through until he reached the second of August. Among the few deaths that day he found three certificates for the Dodson family. He removed the one for James Jr. and looked toward the front desk. She was deep into her magazine, so he folded the certificate and put it in his inside coat pocket.

Harold began his search for James Dodson's grandmother. He wanted the old girl to be long since dead. Sure enough, he found her in the cabinet for '57 through '59. He didn't need to steal this certificate, only to know she was dead and would not be around to complicate things. He left the rows of file cabinets and stopped at the desk.

"I found her," he said trying to look dejected. "She died in '58."

"I'm so sorry. But at least now you can stop looking."

After lunch, Harold returned, went to the cashier's window, and picked up the birth certificates. As he left the building, he gave a long sigh of relief. The rebirth of Jim Dodson was almost complete.

Harold had one more stop to make. The Library of Congress kept copies of all editions of all newspapers published in the USA. He drove into D.C. and went to the library's Main Reading Room. He asked for copies of the newspapers and removed the relevant pages. Then he went home.

Harold called Mac to give him his new name. A woman answered, "MacAssets."

"Is Mac there?"

"Who's calling?"

"Who is this?"

"I'm Barb. I work for Mac."

"Tell him it's the kid."

"Oh, yes. Do you have a name for us?"

This lady seemed to know things. "My name is James Dodson."

"Got it. Just so we know, what do we call you? James? Jim? Jimmy? Jimbo?" She laughed.

"It's Jim. Tell Mac to just call me 'kid' like always."

"Okay, kid." There was a smile in her voice. "We'll talk to you later."

Harold needed a new residence and found a one-bedroom, second-floor, furnished apartment in a small community twenty miles south of D.C.

The next step was the hardest. On his last day at work, Harold called Dottie and gave her the news.

"Dottie, I'm going away for a while. I don't know for how long."

Dottie seemed shaken by this news. "Where are you going, Harold?"

"I can't say just now. It's work-related. A project that needs people with my clearances and skills. I'll miss you."

"Just like that? No notice, no last date, no nothing?"

"I'm sorry. There isn't time. I'm leaving this afternoon. It's been in the planning for a couple weeks, but I wasn't allowed to say anything. I'll see you when I get back."

"Maybe, maybe not," she said curtly. "Goodbye, Harold. Good luck." She hung up.

She was pissed, no doubt about that. He didn't like doing it that way; Dottie deserved better treatment. She'd do okay without him, but he had feelings too, and giving up Dottie wasn't easy.

He spent the next day getting a Social Security card and driver's license. He decided that he would not register for the draft. The Company had arranged a deferment for him while he was employed there. No longer deferred, he was ripe to be called up. He didn't want to be drafted as Jim Dodson. Let them try to draft Harold Sands instead.

At his new digs, he put all of Harold's credentials and papers in a small cardboard box. He took the box to a bank, rented a safe deposit box, and stored it there. Then he opened a checking account in the name Jim Dodson and deposited most of what was left from Mac's cash advance.

Now for the car. His two-year-old Ford was a nondescript family sedan with a high-performance power train. He paid off the loan and sold it to himself. And more traces of Harold Sands disappeared.

He drove into D.C., went to the Passport Office, and applied for a passport.

With his new documents in place, Harold Sands was little more than a stack of papers in a safe deposit box, and Jim Dodson would be ready to start work.

There was one more loose end that might never be tied. He still existed in Dottie's memory and her in his. He couldn't do anything about that. Just knowing her voice was no longer a phone call away left a void in his heart. He already missed her. Maybe he'd get over it.

Chapter 23

Spring was in full bloom in mid-April, and Jim spent the morning shopping and learning his way around his new home town. It was a small town split into two halves by a highway running north-south. Several small shopping centers were there to provide anything he needed. He would be comfortable here, and he settled in.

That afternoon he called Mac.

"Mac, it's Harold. Or was. Jim now. Everything is set up. I'm ready for the next step." He gave Mac his new address and phone number.

"That didn't take long, kid. I'll meet you there for breakfast on Monday. Anyplace in particular?"

"Gloria's Diner at the north edge of town. I haven't eaten there yet."

"Eggs is eggs, kid. How bad can it be? See you there at eight."

Monday morning, Jim met Mac at Gloria's. They exchanged small talk while they ate. Then Mac followed Jim to the apartment. They parked, went up the outside stairway and inside. Mac carried a small duffel bag.

"Nice place. We can get started right after I look around."

Mac walked from room to room and checked out everything in the small apartment. He took hand tools from his bag and searched for surveillance devices.

"Why would anyone want to bug my place?" Jim asked.

"Well, kid, you used to work for the Company. You might have been seen with me. Our enemies ain't exactly stupid. Rather safe than sorry."

"I have enemies?"

"You do now. You work for me."

"You didn't tell me that part."

Mac laughed. After about half an hour, he was finished.

"Okay, kid. It's clean. No bugs. Now, to keep me from having to do this shit every time, put something on the door to see if anyone came in while you were out. Let's set up communications."

He opened the duffel bag and said, "In here is a voice scrambler."

Mac removed a device about the size of a tissue box. He connected it to Jim's telephone.

"When this thing is on, anyone bugging either phone hears only noise. When you come in, if the green light is blinking, call me. See this little harmonica? All but one of the holes are taped off. Give it a blow."

Jim blew into the harmonica. A clear tone sounded.

"If you call me and I don't answer, blow the harmonica into the phone. That sets a light blinking on my box. I'll call you when I can."

"What's the red light for?"

"That says the client called."

"How do you make the red light blink instead of the green?"

"The harmonica hole has two notes. I blow for red, suck for green."

"How does your scrambler know who's calling?"

Mac looked at him and made a face. "It doesn't, kid. I answer the fucking phone and ask who's there."

Jim withered at Mac's rebuff. "You must spend a lot of time making scramblers."

"I have help. I don't understand this shit, so I use a guy who's good with electronics."

Jim looked the box over and made a mental note of how it connected to the phone system.

"Let's talk about clients," Mac said. "I find the clients and put them in touch with you. You only talk to them through me and the two of you don't know who each other is."

"Why all the intrigue? What's the point?"

"Kind of a four-way Chinese wall." Mac drew a rectangle in the air with his index fingers. "There's you, me, the client, and the target," he said, poking at the imaginary edges. "I know you and the client, but I don't know the target. You know me and the target, but you don't know the client. The client knows me and the target, but he doesn't know you. The target doesn't know shit. Nobody knows everything. That way nobody knows enough to compromise anybody else."

"Why wouldn't you know the target?"

"Just don't want to bother with it. The wall protects me and the client. If an operative gets caught, he has no leverage to deal with the cops. He doesn't know who hired him."

That didn't make sense to Jim. "He knows you. Can't he use that to deal with cops?"

"Not a good idea. If somebody sells me out, they don't live to testify."

This brought to mind something Jim had been wondering about. "Mac, does it bother you when you intentionally set out to kill somebody?"

"It used too, kid. But I saw so much of that shit during the war and afterward, I guess I just got immune to it. It's a job. If I don't do it, somebody else will."

Jim recalled the hunting lesson he'd learned from Pop years before. "Like killing a deer?"

"Kind of. Now, moving on. You need a code name. What would you like to be called?"

Jim grinned. "I get a code name? Cool. How about Sandman? My Farm nickname."

"No. Too many people there knew you by that name. Pick something else."

"Shadow? I can be the Shadow. I always liked that radio show."

Mac made an exaggerated nod. "Shadow it is."

Jim paused to let his code name sink in. Then he asked the main question.

"How does the money work?"

Mac grinned. "I knew we'd get to that. A numbered bank account.

You're going to Switzerland. Do you have five grand left?"

"Yeah. Haven't had much expenses."

"Good. You'll need it to open the account. Did you buy a car?"

"Bought my old car from Harold Sands. Gave me a good deal on it." Jim smiled. He was proud of how clever he'd been.

"Not good. The sale is recorded at the DMV and links Harold Sands to Jim whatever-your-last-name-is. It might not come back to haunt you, but that's the kind of loose end you can't afford."

"Didn't think of that. Sorry." Once again Jim had disappointed Mac.

"Well, it's done. Any more questions?"

"How do we know what to charge?"

"You negotiate the fee with the client. I don't get into that. I take twenty percent of whatever you make. Play it by ear. Don't lowball. I have overhead. My only competitor works out of his car. Lives in it too, for all I know. He can take the chump change."

Jim was feeling overwhelmed by all this new information. He hoped he could do the job as well as Mac seemed to think he could.

Mac continued. "I'll send a courier with a letter of introduction to a banker in Zurich and a round trip ticket. Be ready to go."

"You use a courier service?"

"Son of a colleague. Lives in the same building as me, so he's convenient for errands."

"Where do you live, Mac?"

"You don't need to know. Get up against that wall."

That came out of the blue. "What?"

"The wall. Get up against it."

"You going to frisk me again?"

"No, kid, I'm going to take your fucking picture. Now get over there."

Mac took a camera from his duffel bag, stood Jim against the wall, and took several close-up snapshots. "For my files," he said.

Tuesday morning, Jim answered a knock on his door. A boy of about sixteen stood there. He held a small snapshot and looked first at Jim, then at the snapshot, handed Jim a thick envelope, and said, "Mr. Dodson? Package from Mac." The boy looked familiar.

"Let me get you a tip," Jim said, but the boy said, "Not necessary," and ran down the steps to his car, which was idling in the parking lot. Jim recognized Mac's car. Now he remembered. The boy had driven it home after Mac's retirement party.

Jim made sure the boy wasn't looking and followed him to the lot. Jim got in his own car and drove out about ten seconds after the boy left.

Jim followed the car to the highway and then north. They continued north with Jim staying four and five cars behind. After about fifteen miles, they took an exit and drove west for a while, then the boy pulled into a lot in front of an apartment building. Jim pulled to the curb and watched from across the street. The boy parked, got out, and went into the building.

Now Jim knew where Mac lived. It might come in handy later. He couldn't have tailed Mac that way. Mac would have spotted him in less than a mile. He pulled out and headed home.

In his apartment, Jim opened Mac's package. It contained a round trip ticket to Zurich, a hotel reservation, and five twenty-franc notes for expenses. A typed letter introduced James Dodson Jr. to one Herr Brandthof, who Jim assumed was Mac's Zurich banker. A scrawled note said:

> *Take a warm jacket. It's cold this time of year. The room is paid for. Take 5K in cash. Enjoy your trip.*

Chapter 24

The next morning Jim drove to Dulles Airport, checked in, and rode a mobile lounge bus to the 707 for his trip to Zurich.

He arrived in Zurich Friday morning. After making his way through customs and immigration, he picked up his luggage and hailed a cab. When they pulled out of the airport, a brown Citroën fell in behind the cab. Jim couldn't see the driver.

What's this all about? A tail? A shiver ran up Jim's back. He was in a foreign country, and somebody was following him. Was word already out at the Company? Were they zeroed in on a rogue?

The ride from the airport took about half an hour. The Citroën stayed with them two or three cars back, sometimes turning off at an intersection only to rejoin them a block or two later.

Jim recalled Bert Allison's briefing. They put sanctions on rogues. Jim had a lot of training but no experience in the field. He didn't know how to deal with someone who might be coming to deliver a sanction.

What have I gotten myself into?

They drove south from the airport through residential communities with small houses nestled onto tree-lined lots, each house unique and charming. They reached a section of town with stores, restaurants, and hotels and continued through the city until the driver pulled up in front of a small hotel.

The Citroën had followed them to the hotel then sped past. Jim had a brief look at the driver, a dark-complexioned man in a cap, but that was about all he could make out.

Jim's hotel sat a half block from Lake Zurich. A lawn and walkway ran between the lake and the street. He went inside.

The manager spoke English with a German accent. "Welcome to Switzerland, Herr Dodson." He slid the register across the counter to Jim.

Jim signed in and went to his room. It was small and simply furnished. He could imagine Mac tearing up the room, searching for bugs.

The window to the west overlooked the northern tip of Lake Zurich. Long boats motored along the lake in both directions carrying passengers between Zurich and the towns along the lake. He opened the window, put his head out in the cool air and stretched to see a distant range of snow-capped mountains. Alps, no doubt.

Rooftops and turrets of old Zurich topped the buildings to the north. The waves of history and tradition represented by what he could see from these two windows impressed him. Cobblestone streets, stone houses and shops, tiled roofs, sidewalk cafes, cathedrals, and many other buildings, large and small.

And now here he stood, a spy on a trip to Zurich. An orphan from rural Virginia who'd never been anywhere or done anything, about to walk into a Swiss bank with five thousand bucks in his pocket to open a numbered Swiss bank account. And with a tail on him, perhaps to deliver a sanction.

Bond. James Bond.

Dottie would love this place. For a moment, his heart ached.

He put his things away and went down to the lobby. The manager stood behind the front desk. He smiled and waved at Jim.

Jim peeked into the restaurant. They were still serving breakfast. He hadn't eaten since last night. He went into the restaurant and sat at a table.

A long serving table of food stood against a far wall. Steam rose from heated serving dishes, and brightly colored fruits, croissants, rolls, and muffins were heaped on platters alongside. A pretty young waitress came out from the kitchen and to his table. *"Guten morgen, mein herr."*

Jim answered, "Good morning."

She said in English, "Good morning. I thought you might be American, but I did not wish to presume. My name is Elsa."

"How'd you know I'm an American?"

"Your clothing and your haircut," she said. "It's very much American. You may serve yourself. Would you care for coffee?"

"Yes, please."

"Enjoy your breakfast," she said and returned to the kitchen.

While he filled his plate from the serving table, Elsa returned with a pot of hot coffee. She poured him a cup, smiled at him, and went to serve other customers.

After breakfast, Jim went into the lobby and asked the manager for directions to the bank. When Jim came out of the hotel, he saw a man standing across the street, leaning on a lamppost and watching him. The man looked away abruptly when Jim caught his eye. Jim couldn't make out his features from that distance, but he was older than Jim and wore a leather jacket, cap, sneakers, and blue jeans.

Jim strolled north and then west across a bridge. He walked through the park, constantly watching for the man in the cap but didn't see him again. His walk took him through a shopping district to the financial district.

The bank was an imposing building, several stories high with a granite face and huge leaded windows. The bank's name was engraved on a brass plaque beside a large glass revolving door with brass frames and fittings. He went inside. The lobby had mahogany walls trimmed in brass with oak inlays. It had high ceilings, floor-to-ceiling maroon velvet draperies, and a marble floor. The walls displayed framed portraits of stuffy-looking old men posed in three-piece suits and with grim faces. Plush leather chairs sat empty around the room, and several large potted plants occupied places of prominence next to marble columns. It looked like something out of an old movie.

A huge reception desk stood in the middle of the lobby, and a tiny elderly woman sat behind it. She seemed out of place, dwarfed by the majesty of her surroundings. He walked to the desk, his footsteps echoing throughout the lobby.

"Good morning, sir. How may I help you?"

The natural reverberation of the cavernous room gave her voice a boom that made it larger than it ought to be.

"My name is James Dodson. I wish to see Herr Brandthof."

"Yes, Herr Dodson. Would you please have a seat over there?"

Jim sat in one of the leather chairs, deep and comfortable. He sank down and hoped he'd be able to pull himself out gracefully when the time came. He hadn't slept since arriving in Switzerland, and jet lag had begun to kick in. He had to concentrate to keep from dozing off.

He came wide awake when the brass elevator doors parted, and a young woman stepped out and walked toward him. This was one choice tomato, as Mac would say. She wore a dark green suit and high-heeled shoes. Her strawberry blonde hair was pinned up, and she wore flawless makeup applied as if by a professional makeup artist. Stunned, Jim didn't have the presence of mind to turn on the old charm; he just watched her walk in his direction.

The young lady drew near and, in a soft tone with a slight German accent, said, "Good morning, Herr Dodson. Herr Brandthof will see you now."

He struggled out of the deep leather chair and followed her to the elevator. Always at ease with women, even as a boy, he felt like a bumpkin in town for the turnip festival in the presence of this exquisite creature. Her perfume was exotic and hypnotic, particularly in the close confines of the elevator, which carried them to the seventh floor.

He finally managed to stammer out, "What is your name, miss?"

"It's *frau*. Mrs." She said with an understanding smile. "Please call me Maria."

She walked in front of him out of the elevator and down a corridor.

"Herr Brandthof's office is just a few doors down."

Jim imagined a huge executive office with a mahogany desk and paneled walls. He pictured Herr Brandthof as a stately gentleman who resembled Claude Rains and who spoke with a fine, deep cultured voice and wore a tailored three-piece suit with a gold watch chain draped across his belly. Like the old guys in the lobby portraits.

Maria led him to a small office where a small elderly man sat at a large cluttered time-worn roll-top desk. The desk was against a wall. The room had books and papers in seemingly random piles stacked every-where on the furniture and on the floor. Its elderly occupant was bald and wore a green eye shade and reading glasses with rectangular lenses that slid down to the tip of his bulbous vein-speckled nose. He had bushy gray eyebrows and a bushier gray mustache tipped brown at the ends from dried coffee. He wore a rumpled wool suit that looked like it was overdue for a trip to Goodwill.

Not Claude Rains. More like Walter Brennan.

The elderly man pored over papers, which would fall to the floor around his chair when he shuffled them. Each time a page floated to the floor, he reached down and picked it up. Every now and then he'd punch buttons on a giant adding machine tucked away among the piles of pa-pers. He'd pull a handle on the machine, more papers would drift to the floor, and he'd patiently pick them up and return them to the pile.

Maria led Jim into the room. The old man swiveled around in his chair with a squeak and looked up. Maria introduced them and left the office.

Herr Brandthof pulled himself up from his chair with some effort and vigorously shook Jim's hand. He spoke English but with a thick German accent.

"So good to meet you, Herr Dodson. Please sit down."

He directed Jim to a straight-backed chair against the opposite wall. He sat in his own chair and smiled.

"And what can we do for you today, Herr Dodson?"

Jim handed him the letter of introduction.

"Ah, one of Herr Mac's accounts. He sent word you'd be coming. I have the paperwork completed. Did you bring money to deposit?"

Jim opened his briefcase and handed the five thousand dollars to Herr Brandthof, who counted it, scribbled something on a note pad and opened a desk drawer. The old man had difficulty opening and closing the drawer because of the papers jammed in. He stuffed Jim's money in and around the papers, and Jim hoped his money wouldn't be lost in there. When he closed the drawer, Jim could see the corner of a hundred dollar bill sticking out. The old man rummaged around on his desk, found a battered old green and gray, cloth-bound ledger, opened it, and made an entry.

"This ledger goes in the vault when I leave each day. I learned that from Herr Mac and Herr Snuffy many years ago. And to make sure everyone who sees it knows it is not left out. Perhaps he told you."

"No, sir, that's one I haven't heard."

Herr Brandthof referred to the ledger and scribbled something on a slip of paper, which he handed to Jim.

"These are your account numbers. Do not lose them. You access your account only with these numbers. Without them, we don't know you. Is that understood?"

"Yes, sir." Jim read and memorized the numbers.

"The first number is your private number. The second is your public number for others to use when they transfer money to you."

Jim put the paper in his briefcase. "Is that all there is to it?"

"That's all. I hope you have time to enjoy our city while you are here. Thank you for your business."

He picked up the phone and spoke into it. Jim hoped Maria would return to escort him to the lobby. He wasn't disappointed. She walked with him to the elevator.

That perfume again. Jim should ask her what it was so he could buy the same kind for Dottie. Then he remembered. He had dumped Dottie. He wished he could at least send her a post card.

As they descended, Jim asked Maria, "Is Herr Brandthof president of the bank?"

She laughed. "Oh, no. He's not even a vice president. But he is a legend in international banking circles. He knows many important and powerful people and manages many accounts." She lowered her voice. "You wouldn't believe the famous people I've escorted to and from Herr Brandthof's office. Movie stars, royalty. Of course, I cannot tell you who they are."

She walked with him from the elevator to the front door.

"Goodbye, Herr Dodson. Perhaps we will meet again."

In my dreams.

He stopped at a street vendor's cart and bought a large sausage and a bottle of beer. He sat on an abutment overlooking Lake Zurich and ate his lunch.

The man in the cap sat at a table at a sidewalk café about a block to the north.

Should Jim try to shake him? Then he'd know Jim had busted him. Better wait.

He returned to the hotel and slept until dinnertime. After dinner at the hotel, Jim strolled south for about a mile through a park. The man in the cap was nowhere to be seen, but the area was dark, and he could be anywhere. Here and there young people clustered around small fires, chatting and laughing. Jim wondered what they were talking about. Occasionally a passenger boat slipped by, its lights reflected in the lake, its motor chugging with a steady rhythm as the sounds of passengers' voices drifted across the water. He was lonely, so he turned around and headed for Zurich's night life.

He walked into the old district and found a bar that featured a jazz trio. He had one drink and left.

He hit several more bars, having one drink in each, but he switched to Coca-Cola. The mysterious man in the cap didn't show himself that evening.

Jim had trouble getting to sleep that night. His thoughts and later his dreams meandered from the man in the cap to Mac to Zurich to Dottie to the Farm and back again. Everything swam around in his mind in random order. He slept fitfully.

The next morning after breakfast, Jim walked north toward the old section of Zurich. The morning air was nippy, and he wore his jacket. His route followed cobblestone streets between and around stone buildings of all shapes and sizes. Occasionally, he came across small open courtyards with street vendors hawking their wares from kiosks. Tourists pored over the displays of jewelry, clothing, bric-a-brac, and chocolate, lots of chocolate. They haggled with vendors over prices. He purchased a chocolate bar and ate it while he walked. Dottie had always enjoyed chocolate, his traditional gift to her on birthdays and holidays. He wished he could bring her some from here.

He kept a watch over his shoulder for the man in the cap but didn't see him. He climbed the towers of *Grossmünster* and *Fraumünster,* both of which provided stunning panoramic views of Zurich. Once again he bought lunch from a street vendor, then walked across the river to visit the outdoor shopping plaza.

Jim didn't see the man in the cap all day Saturday. Either he was good or he'd taken the day off.

Jim spent Sunday riding trains around the country. On his first trip out of Zurich he spotted the man in the cap on the train platform several cars back. Jim had planned to go to Geneva, but when he boarded the train, he watched the platform through his window, and the man in the cap boarded too, but in a different car. When the train started moving, Jim jumped onto the platform and ran toward a different train boarding for Lucerne. The Geneva train sped up, and the man in the cap sat looking at Jim from a window. Jim boarded the other train.

He visited Lucerne and Bern and returned to Zurich on Sunday evening, had dinner in the hotel restaurant, and retired early. Tomorrow would be a long day.

Monday morning, he arose at the wake-up knock on his door. He packed for the trip home but kept his jacket out. It would be chilly. He went down to the restaurant for breakfast. Elsa brought his coffee.

"I'll be saying goodbye this morning," he told Elsa. "I'm going home."

"How exciting. I've always wanted to see America."

"What do you think you'd find there?"

She paused and looked at the ceiling. "Big cars, ponytails, beaches, cowboys."

He had to laugh. "That's what you'd find all right."

After breakfast, he went into the lobby and checked out. The manager looked around and lowered his voice. "Please give our regards to Herr Mac."

Outside, he turned and took one final look at the hotel. This was his first time as a world traveler, and he didn't want to forget anything. Maybe he'd have a chance to tell Dottie about it. Maybe someday he could bring her here. If only...

The man in the cap stood across the street leaning against the same lamppost. Jim put his luggage in the hotel lobby then came outside and walked north toward the old town. The man fell in behind him about a block back. Where the street bent off at an angle, Jim took advantage of the bend to put a building between him and the man. Then he ducked into an alleyway and stood close to the corner with his back pressed against the wall. He watched to see when the man would pass his position. His heart pounded. He intended to tail the man to see where he went. With several hours before his flight, he had time for this cat and mouse game.

He waited. The man didn't appear. He waited some more. Nothing. He inched toward the corner of the building to look in the direction from which the man should be coming.

A voice came from behind him. "Are you looking for me?"

Jim spun around. The man in the cap stood about six feet away. He had come around the block and snuck up on Jim.

Jim braced himself. "Who the hell are you?"

"Relax, Jim. I'm Paulo. Mac asked me to keep an eye on you."

Jim looked the older man over. He could have been Spanish, Italian, Indian, or from any of a number of cultures.

"That's a relief. You sure had me going. Glad to know you." Jim reached for the handshake.

"Let's get coffee," Paulo said. "You have time?"

"Sure."

They walked to a sidewalk café and sat at a small table.

"*Zwei coffees bitte*," Paulo told the waiter.

"Mac asked you to keep an eye on me? Why?"

"To keep you out of trouble. Give you experience being tailed. And just because he's Mac."

"You work for Mac too?"

"Sometimes. I was his handler over here. When I retired, I stayed and freelance now."

"What kind of trouble were you supposed to keep me out of?"

"Mac worries about competition. And the Company. They don't exactly approve of what he does. Some think he's running a rogue operation. He worries they'll sanction his people. I don't think so, but Mac doesn't take any chances. I'll let him know you're okay."

They finished their coffee. Jim thanked Paulo and said goodbye. He returned to the hotel and retrieved his luggage. Several taxicabs lined up at the curb. He took the first one in line and asked to be taken to the airport.

On the way, he said to the driver, "Stop at that shop, please. I need to get something."

He went into a small confectionery shop and bought a big box of dark Swiss chocolate bars. He chose the most ornate embossed box with pictures of the Alps and colorful lettering. Dottie's birthday was in November. Maybe he could give this to her then. Or sooner.

The first leg of his flight home was on a four-engine propeller airplane, Zurich to Paris. Then he boarded a 707 for the long haul across the ocean to New York. He managed to sleep, but with a full passenger capacity, he couldn't stretch out, and he slept in small increments. From New York, he caught a commuter flight to Dulles Airport, picked up his car, and drove home, exhausted.

He unpacked, put the chocolates in the refrigerator, and went to bed. He lay awake and thought about the trip, the people he'd met, the places he'd seen, and what life held in store, all the while not knowing what form it would take or what he would have to do. But his thoughts raced through the possibilities.

He gave up trying to sleep, pulled himself out of bed, and sat at the kitchen table in his underwear and bare feet, drawing diagrams of an idea he'd been knocking around.

He had decided to build a camouflaged sniper's rifle. It would give him something to do while he waited for the phone to ring. Hours later, he took the diagrams to the couch, turned on the lamp, laid back, and studied them. His idea was taking shape.

He awoke with a start, unsure of where he was. His diagrams were scattered on the floor beside the couch. Light streamed in through the living room window. He looked at his watch. Noon on Wednesday. Time to do something constructive. He needed a project. Perhaps his newly-formed design could occupy the time until he heard from Mac. He hadn't planned on this endless waiting for the scrambler to blink.

Chapter 25

May burst on the scene with splashes of pink, white, purple, blue, and green pastels. Spring was in full bloom. Dogwoods, mountain laurel, magnolia bushes, and lilac trees blossomed everywhere. Colorful wildflowers peppered the countryside, and soft, cool breezes drifted over the land effortlessly. Mockingbirds, blue jays, and cardinals in the tall pines added dots of color and pure tones of music to the scenery. Virginia was a nice place to be this time of year.

Jim wondered how long it would be before he broke his silence and called Dottie.

You never know what you had until you've lost it.

With his identity change and a numbered account, Jim was ready to go with nothing to do. Just like in the Company. Well-prepared and no assignment.

But he had his sketches and diagrams to keep him busy. His design looked good on paper and had been inspired by James Bond's attaché case, which, in the books, contained a weapon, silencer, and other gadgets. In Jim's design, the case would not only carry the weapon, it would be an integral part of the weapon.

People would notice a guy with a rifle but not a guy with a briefcase. Hiding a rifle in a briefcase was nothing new. Many weapons could be dismantled and stored in cases. The problem was the time it took to remove and assemble the weapon and to reverse the procedure after the shoot. His design would solve that problem.

Jim cruised pawnshops looking for a suitable rifle. Eventually, he found a Savage Model 219. The gun was ten or fifteen years old, had a scope, and cost twenty dollars. Jim bought it and went to Sears and bought a briefcase.

The silencer wouldn't be that easy. Jim would have to build and test it. He knew how—several manuals in the Farm's library had explained the materials and process—but he'd never built one.

He couldn't wait to have the weapon built so he could test-fire it and put it to real use someday in an important and exciting mission.

He needed a secluded workshop with machine-shop tools. He looked in the Yellow Pages under *Gunsmiths*, bypassing the big flashy display ads and concentrating on simple one-liners with a name and address.

Jerry Matthews had such a listing with his business located on a street in a nearby wooded residential area. Jim drove to the address and found a small house with a detached two-car garage on a side street set in a stand of trees. A sign over the side door said:

J. Matthews, Gunsmith.

Another sign said the premises had a security alarm system. Jim examined the doorway for leads and sensors that would trigger an alarm. He didn't see any. He tried the door. It was unlocked, so he opened it and went inside. A man in his mid-forties sat at one of two workbenches. Jim entered the shop, and the fellow looked up and turned toward him.

"Hello. Can I help you?"

Jerry Matthews had balding gray hair matted into a slick comb-over and a slender frame. He wore thick bifocals and had a jeweler's glass mounted on his glasses, swiveled up and out of its viewing position. His loose-fitting overalls covered a long-sleeved plaid shirt. He had the hands of a working craftsman, gnarled and scarred, with dirty, untended fingernails. His mustache needed grooming, and his pipe impregnated the room with its thick, sweet aroma.

"My name is Jim Dodson. I'd like to talk to you about renting workshop space."

"Rent? Never rented out any space. I need most of it for my own work. What did you have in mind?"

"I need it during off hours. Evenings and weekends, or whenever you aren't using it."

Jerry took a moment before answering. He rubbed his jaw and pursed his lips. Then he said, "I have a day job. I work here evenings and weekends. I could maybe rent you some space on weekdays when I'm at work."

"That would do. Is anyone here during the day?"

"No, I live alone. I'm here today because I got behind on a project."

"I see. Do you think we can make a deal?"

"I sure could use the money," he said. "How's fifty bucks a month?"

"That's fine." He gave Jerry cash for the rental. Jerry wrote him a receipt and gave him a key to the door.

Jim looked around the room. "Any of those storage cabinets available?"

"Sure. Use the one by the ice box. I'll clean it out."

"How does the alarm work?"

"No alarm. Just that sign on the door so people think I have one."

Jim smiled at that. "Well, I guess that's it. I'll be back on Monday morning to start work."

"Don't park on the grass behind the building. The septic tank and drain field are there. I'm glad to meet you, Jim, and thanks for the business."

They shook hands, and Jim went outdoors and looked around. If he pulled his car alongside the workshop away from the road, passing motorists would not see the car. Everything about this arrangement fit his requirements.

Monday morning Jim packed a lunch, loaded his car, and drove to Jerry's place. His car made crunching road noises when he drove over the gravel driveway. No one could sneak up on him while he worked, at least not in a car.

A sign on the workshop door said:

Closed. Open after 6:00 p.m. Mon-Fri and all day Sat.

Jim parked and carried his load into the workshop. As promised, Jerry had cleaned one workbench and emptied the storage cabinet.

Jim spent the first day planning, measuring, making drawings, and keeping notes. His design was taking shape, and he made a list of additional materials he would need. At four in the afternoon, he locked everything in the storage cabinet, turned out the lights, and locked the door behind him.

For the next several weeks, Jim repeated this routine, arriving at the workshop each morning after Jerry had gone to work and leaving before he returned. Jim didn't hurry his work, but took a deliberate and methodical approach. Progress was slow because he took his time. He would sit in Jerry's rocking chair for hours at a time, reading and drawing sketches of other things he might build.

From time to time Jim would stop and consider the path he was paving for himself. He was conditioning and equipping himself to be an assassin for hire. So far his plans and preparations had focused on the raw accoutrements of killing—guns, scopes, ammunition—but he still had to deal with the reality of the deed, ending a life without passion, ideology, or agenda other than collecting a fee.

Chapter 26

May gave way to June and hot, humid weather. On the first Monday when Jim came in from the workshop, the green light was blinking. He went to the phone and dialed Mac's number.

"Hi, Mac. It's me."

"Hi, kid. Flip the switch on your box. We can test this thing."

The receiver clicked, and there was static. He reached over and flipped his switch. The static changed into Mac's voice, "—coming through okay?"

"Loud and clear." The muffled sound had a small buzz to it, but the words were clear, and Jim could recognize Mac's voice.

"You enjoy Zurich?"

"Yes. I met your friend Paulo."

Mac laughed. "He said you did okay. Busted him right away. But then he snuck up on you. Good practice for you."

"Don't do that again. What if I'd killed him?"

"That would have been good practice too. Okay, kid, I got a job for you."

"What's the job?" Jim hoped he didn't sound too eager. He carried the phone and a notepad to the dinette table.

"A simple B and E," Mac said, using law enforcement lingo for *breaking and entering*. "The client is bidding on a government computer job. There's only two bidders, so he wants to find out how much his competitor is bidding so he can underbid them. Interested?"

Jim took notes. "Yes," he said. "You know the setup?"

"A small defense contractor in suburban Maryland."

"How secure?"

"Not very, although they lock the doors at night. And they might keep sensitive documents in a safe. The target mustn't know his security has been compromised, so you can't just blow a safe and steal documents."

"Good. I don't know how to blow a safe. How would I get the combination?"

"It's called *intelligence* for a reason, kid. Everybody writes down their combinations. You have to find it."

Jim was glad Mac couldn't see him blushing.

Mac continued. "You'll make copies of the pages he wants and leave everything looking undisturbed."

Jim looked at the calendar. "Deadline?"

"You have about two and a half months before you go in. The bids are due on the fifteenth of August."

"Let's go for it."

"I was hoping you'd say that. When's a good time for the client to call? Have to be during business hours."

Jim looked at the calendar again. "Tomorrow. I'll stay home. What's his code name?"

"Abercrombie. Don't laugh. That's what he chose."

"He wants copies of documents. Do you have one of those little cameras for shooting pictures of pages?"

"Minox B. The spy camera. I have several."

"Good. I'll need one."

Jim hung up the phone and felt a rush. His first assignment, and he would set the fee. He figured he'd need seventeen-five to pay Mac and have something left over.

Jim's phone rang at two p.m. on Tuesday. The blinking red light meant the client was patched through. Jim switched on the scrambler and picked up the receiver.

The voice on the other end said, "This is Abercrombie. Who is this?"

"Shadow here." Jim flushed with excitement. The first time he'd used his codename. "Tell me about the job."

"You know most of it from what Mac told you. About all you need is the name of my competitor and where they are."

"What does the job pay?"

"What's your fee?"

"What's your budget?"

"I can pay fifteen grand."

Not quite enough. "Make it twenty and we have a deal." Give the buyer room to negotiate.

Abercrombie was ready with a counter-offer. "Seventeen-five and you're on."

Amazing how that works. Right on the money.

Jim sat back in his chair, relieved. "Done. You tell me where the target is. I case the setup. If it's doable, we proceed. If not, like maybe it's Fort Knox, I let Mac know, and he takes it from there."

"Good. What I need is my competitor's cost information. I need it the morning the proposal is due, which means you have to get it the night before."

"Understood. Who's the target?"

"Pine Hill Software in Bethesda."

Abercrombie read off the address and phone number, and Jim asked, "What's the guy's name in charge of the project?"

"It's a woman. Mrs. Sarah Weston."

Jim jotted her name down.

"What's the document?"

"A proposal for a small job called NAVAMS. Navy Vehicle Automated Maintenance System. I need their cost breakout, all their numbers, labor hours and costs, expenses, profit, overhead, G&A, and all that stuff."

Jim didn't know what all those words meant, but he'd learn. "Can do," he said. "Here's how you pay." Jim read off his public account number and the phone number in Zurich. "Unless something changes or

I have questions, we won't need to talk again. Mac will handle the drop."

Jim hung up, picked up again and dialed Mac's number.

After a few seconds, "Hi, kid."

"The job is on. Target's in Bethesda. Man, this is so cool."

"Okay. What do you need from me?"

Jim referred to the list he'd made while talking to Abercrombie. "Send me the little camera. And on the night of August fourteen, I need you nearby waiting."

"Can do. Why me and why nearby?"

"You have to handle the drop face-to-face. And we need a place close to the target with running water to develop film."

"I keep a safe house over there."

"Can I live there?"

"Sure. For the duration if you want."

"Good. No commute."

Mac chuckled. "I guess you're not going to break in, are you?"

"Not if I can help it. I'm going to walk in through the front door. Get a job and have a key. Even if I have to be a janitor."

Mac laughed. "A mole. That's what I like about you, kid. You always look for the least complicated way to do shit."

Jim beamed when Mac complimented him. Mac's approval meant a lot.

Mac said, "The courier will be there tomorrow morning with what you need. Your previous job is with MacTech. It's on that list I gave you."

"Okay. Just tell them I walk on water. How soon can I get in the safe house?"

"Right away. It's a fleabag, but it'll do. Take your scrambler."

That evening Jim pulled his typewriter down from the closet and typed his cover résumé, which documented a background for a consult-ant Pine Hill Software would want to hire.

This was what he'd been waiting for. A real intelligence assignment with a real purpose. Maybe not as important or dangerous as what his counterparts at the Company did, but it was a start.

Chapter 27

Early Wednesday morning Jim answered the door. Mac's courier handed him a package that contained keys, the address of the safe house, a Minox B camera, and its manual. He packed everything he'd need in a duffel bag, locked his apartment, and went to his car.

An hour later he pulled up in front of a two-story frame house on the north edge of D.C. He parked on the street and took his things around back. An exterior stairway led to a door on the second floor. He climbed the stairs and went in. His new digs consisted of a one-room efficiency. Sparse but livable.

Jim was excited. His first assignment would start soon. He picked up the phone, dialed the number for Pine Hill Software, and asked for Sarah Weston.

A woman's voice came on the line. "Sarah Weston."

"Good morning, Mrs. Weston. My name is Jim Dodson. I'm a freelance computer programmer and tech writer. I have the next couple of months free, and I'm calling around to see if any local companies have contract work."

"What's your specialty, Mr. Dodson?"

"Computer programming. Software tech writing. Program documentation, operator's manuals, system requirements, proposals, and like that. Mostly government projects."

"We might have something for you. Can you drop by today for an interview? Say, two o'clock?"

"I'll be there."

He changed into his best suit and headed out. He bought lunch at a carry-out burger joint and ate in his car. Then he drove to the Pine Hill address. A three-story office building sat back off the street with a small visitor parking lot in front and an employee lot in back. He drove around the building and cased the exits. He remembered Mac's first rule of facility penetration: *getting out is more important than getting in.*

He parked in front and went in. No receptionist. He looked for signs of an alarm system and found none. He entered the lobby, checked the office register, took the elevator up, and found Sarah Weston's office.

She sat at her desk reading documents. A pretty woman in her mid-thirties, she wore horn-rimmed glasses, a dark blue business suit, and basic makeup. Her auburn hair was pulled back and pinned into a twisted bun. She wore basic jewelry, fitting for a businesswoman: a wedding band, small pearl earrings, and a gold chain around her neck with an opal pendant near the hint of cleavage at her blouse's open collar. To Jim's eye, she wasn't bad looking if she'd lose the glasses and let her hair down.

He did a quick scan. The office door had a simple lock, easy to pick. A padlocked filing cabinet stood against the wall. Nothing about the room and its contents looked super secure.

He tapped on the door and poked his head in. The woman looked up.

"Mrs. Weston?" he said.

"Yes. Mr. Dodson?"

"That's me."

Sarah Weston gazed at him for a few seconds.

"Please come in and sit down. Did you bring a résumé?"

"Yes, ma'am." Jim sat at the table in front of her desk and handed his résumé across to her.

"Impressive," she said. "Your last assignment with this, uh, Mac-Tech used the same computer this project will be using. Do you happen to know anything about vehicle maintenance?"

He leaned forward. The truth would work. "I worked as a mechanic's assistant in high school. Had a part-time job evenings at a local gas station. Minor repairs."

He sat back in his chair, satisfied with his answer.

"Did you ever work where commercial vehicles had regularly scheduled maintenance based on government regulations?"

Again, his real experiences would apply.

"Yes, ma'am. I was a line boy at a small airport. I helped the mechanic with inspections and repairs. I did all the paperwork, FAA forms, aircraft logbooks, and like that."

"Where was that?"

Now he had to lie. He looked past her face out the window, took a breath, and concentrated on his contrived background.

"Tazewell, Virginia."

"Were you born there?"

"No, ma'am, I was born in Pennsylvania."

"You don't have a Pennsylvania accent."

"No, my parents died when I was a child. Relatives swapped me around until I wound up in an orphanage in Tazewell. They say I don't have a southern accent either. Kind of a hybrid."

Sarah smiled at him. "I guess. Anyway, everything about your experience fits what we need."

Jim spent the next hour with two men in a conference room adjacent to Sarah's office. Both men were older than Jim. Martin, the younger of the two, was perhaps thirty. He wore thick glasses, was overweight, and had bad teeth. Brent was maybe forty, gray at the temples, and trim. His questions suggested he was management, less technical, more of a high-level guy. Martin was a programmer.

They grilled Jim at length about his knowledge and experience. At the end of the interview, they asked him to wait and walked out. Jim heard Martin say, "What do we need this guy for?"

About ten minutes later, Sarah Weston came in and sat across from Jim. She crossed her legs in a way that would make him notice, which he did, but he tried not to be obvious about it.

"Are you interested in full-time employment?" she asked. "We do government work for the military. You'd need a security clearance."

Jim didn't want security investigators poking around his background. "Maybe later. I have a commitment in September that runs several months. After that, I might be interested."

"I can work with that. I want to use you on this project. Brent was impressed by your interview. Martin seemed less so, but don't worry about that. I called your previous job, and they said you walk on water."

Jim laughed. Had Mac really said that?

"Here's a nondisclosure agreement."

She handed Jim a document. The agreement prevented him from disclosing any proprietary information he might learn as a result of working there. He considered the irony. *If only she knew.*

He signed the agreement and passed it back to her.

She gave him a key ring with two keys. "The front door and your office." Sarah leaned closer. "Your job is to help us write a Navy proposal, but our sources tell us that whoever wins has a leg up for a bigger intelligence project coming down the pike."

Sarah stood to leave the conference room. Jim stood too.

"Welcome aboard, Jim. Nine o'clock Monday morning. See you then."

He watched her walk away and out the door. Nice figure and a sensuous walk, even in the conservative clothing. And he recognized the way she had smiled at him when they talked about his background. The orphan bit got them every time.

After the meeting with Jim, Sarah made a call.

A man answered. "NAVINT Headquarters. Lieutenant Commander Rod Bales."

"Rod, it's Sarah. I need a favor."

"Name it."

Rod was Sarah's worm in Navy intelligence.

"Can you check up on someone? His name is James Dodson Jr. I'm taking him on as a consultant for NAVAMS, and I'd like to know a little more about him."

"I can do that, but it will take time."

"No hurry. He's only here for the proposal, but I'm thinking about him for later, and I'd like a little heads up before I invest any time bringing him up to speed. He's a bright kid, but he might need nurturing."

Jim Dodson had brought out the mother in her the minute he walked into her office. Between that boyish smile and him being an orphan, she wanted him on her team. His knowledge and experience sealed the deal. But she didn't want disappointments.

"Okay, doll. Tell me what you know about him. I'll let you know when I have something."

Sarah read Jim's background information to Rod, and they hung up.

Sunday evening, Jim left for the safe house. On the way, he stopped to have duplicates made of the Pine Hill keys and to check his post office box. He was surprised and almost delighted to find a letter from Dottie. He stuck it in his pocket and continued to the safe house.

He sat in the easy chair and read Dottie's letter. It was dated a week earlier. She wrote about her disappointment that he hadn't tried to contact her:

> If I don't hear from you soon, I will move on and maybe accept some of the tons of offers I've had to go out.

The letter troubled him. He missed Dottie and was mad at himself for caving in to Mac's instructions and letting her go. He didn't like her dating other men, and his own feelings surprised him. He almost reached for the phone, but he resisted the impulse. He could always find someone else if he needed female companionship. But Dottie. She'd be hard to replace.

He wondered about her promise to move on. If she didn't, he might have to persuade her to get off his trail. But he'd rather not close the door on seeing her again.

He sat at the table and reread her letter. He pulled down his typewriter, addressed an envelope to her, and typed:

> Dottie, I received your letter. I'm in deep cover. Please don't try to contact or find me. I'll be in touch later. H.

He set the letter aside to consider whether he should send it. No point in asking Mac. He'd say definitely not. There was no hurry. Plenty of time to send it. If he was going to send it.

Jim arrived at the Pine Hill offices early Monday morning. He put his things in his office and wandered around getting the lay of the office complex.

The men's room had one toilet and a deadbolt on the door. The overhead light shone bright enough that he could take pictures of document pages there.

At nine o'clock he walked to the conference room and found Martin and Brent already there. Two women sat across from them. Brent introduced Jim to Maggie and Jennie. Maggie, a pretty woman in her mid-twenties, had bright red hair and a nice figure. Jennie was in her mid-to-late thirties and slightly overweight. They both wore wedding bands and greeted him cordially. Martin just stared at him.

A few minutes later, Sarah Weston came in and closed the door. She looked as good today as she had the day Jim met her. She started right in.

"Everyone, welcome to the team. A special welcome to Jim Dodson. He'll be joining us."

Sarah pointed out each person when she introduced them.

"Maggie is the team typist. Jennie is responsible for the cost proposal. You already met Brent and Martin."

Jim took note of all this. At different times any of these three women's offices might contain the pages he needed.

Sarah handed out a schedule. It included writing assignments and due dates. The schedule would tell Jim when to look for pages to copy.

After the kick-off meeting, Jim initiated his preparations. He would stay later each evening than the others, even when he had nothing to do, to accustom them to him working late. To justify the extra hours, he did real work. Martin's limited understanding of the hardware and software architecture had Jim making comments about and corrections to his work.

Eventually, Jim rewrote major parts of the technical proposal, and

Sarah welcomed that kind of initiative. Martin's resentment of Jim, however, became more evident each day.

In the second week, Jim used his overtime hours to set up the theft. He went into Sarah's office to crack the combination to the file cabinet's padlock. A simple but tedious procedure, it took about ten minutes. Jim wrote down the combination.

While he had the filing cabinet open, he looked for various parts of the document, which might tell him where to find what he needed later. Then he closed everything and left it the way he found it.

On subsequent nights, Jim broke into the offices of Jennie and Maggie. One such evening, Jim had just picked the lock to Maggie's desk when something caught his eye. A moving light shined through the window onto the far wall. He switched off the penlight and went to the window. A car pulled up to the back door, and Martin got out. Jim couldn't figure what Martin was doing there that time of night.

Martin looked toward Jim's car in the parking lot and then up at the light in Jim's office.

Jim couldn't risk being caught in Maggie's office. He opened the door a crack and looked down the darkened hallway, lit only by a dim night light on the wall halfway down the corridor. The elevator made its noisy running sounds, which meant Martin was coming up, so Jim closed the door behind him and crept to his own office, hugging the wall, hoping to be inside before Martin spotted him. He made it to the door just as the elevator opened. He went in, closed the door, sat at his desk, and waited and listened.

Martin's steps echoed up the hall and stopped in front of Jim's office. There was a tap on his door.

"Come on in, Martin."

The door opened, and Martin came in and slumped down into Jim's guest chair. "What are you doing here so late?" He asked, his words slurred. He'd obviously been drinking.

"Catching up on some work. What brings you here?"

"How'd you know it was me at the door?"

"I saw you pull in through my window. What brings you out?"

"You do, Jim." The booze had bolstered his courage. "You show up out of nowhere and make me and my work look bad. Then, when the job's done, you'll be gone, and I'll have to work with these people. So, I figure I need to keep an eye on you. Nothing personal. Just looking out for myself."

Jim didn't need this. He had to discourage Martin from making these late night visits. Perhaps if he could convince Martin he wasn't a threat...

"Martin, you have it all wrong. I already told Mrs. Weston if we win this job and she hires me, I want to work for you."

Martin perked up at this news. "You did?" He sat on the edge of the chair and looked straight at Jim.

"Of course," Jim said in his most schmoozing voice and with a forced smile. "You have the most insight into the technology of anyone here. Your general understanding of big computer systems is way beyond mine. You have years more experience than me, and I know I can learn a lot from you."

"You can?"

Jim had him now. "Yes. So let's forget this silly rivalry and be friends."

"Yeah, let's. What say we go somewhere and get a drink?"

Jim looked at his watch. "Bars are closing. Let's do that for sure when the project's over."

"Well, okay. Um. Thanks, Jim." He reached out to shake hands. "I'll see you tomorrow. I'll probably be in late."

"Goodnight Martin. I'm glad you came by."

"Me too."

Martin left, and Jim breathed a huge sigh of relief. He'd have to butter up Martin until the job was over, but it would be worth it.

Chapter 28

After his father died, Jamey Barrett had no job. He'd tried running the gas station, but business had dropped off, the oil company canceled the franchise, and the bank foreclosed on his house. Now he lived on the streets, panhandled, and slept in alleys, in abandoned buildings by the waterfront, and on grates. He stayed a step ahead of the cops most of the time. He'd loiter or beg for spare change, and they'd chase him and throw him in the drunk tank to sleep it off.

Jamey longed for the days in high school and for his friend, Harold Sands. Harold was smart and could do anything. They had worked on cars at the gas station and airplanes at the airport. Jamey had enjoyed the few months Harold lived with him, and it made Jamey proud when people thought they were brothers.

He hadn't seen Harold since the time they bumped into one another on the street. Harold had talked to him for a while and had given him some money. He wondered what Harold was doing now.

Tonight Jamey chose a dark corner of an abandoned warehouse to sleep in, one of his regular places. The dark concrete block building provided cooler bedding than the streets in July. He took a final pull on his bottle of wine and lit his last cigarette.

As he settled in, the sounds of people echoed from across the dark warehouse. He pulled himself to his feet and staggered toward the sounds. A young couple sat against a pillar across the warehouse on the concrete floor, groping with one another's clothes. He backed away and looked out an open door. A red Corvette convertible stood unattended in the alley with its top down.

Jamey walked out and looked in the Corvette. The keys were in the ignition. He climbed in and lowered himself into the bucket seat. He had never driven a Corvette, and he admired the sporty instrument cluster, floor shifter, and pleated leather bucket seats. He pushed in the clutch, turned the key, pressed the accelerator, and the engine came alive with a deep rumble. He put the car in reverse, backed out, put it in first, and drove out of the alley.

As he drove away, the young couple came running out of the warehouse. The boy stumbled along, pulling on his trousers. The girl wore a slip and was barefoot. They yelled after the Corvette, but Jamey ignored their calls.

The effects of the wine started to wear off, and he wondered where he could find more. He turned onto the freeway and headed south.

His mind clouded up for want of alcohol. After a few miles, he came to the exit to where he'd lived as a boy. In his confused state, this road led home. He took the exit right and immediately turned south on a narrow two-lane road that wound through the woods. He stopped in front of a small house, the house where he had grown up and that the bank had taken away from him. He didn't remember that, though. To his mind, he was home. That was all he knew.

He started to shake for want of a drink. Maybe he'd find something in the house. He turned into the driveway, killed the engine, and walked to the rear screen door. It wasn't latched.

Jamey went into the kitchen. He hoped in his haze he wouldn't wake his father. He went straight to the pantry where they kept the whiskey and wine.

His hands shook and he reached for the string that hung from an overhead light bulb. He pulled the string, and the naked bulb bathed the pantry in bright light. He searched the shelves, pushing jars, cans, and cereal boxes around, looking for a bottle.

FBI Special Agent Amos Lincoln had purchased the little house from a bank foreclosure several years before. The rural community was populated mostly by government employees and their families. Marge Lincoln liked the isolated location with its surrounding woods, shade trees, a place for her rock garden and flowers, and, best of all, the elementary school less than a mile away.

Amos had fourteen years at the Bureau, having joined right out of college. He was short and of medium build, had a brown crew cut, graying at the temples, and was clean-shaven with the pale complexion of someone who didn't spend much time outdoors. He disliked field work, preferring instead the meetings, paperwork, bureaucracy, and politics of a desk job at headquarters.

On this night, Amos had awakened to the sound of a car in his driveway. When he looked out his bedroom window, he could see the reflection of headlights in the trees, but the driveway was on the other side of the house. He couldn't tell who was there.

"Marge. Wake up."

She awoke with a start and sat up in bed, "What is it?"

"I heard a car drive in."

"Who'd be coming here this time of night?" Marge pulled the covers up around her neck. The kitchen door made its usual loud squeak when it opened.

"Somebody's in the house. Stay here."

He took his revolver from the nightstand and went into the living room. He could see the glow of the pantry light on the kitchen linoleum. He inched forward, staying in the shadows of the living room.

The silhouette of a young man, dirty, unshaven, and in ragged clothes, stood in the glare of the pantry light.

Amos leveled his weapon at the man and yelled, "Stop! FBI!"

The intruder faced him and froze. Then he ran toward Lincoln. Amos shot without hesitation, and the intruder stopped in his tracks and slumped to the floor, fatally wounded.

Marge called from the bedroom, "Amos, are you okay?"

"Yes, honey. Stay in there." His children were crying.

He walked to the intruder, bent over, and felt for a pulse. There was none. Blood drained from the chest wound and pooled onto the linoleum. The intruder's open eyes stared past him. Amos checked the man's clothes and around him for a weapon. Nothing. He looked for a wallet or anything to identify the intruder. He found only a greasy pack of playing cards in the dead man's pants pocket. He returned the cards to the pocket.

He felt foolish standing over a dead man, a gun in his hand, wearing only boxer shorts and a T-shirt. He had never taken his weapon out of its holster in the line of duty, much less fired it. Now, off-duty and at home, he'd used it to kill a man. He had done the right thing to protect his home and family. Even so, he had a dead man on his kitchen floor. His left eye started to twitch, which usually happened whenever he faced a stressful situation.

He found Marge in the children's room, sitting on the lower of two bunk beds, holding the children close, their crying reduced now to whimpers, their eyes wide and scared.

"Good. Stay with them." He went into the living room and called the county police.

"This is Special Agent Amos Lincoln, FBI. I just shot an intruder in my house. He's dead." He gave the dispatcher his address.

Then he called FBI Headquarters and spoke to the duty officer.

"This is Special Agent Lincoln. An intruder broke into my house tonight, I shot him. He's dead. I notified the county police."

Amos dressed and waited in the living room, not ready to go in the kitchen and see the face of the man he'd just killed. His left eye continued to twitch.

Marge came into the living room. "I killed him, Marge. I called the cops and the Bureau. They'll be here soon. Keep the kids out of here."

"They're okay now. I'll stay up and wait with you. Should I make coffee? I sure could use some."

"No. I don't want you going in there and stepping over a dead body."

"Well, then, Amos, you go in there and step over the damn body and bring me the coffeepot and makings. You need coffee. I need coffee. People are coming here who will want coffee." He gave in and went into the kitchen, taking care to step around the body. After he returned, Marge set up the coffeepot and then sat with him and held his hand while they waited for the authorities.

The phone rang. It was the FBI duty officer.

"Sir, a supervisor is on his way and will arrive soon. If the police get there first, identify yourself and ask them to wait for our guy to establish jurisdiction before proceeding."

"I suppose that's necessary. But this is just a case of a homeowner shooting a burglar."

"Probably. Don't answer any questions. You're officially under the Bureau's supervision from this point forward in this matter, and the supervising agent has full authority."

"Understood. Thank you."

As he hung up, a county police cruiser pulled into the driveway, its lights flashing. He went out to greet the policeman. A shiny red Corvette convertible sat parked in his driveway.

The policeman stepped out onto the driveway and introduced himself. "I'm Officer Robert Marshall, sir. What happened here?"

"Good evening, officer. I'm Special Agent Amos Lincoln, FBI." They shook hands, and Lincoln showed him his credentials. "I shot an intruder. He's dead in the kitchen. An FBI supervisor is on his way. We are asking you to wait for him before proceeding."

Marshall looked around the premises and asked, "When will your supervisor get here?"

"Any minute now. I called in right after I called you."

"I think we can wait. You're sure the intruder is dead?"

"One through the heart and no pulse."

"Understood. I'll call my shift commander."

The policeman went to his car. He returned after a couple of minutes and said, "We can wait. The coroner's wagon is on its way. They'll get the body out of the house and to the morgue. After your guy is done, of course."

A blue sedan pulled into the driveway behind the police car. A sleepy-looking fellow in a rumpled brown suit and no tie stepped out. He walked up to them.

"Special Agent Lincoln?"

"Yes."

"I'm Supervisory Special Agent Andrew Franks. Tell me what happened."

Franks was taller than Lincoln and about the same age. He was balding and had a slight paunch. His well-tanned face gave him a hardened look.

Amos explained, "I was in bed and heard a car pull in. The kitchen door opened. I went to investigate, called to the intruder to stop, and he rushed me. That's when I shot. I called the police and the Bureau. That's about it."

The cop scribbled notes on a notepad. Franks didn't take notes.

Franks asked Marshall, "Have you been in there yet?"

"No."

"I'll be right back," Franks said. "I want to see everything before we go stomping through the crime scene."

He went into the house through the kitchen door. A minute later he returned.

"Let's go have a look."

Marshall went first. Franks held Lincoln back until the cop was out of earshot.

"I dropped a piece on him."

They went through the back door into the kitchen. Franks carried a camera. He took several pictures of the fallen man.

"Do you mind if I turn him?" he asked the cop.

"No, go ahead."

Franks kneeled down and turned the body face up on the floor. A small revolver was on the floor where the dead body had been lying. He picked it up with his pencil through the trigger guard.

"You got an evidence bag?" he asked the cop.

"I'll get one." He went out the kitchen door.

"This piece is not in the system," Franks said. "And now it's covered with that stiff's fingerprints."

"Thanks." Lincoln's eye stopped twitching.

Franks took a picture of the dead man's face.

Officer Marshall returned and put the gun in a small paper evidence bag, which he sealed. He scribbled something on a white tag on the side of the bag.

Franks asked Amos, "You know this guy?"

"Never saw him before."

"What? Did he just wander onto your place?"

"Maybe in that Corvette. It's not mine."

Franks said, "Oh." Then to the policeman, "Other than getting his prints, I'm done here. I don't think we need jurisdiction, but if you decide to file charges, we need to be in the loop. Here's my card."

"I doubt there will be charges filed," Marshall said. "I'll run the plates on the Corvette. Maybe that will identify the guy."

Franks said, "From the looks of that guy, I'd say he stole it. Nice car."

A black hearse with county markings pulled up. Two men rolled a gurney up the walkway and parked it next to the kitchen door. Then they went inside. Amos Lincoln shook hands with Franks and Marshall. Franks walked out to his car for his fingerprint kit. The policeman went to talk to the men from the coroner's office, and Amos returned to his house to see to his family and figure out the day ahead.

Chapter 29

The heat of July in northern Virginia smothered everything. Nothing moved. Mac had all his windows open, but with no breeze, there was little relief. A whippoorwill in a nearby patch of woods had kept him awake half the night. Now some other kind of noisy bird chirped its brains out in a tree just outside his window. He looked at his alarm clock. Eleven o'clock. Just about time to get up. Then the phone rang. Mac pulled himself out of bed.

"Mac, Bert Allison."

"Hi, Bert. How's by you?"

"One of our boys bought the farm a couple of nights ago."

"Who?"

"Harold Sands."

Mac's heart sank. "Shit. How'd it happen?"

"He broke into a house. The resident is FBI. He found Sands in his kitchen in the middle of the night and shot him. Do you have any idea why Sands would be in an agent's house? He was carrying a twenty-two revolver, driving a stolen Corvette, and looked like a hobo. Maybe a disguise. Was Sands working for you?"

"No," Mac said. "Deep cover?"

"I think I'd know about that. Do you suppose he went rogue?"

"Not likely. How do they know it was him?"

"His prints. The homeowner being FBI, they did a priority search and found him in the file of Agency job applicants."

Mac gave a silent sigh of relief. The body wasn't the kid. "Where'd

149

this go down?" he asked.

Allison gave him the address of the Lincoln house.

Mac wrote that down on his bedside notepad. "How'd you get involved?"

"The FBI notified the Agency. Right away I thought about you."

"Thanks. The kid was kind of special to me."

"The coroner wants a positive ID. I don't know why since they have the prints."

"Probably just a formality."

"I can't do the ID for them, Mac. We have to keep our distance on this one. We don't know what's going on. I told them he doesn't work for us any more. Did he have family?"

"No. He had a girlfriend at the Agency, but I don't know who she is."

"I'll ask around. Can you identify the body? I don't know who else to ask."

"I'll do it."

Mac went into the kitchen to make breakfast. He finished eating, went to his car, and drove to the county morgue.

Mac walked into the county building's main entrance, found his way to the morgue, and approached the receptionist. "I'm here to identify one of your guests."

She directed him through metal double doors. An attendant in a white lab jacket met him.

"I understand you need an ID on a Harold Sands," Mac said.

The attendant led him to a wall with shiny steel drawers. He checked the labels under the drawer pulls, opened a drawer, and pulled it out. He pulled back the shroud that covered the face.

Mac took a close look and said, "I guess that's him. His face looks different." Mac played dumb.

The attendant explained. "That's from rigor mortis. This fellow has been dead at least a day and a half."

Mac was sure now. The corpse resembled the kid, but it wasn't him.

He made a snap decision.

"It's Sands," he said.

A woman's voice behind him said, "Is that Harold?"

Mac turned. A pretty young woman stood there clutching a handkerchief.

"Yes, miss, it's Harold Sands, I'm sad to say. Who are you?"

"I'm Dorothy Mills. Mr. Allison at work called me and told me about this. Harold and I were—" She choked back a sob.

"Yes. He spoke of you often. My name is Mac. I used to work for Allison."

Dottie hesitated. She knew better than to discuss Agency business on the outside. She turned to the attendant. "May I please see the entire body?"

"Well, that's not the usual procedure, miss. Respect for the dead and all."

"It's okay. He doesn't have anyone else. And it's important. Please."

The attendant looked around to be sure no one was looking. He pulled the drawer out, folded back the shroud, and exposed the corpse's naked body.

"Thank you. You may cover him now."

"He's all yours," Mac told the attendant.

"Do you want his personal effects?"

"He had some?"

The attendant went to a file cabinet and removed a small manila envelope. He took a soiled and tattered deck of playing cards in its box from the envelope.

"This was in his pocket. The cops have his gun. That's all there was."

He handed the box to Mac, who looked at it, shrugged, and put it in his pocket.

Dottie turned to Mac. "May I walk out with you?"

"Sure, come on."

They went out into the lobby and to the receptionist. Mac filled out a form, and they went out into the parking lot.

"I'm glad to meet you, Mr…"

"Call me Mac. It's good of you come down here. Harold would have appreciated it."

"But I'm not sure it's him. It doesn't look like him."

"But you're not sure." Mac wished she'd agree the stiff was the kid.

"No, I'm not. Although you'd think I'd know my own boyfriend."

"Sure looks like him to me." Mac didn't know just how to handle this situation. "They identified him from his fingerprints."

"Yes. But those things can be fixed. I don't know who you are, but I work for the Agency too. I'm just a number cruncher, but I know some of what goes on out there. I think it's time somebody let me in on it."

Mac looked out at the traffic passing by. He needed this pretty girl out of the picture and wasn't sure how to do it.

"Your guess is as good as mine, Miss Mills. I've been retired a while now. But, based on how things work, I suggest you don't make an issue of it. If something's going down, they don't want anyone stirring the pot. Might compromise an operation."

"I suppose so. Mr. Allison didn't mention anything about Harold being on assignment."

"He wouldn't. Need to know."

"How do I reach you?"

Mac gave her a card.

She wrote her phone number on a piece of notepaper from her purse and gave it to him.

"Please call me if you learn anything. I've been trying to find Harold. I sent him a letter to his forwarding address, but I haven't heard back. I was worried. Now I don't know how to feel."

She drove away. Mac drove to his apartment. He'd have to call the kid and tell him.

Never called a dead guy before.

Chapter 30

Jim left the safe house in the early evening, walked to a nearby mailbox, and mailed the letter to Dottie. She'd probably give up on him. He couldn't blame her.

When he came into the safe house, his phone was ringing with the blinking light announcing Mac was calling. Jim picked up right away.

"What's up, Mac?"

"Guess what, kid. Bang. You're dead."

"What?"

"A couple nights ago a burglar was shot and killed in a break-in. The burglar's prints are on file with the FBI under the name Harold Sands. Forget ever being Harold Sands again, kid. He's officially dead. And it worried me at first. I went to see. The stiff looks just like you. A dead ringer, so to speak. I thought I'd lost a valuable asset."

"I guess that was Jamey. Give me a minute." Jim took time to reflect on the loss of what had been his best friend from several years ago. He should feel more grief, but he didn't. Jamey's life had been wasted. Jim spoke again. "No one will miss him. No family."

"He stole a car, drove to a little community south of here, and broke into a house. He had a gun."

Jim sat on his sofa, surprised by this news. "A gun? Jamey didn't like guns. He was afraid of them."

"An FBI guy lives there. That's who shot him. He probably dropped the piece on the stiff to make the shoot look righteous."

That made more sense. "Where'd it go down?"

"Hold on." After some shuffling of papers, Mac read the address.

"That's where Jamey grew up," Jim said. "I lived there for a while. He probably didn't mean any harm, didn't know what he was doing. Well, that's a damn shame. I guess being dead and all I won't be getting my tax refund."

Mac snickered. "Kid, you got ice water in your veins. By the way, I met your girlfriend at the morgue."

"What girlfriend?"

"Dorothy Mills. Your bird from the Agency. Allison told her you'd taken a bullet, and she came down to see for herself."

"Dottie was there?" Jim's pulse quickened. "Didn't she know it wasn't me?"

"She wasn't sure. Rigor has a way of making you better looking. She asked to look at your dick to see if it was you. Even then she wasn't sure. I guess you have an average dick. You think we ought to go to the funeral?"

"You can go. Not me. Shit. This is going to get complicated."

"How so?"

"She's been trying to find me. She sent a letter to my post office box. I wanted to put her off the trail, so I sent her a note saying I was under deep cover and to back off."

"That was stupid, kid. I told you to break off all personal contacts. For a smart kid you sure do some dumb shit sometimes. When did you mail the letter?"

"This evening." Jim felt a large helping of remorse. He'd stepped over the line.

"Nuts," Mac said. "I'll hear from her now for sure. Lucky for us she's with the Agency and might be able to understand." Mac paused for a moment. "So, kid, now that you're dead, your tomato is available. She's good to look at. Do you think I have a shot?"

"Sure, Mac. Go for it. Might solve my problems. Get her off my trail. And off my mind."

"Just pulling your chain, kid. Continue doing what you're doing, and let this shit sort itself out. I'm looking for something else for you to do when this job is over."

Jim hung up and sat back. He stared at the telephone and remembered Jamey, all the fun they'd had as kids, how Jamey had taken him in when he needed a place, how he had sunk into alcoholism and destitution without someone to watch over him, and how now he'd gotten himself killed. Maybe if Jim had spent more time with him after Mr. Barrett died, Jamey would have turned out different, better. Maybe if...

Jim put that sad story out of his mind and considered Mac's parting words instead. Jim was ready for that something else Mac had promised and hoped the next assignment would be more of a challenge than just stealing documents. Something important that would make it worth giving up his personal life.

Chapter 31

Sam Montague sat in his office and stared at the wall. This had been a bad morning. He had just left a conference at the Pentagon with a three-star general.

When Sam left the Company after the Bay of Pigs, he joined up with a tech firm in the military-industrial complex, had risen rapidly through the ranks, and was now its CEO.

Today Sam had pitched the concept of a van-mounted computer system for battlefield applications, not a new concept but one that until now had been considered impractical given the size and power requirements of contemporary computers.

Sam had learned that a major computer manufacturer would announce a new, more powerful and more compact computer system next year.

That inside information had come by way of Mac. At Sam's request, Mac sent a mole inside a manufacturing facility to steal design documents for the widely rumored computer. Based on the specifications, Sam calculated that the system could be fitted into three standard van-trailers and would meet military requirements for mobile computing in the field.

US involvement in Vietnam was heating up, and the Army would need computers on the battlefields and in rear echelon positions. With his company well-positioned to provide van-mounted computers, there were hundreds of millions of dollars to be made.

But today's conference had been a major letdown.

Sam had pitched his concept with a slide show. The general had interrupted the briefing frequently to ask questions. Then he asked the question no one wanted to hear.

"What use would these systems be if no war is being fought, no enemy, no battlefields? What advantage do they have over conventional indoor fixed-installation computers?"

Sam cleared his throat and tried to address this concern. "Well, readiness, of course. Develop them now, and you're ready the next time something breaks out."

"That's true of anything," the general said. "However, given that the president is planning to wind down US involvement in Vietnam, I don't see an immediate need for computers in the field."

Now in his office, Sam considered this problem. To Sam's way of thinking, the real problem sat behind a desk in the Oval Office. Sam's years in CIA had taught him that to solve such a problem, you empty that chair. His associations with executives and operatives at CIA had given him a cynical outlook on how to deal with difficult and powerful people in difficult times.

He had no love for Kennedy. His job as Miami station chief during the Bay of Pigs and its subsequent consequences to Sam's career had finished off any respect he had for the president.

Kennedy had blamed CIA for the mission's failure and vowed to dismantle the Agency. After the Cuban Missile Crisis, Kennedy had flip-flopped on that position, but there were those in CIA who would silently support his removal. They didn't trust him not to turn against the Agency again the next time something went awry.

Perhaps he could involve a few of his former Company colleagues in the solution. Sam was thinking about Murphy. He reached for the telephone.

Mac awoke to a knock on his door. The whippoorwill had been quiet this night, and Mac had slept. He dragged himself out of bed, pulled on his robe, stepped into his slippers, and lit a Camel. He found his eyeglasses, wrapped them around his face, and went to the door.

Murphy leaned against the wall in the hallway, smoking a joint.

Murphy was about forty, six feet tall, slim and muscular, with sandy, close-cropped hair and a ruddy complexion. Tight blue jeans, motorcycle boots, a thick leather belt with a silver buckle, and a maroon Redskins T-shirt all combined to complete the picture. A heavy chain dangled from his belt to his right pants pocket, and a leather pouch on his belt suggested an oversized pocket knife. But anyone who knew him recognized the pouch as his stash.

Smoke curled up from the joint he held between his thumb and forefinger. He was taking a drag when Mac opened the door. He held his breath for five seconds, exhaled a plume of smoke, and smiled at Mac. He came in and plopped down in a chair.

"Hey, Mac. Want a hit?" He held out the joint.

Mac waved off the offer.

"Sam will be calling you," Murphy said. "He wants someone to whack the big guy."

"What big guy?" Mac asked.

"Kennedy."

"Kennedy?" Mac whistled. "Isn't that more down your alley?"

"I turned it down. I want to keep living here. Whoever does this one expatriates. I'm a proud American. I recommended you. A finder's fee would be nice."

"If I do the job, you'll get a taste."

Murphy gave Mac a thumbs up, turned, and left.

Mac went into the kitchen to make breakfast. Montague would call soon. He cracked two eggs into the skillet and dropped bread in the toaster, and the phone rang.

He turned down the burner, picked up the telephone, and said, "Mac, here."

"Mac? Sam Montague. I have a job for you."

"Hello, Sam. Good to hear from you. I'll need to get a box installed there. Danny will bring it as soon as I can round him up."

Mac had Jim in mind to be the mechanic. After hanging up with Sam, he called Snuffy.

"Snuffy, I need Danny if he's available."

"Sure, Mac, he'll be right there."

Danny was at the door in less than a minute. He sniffed the air. "You been smoking shit in here, Mac?"

"Naw. Just burning toast."

Mac dispatched Danny with a scrambler to Sam Montague's office. Then he finished breakfast and waited for Danny to report. He was back in less than an hour.

"The scrambler is installed, Mac." He sniffed the air again, smiled, and went downstairs.

Mac dialed Sam's number.

"Sam? Mac. Hit the switch."

Mac waited until the click sounded, then he threw his switch.

"Okay, Sam, what have you got?"

"A big hit. Public figure, heavily guarded. It's worth a lot to us to have him out of the picture. What do you think?"

"I think I can handle it. I have the perfect mechanic for it. He'll be available to start next month. Is that soon enough?"

"Have to be."

"Keep the scrambler. We'll be in touch when we're ready. Assuming the target is still a target by then. Let me know if anything changes."

Mac hung up, left his scrambler on, and called the safe house, Jim wasn't home yet, so Mac blew into the harmonica.

Jim called at lunch time. "What's up, Mac?"

"Hi kid. Are you going to be finished with the current job on schedule?"

"Yes. Why?"

"I have something else. It's big. A high-profile hit."

"Big money?"

"Huge money. Interested?"

"Definitely. I'm working on a rifle that fits in a briefcase. Rapid assembly and disassembly. In and out in less than a minute. Maybe I can use it on this job."

"Maybe you can. I'll get back to you."

Mac sat back. This mission would be the biggest job he'd ever booked. He wasn't sure Jim was up to it. The kid had never done a hit, and Mac didn't know whether he had the stones to go through with it. Mac would stay on top of this one. They'd both make a lot of money, and the kid, with the hit of the century, would be inducted anonymously, Mac hoped, into the assassin's hall of fame.

Chapter 32

Sarah Weston was busy with the draft technical proposal when her phone rang.

"Sarah, it's Rod. I've got information on the guy you wanted me to check on."

Sarah had been waiting for this call.

"What did you learn?"

"Well, it's what I didn't learn. I didn't learn who he is. More like who he isn't."

"What do you mean?"

"We searched public records for the town where he said he grew up. Nothing there about him."

"I see. Do you plan to take it further?"

"No. I did all this outside any budget. Called in some favors. Be careful. He might be trying to get access to classified data related to the next project, so maybe he's working his way into your confidence now."

"I don't know, Rod. But I want to keep him on board at least until the proposal is finished. He's doing good work, and we don't have any classified documents. Do you mind if I kind of spring this on him? See how he explains it? There might be a reasonable explanation."

"No. I don't mind. He might just disappear once his cover is blown. Do we know where he lives?"

"Not really. Somewhere near here."

"I'll find him if we need to, Sarah. I'll talk to you later."

She sat at her desk, swiveled around, and looked out the window.

She wondered what to do. She dialed Jim's extension.

"Jim, could you come talk to me?"

He was in her office right away. "What's up?"

"We have a situation here. Close the door. I don't know where to start. You're doing such a good job, and you're so well matched to what we're doing, that you seem, well, too good to be true. So, I did some checking up."

Jim drew a breath. "What kind of checking up?"

"Your background. Never mind how. But…" She took a moment. Then said, "There's no record of a James Dodson growing up in Tazewell. So maybe you aren't who you say you are?"

"This is a bit of a surprise. May I please take a few minutes to decide how to discuss this with you? It's a personal thing."

She wondered if he was stalling for time.

"Sure, Jim. Come back after lunch. I need to decide whether we can keep you on. I hope so. I like having you around."

As he left, she turned her attention away from him and to her document. But her focus was divided. She really did like having him around. More than she cared to admit to herself.

An operative's worst nightmare. A blown cover. All efforts to build credibility, gain confidence, fit in, maximize the mission's opportunities, all down the drain. You have to defuse the situation and explain the anomaly, come up with a viable alternative, or abandon the mission and avoid capture.

Jim went to his office to think. Should he bring Mac in on it? Pine Hill might terminate his consulting agreement. That shouldn't prevent him from fulfilling the mission. He already knew what he needed to know.

He drove to the safe house and called Mac.

"Small problem, Mac. The target blew my cover."

"How the hell did they do that?"

"They found out nobody named James Dodson ever lived in my cover's home town. Maybe they put their Navy spooks out there to sniff me out."

"You bet they did. This could compromise the assignment. If they suspect a mole, they'll lock down. You need to convince them that what they learned is a misunderstanding. After the job is finished, you need to lose that identity. It's tarnished."

"Thanks, Mac. I'll let you know how it turns out."

Jim felt a lot better having discussed it with Mac. He pulled out his notes and newspaper articles about James Dodson's life. He made a quick scan of everything and tried to contrive a believable explanation.

The success of this small mission could depend on how well he pulled off the deception.

He returned to Pine Hill and went to Sarah's office. She was still reading documents. He tapped on the door, and she looked up.

"Come in, Jim."

He went in, closed the door, and sat. "Where to start?" He fiddled with a pencil and looked everywhere except at Sarah. "This is difficult. You're going to think I come from a wacky background."

He put the pencil down and walked past her desk to look out the window. He felt her gaze following him.

"I'm hoping I can keep my job, but I'll understand if I can't. I'm enjoying the work and need the money." He turned and looked at her. His story had to be convincing, not only in the details but his delivery too. He returned to the table and continued, mixing truth and lies to form what he hoped would be a believable story.

"My parents died in a car crash when I was an infant." He fiddled with the pencil again. "Of course I don't remember any of that. After the accident, my grandmother went to a nursing home. I was passed from relative to relative, then to an orphanage, and then foster care. At least that's how it was explained to me. I lived in Tazewell, but nobody ever documented it."

"Why ever not?"

"My foster parents believed in teaching children at home among other unconventional things. Mountain people. Appalachia. They didn't trust the school system or anything else about the government. I guess you could call them benign anarchists. So they never registered me any-where. I doubt you'd find any records of them either."

Jim knew none of this would stand up under close scrutiny. He just hoped it would buy him another week.

"That's about it. You can take it for what it's worth."

He waited for her reaction. He had told a complicated lie, and now he counted on his charm and powers of persuasion to sell the story. He made his saddest face and waited for her to speak.

"That's quite a story, Jim. Raised by a hillbilly cult...I'm sorry. I didn't mean to disrespect the people who raised you. And I do believe you. What else could it be? Let's keep this between us. The others don't need to know."

"Do you think the investigators will want more details?" He didn't want them poking around any more than they already had.

"Not now. Maybe later when they do background checks." She smiled. "There are things in my past I'd rather not have anyone know. But that's another story. And no, I won't tell you about them someday. Get out of here and get to work."

As Jim started out the door, Sarah said, "Jim, come back in and close the door. There's something else."

He sat across from her. She got up from her desk, walked around it, took off her glasses, and sat next to him. She turned toward him and her knees brushed the side of his leg.

Sarah said, "This is outside the scope of our present business ar-rangement and cannot be allowed to affect anything we do here."

She tilted her head, looked into his eyes and, lowering her tone, asked, "Would you like to meet me this evening for a drink after work?"

She opened her legs a small distance so her knees moved across his thigh again. His pulse quickened. He drew a breath and looked at her knees.

She went on. "There's more work coming along. But we shouldn't discuss that while the meter is running for this project. It would have to be off the clock."

Jim had sensed Sarah felt an attraction for him from the day they met. One thing for sure, that attraction was the only reason he still worked here. If the boss had been a man, Jim would have been out on his ass as soon as his cover was blown.

"Sure, Sarah. We can meet. Where?"

"Nowhere nearby. If anyone saw us, they might misunderstand. Do you know Cholly's?"

"Near Dupont Circle?"

"That's it. I'll meet you there at about seven-thirty. That'll give me time to change, feed my kids, and drive down."

Jim returned to his office. This was a tough call. His instincts told him getting romantically involved with a target meant bad business. But turning her down might get him the boot. He needed Mac's advice. He returned to the safe house and called Mac. The line was busy. He'd try later.

Mac had been shooting baskets with balled up wads of paper and the trashcan when the phone rang. The trash can was across the room, and he was hitting about one out of three. Crumpled wads were all over the floor.

"Mac, it's Dorothy Mills."

Mac had been dreading this call. "Hi, Dorothy, what can I do for you?"

"For what it's worth, I am absolutely sure the body at the morgue wasn't Harold."

"Are you sure that's not just wishful thinking?"

"Yes. I am sure."

"How can you be?"

"This is kind of embarrassing." She paused. "Well, here goes. I didn't know whether rigor mortis could make an uncircumcised man look circumcised. I've since learned it cannot. Harold wasn't circumcised. The body we saw was."

"Well, maybe he got trimmed since you last saw his, uh, I mean, him." Mac was grasping at straws and trying not to laugh.

"I'd almost believe that except for one thing. I got a letter from him.

It was postmarked two days after that man was killed. Harold said he was in deep cover."

More straws. "He did get shot in an FBI agent's house. Can't get much deeper than that. Maybe someone else mailed the letter and didn't get around to it right away. Maybe it wasn't from him."

"Well, I don't believe all that. And, quite honestly, I think you might know more than you're letting on. I don't know where to go from here. Do I tell the Agency about my suspicions?"

"No. If he's in deep cover, he might need to stay dead. You could put him and his mission at risk."

"I guess you're right. But my life is upside down now. I don't know whether to write Harold off or wait and see."

"Do what's best for you, Dorothy. We don't know what's best for him. But if I hear from him, I'll let you know."

"I'd appreciate that, Mac. You've been a friend in all this."

Mac hung up the phone. All his life people had said he was their friend, and most times, like now, it was right after he'd lied to them in the interests of some greater good.

But it was okay. The good this time, like all the others, was indeed greater. Or so he'd convinced himself.

Mac went into the bathroom for his afternoon constitutional. He settled in with a magazine, and the phone rang again. He had an extension on the bathroom wall for such occasions.

"Mac, it's Jim."

"Hi, kid. I'm on the crapper. No box in here. Watch what you say."

"There's a small problem. The boss wants to take me out for a drink."

"There's a problem with that?"

"She's a woman. A damn fine-looking woman."

"Gee, kid. I wish I had your problems."

"Couldn't this upset things?"

"Of course it could. What do you think you should do?"

Mac farted, and it resonated loudly in the echo chamber of the porcelain toilet bowl.

Jim laughed and then said, "I was hoping you had some advice. If I turn her down, I might be out of there. If I go for it, I might have her in my hair after the job is over. She's a married woman. That can complicate a guy's life."

"What? A jealous husband? A guy with your skills ought to be able to handle that." Mac chuckled.

"I need this lady off my case, Mac."

"Hold on a second. I'm getting off the hopper." Mac put the phone on the toilet tank so he could finish up. Then he stood, pulled his pants up, and flushed the toilet. He picked up the phone and said, "Well, kid, there's a way to have the best of both worlds."

"What's that?"

"Fuck her, but don't be real good at it."

"Huh? What do you mean?"

Mac held the phone between his head and his shoulder while he washed his hands.

"Hold on until I get to the box." He put the phone down, went into the living room. picked up, and said, "Hit the switch."

He turned on his scrambler and waited for Jim to do likewise. "It's easy kid. Do what so many husbands do, which is why these married tomatoes are out looking in the first place. Make it eminently forgettable. No foreplay, keep your socks and undershirt on, stay on top, get your carrot waxed, get your rocks off before she can, wipe your dick on the bedspread, burp, fart, leave her in the wet spot, roll over and go to sleep, snore, and let her walk herself to the car."

Jim's telephone hit the floor. When he recovered it, he asked between spurts of laughter, "What good would that do?"

"You laugh, but it would accomplish two things. First you didn't reject her, so she won't be pissed about that. Second, you were a bum fuck, so she won't be stalking you wanting to varnish your cane again. I bet the next day at work she'd be real businesslike. You won't even get a smile out of her."

"Mac, you're something, you know that? I just don't know."

"Well, do what you think is best, kid. You already said they blew your cover. Have a good time, and when you get a new identity, she shouldn't be able to find you."

"Thanks, Mac. I'll play it by ear."

"That's not the appendage I'd use, but whatever swings your clapper. By the way, your girlfriend just called. She got your letter. I told her to cool it for a while, but I don't know what she'll do. You sure know how to get a lot of chippies involved in your work."

Jim changed into casual attire and ate a sandwich. Then he went to his car and headed into town toward Dupont Circle. He arrived at quarter after seven and found a parking space on a side street. He walked to Cholly's, went down the stairs and through the entrance, and took a seat at a small table away from the door. He ordered a beer and waited.

She was five minutes late. He almost didn't recognize her, she was that different. She had let her auburn hair down so it hung just below her shoulders. No horn-rimmed glasses to obscure her deep brown eyes. She wore carefully-applied makeup, more than the dab of lipstick she wore at work. Her provocative outfit, a loose-fitting blouse open down to some significant cleavage and a knee-length, tight-fitting skirt that showed off her figure when she walked, left little to the imagination. Nylons and high heels completed the outfit. No doubt about it. Sarah Weston was a beautiful, alluring woman, and tonight she had dressed to show herself at her sexiest best.

She sat next to him, said hello, and touched his arm. The waitress was there right away, and Sarah ordered a glass of red wine.

"Have you eaten?" she asked.

"Had a sandwich at home."

"Me too. If we get hungry later we can have dinner somewhere. So, Jim, how do you like working for me?"

"I like it fine. Interesting work, smart people, and no pressure."

"I hope you'll come with us if we win the bid." She took a sip of wine. "By the way, what'd you do to Martin?"

"What do you mean?"

"He's done a one-eighty on you. When you first came here, he bad-mouthed you all over the project. Said we didn't need you. Brent told me about it. Now, he's telling me I need to hire you right away to make sure you're on staff for the job. How'd you do that?"

Jim smiled. "Must be my country-boy charm."

"Well, that's for sure. Anyway, maybe you can come to work for us. And, if not, well, maybe we can just see each other occasionally."

"I hope so. I have to say, Sarah, you look good. I've never seen you look so, well, so attractive. You don't look like the boss lady now."

"Why thank you, kind sir. I try to stay businesslike on the job. But when I'm out, I prefer to let my hair down and relax."

"I like the relaxed you better."

She turned in her chair so her knees were touching his leg like she had at the office. She slowly raised and lowered her leg so her knee moved up and down stroking his thigh. She looked in his eyes and took a sip of wine. "Jim, do you know what's upstairs in this building?"

"It's a hotel, I believe."

"Yes, it is. Suppose you wait here while I go see if they have a vacancy." She looked into his eyes with mock concern. "I'm not being too forward, am I?"

"No, I thought you'd never ask," he said. "Need cash for the room?"

"No thank you. This one's on me." She leaned closer and looked in his eyes again. She almost whispered, "Next time you can be the host. If there is a next time. Do you think there will be a next time?"

"I don't know. I don't have much experience with office romances. I've always heard they're a bad idea."

"They can be. I don't do this as a rule. But you won't be in the office much longer, so I can bend the rules."

She put her hand on his arm and took a serious tone. "Jim, I don't want to break the mood, but I should say this. Afterward, one or the other of us might not want to continue while the other one wants to. You have to promise me if I need to call it off, you'll respect my wishes."

"And if I refuse to promise?"

"I'll take that chance. Don't go away. I'll be right back."

She leaned over and kissed him lightly on the lips. Then she went across the room and up the stairs.

Three hours later, they lay spent in the king-sized bed.

"That rarely happens," Sarah said.

"What's that?"

"I got off twice. And I think I could do it again." She turned on her side to face him. "You're something else."

"I'm getting hungry. Room service?"

"I have to get home. I wish we had time to try for another one, but it's late. Stay here as long as you like. The room is paid up for the night. This was a lovely time, Jim. I hope we can do it again. Maybe after the project is over."

"I hope so too."

But he didn't hope so. The sex was more than good, but he needed to put distance between himself and this beautiful lady, the one who came so close to blowing his cover.

He stayed in the bed with the covers pulled up to his chin while she went into the bathroom to wash up. Then he watched her dress, which was every bit as nice as watching her undress three hours earlier. She moved with grace and style. She came to him and kissed him passionately.

"There's lots more where this came from," she said.

He pulled her down on the bed and continued the kiss. When he released her, she reached down and touched him.

"Again? I'm already dressed. How about just this?"

She stroked him gently then poked her head under the blanket.

The humor of the situation got to him. Here he'd been worried about getting his cover blown, and now he was getting blown under the covers. He laughed.

She stopped. "And what's so funny?"

"Nothing, nothing. Don't stop now."

She dove under the covers again.

Afterward she kissed him and ran across the room to the door. "See you tomorrow," she said.

So much for Mac's advice. He doubted he could have done it anyway. Maybe after he was Mac's age.

Jim turned out the light and lay in bed thinking about next week when he'd complete this mission and move on to the next one. He wondered whether tonight's rendezvous would have consequences. For now it didn't seem to matter. But later...

Chapter 33

A week had passed since Jim and Sarah met for drinks. She hadn't mentioned their dalliance. In fact, she hadn't said much more than good morning and good night. He hoped their interlude was, to her, just another one-night stand.

Jim sat with Martin, Brent, Maggie, and Jennie around the conference table in Sarah's office for the project wrap. Glad the project was nearly over, he was ready to move on to his reason for being there. He looked across the desk at Sarah. She busied herself with a stack of papers. She was indeed one fine-looking woman. He remembered what she looked like a week before at Cholly's and later in the hotel room. He would like to see Sarah that way again, but he knew better.

Sarah said, "Thanks everyone for your work. I think we have a solid proposal and a good chance of winning. And we have a job well done. Win or lose, I call this a success. Thank you again."

The team filed out of the office. Sarah gestured for Jim to stay behind.

"Close the door, please." He did.

"Jim, obviously we don't need you after today. I'll miss having you around. Here's a check for through the end of the week. You've earned it. I'll need your keys. You should take anything personal from your office with you now."

Jim removed the two keys from his key ring and gave them to her.

"Sarah, thanks for the work and for your understanding and discretion with the issue related to my background."

"As I said, Jim, I'll miss you. Maybe one day soon we can get together and discuss the future. I'm sure I can use you on other projects. And if we win this bid, there is a place for you here. May I call you in a week or two? Maybe schedule another staffing meeting at Cholly's?"

"Yes, Sarah, I'd like that."

He'd be out of the area soon, and she wouldn't find him. He was almost sorry about that. She was one hell of a woman. He went to his office, put his things in his briefcase, and left. He wanted to be out of there before Sarah realized she didn't have his phone number.

He drove to his apartment, changed into work clothes, went to the workshop, and piddled around, working on the sniper rifle. He had it almost ready for a test firing. At four, a truck pulled up outside the workshop. He looked out. A tanker truck with a septic tank service logo sat in the driveway. A man in work clothes walked toward the door of the house.

Jim yelled out the door, "Need me to move my car?"

The man yelled, "Here to drain the septic tank. You know where it is?"

"Between the house and the garage, I think."

The man walked around and looked. "I can reach it from here."

Jim went outside to watch. As with most things, his curiosity drove him to learn whatever he could about how things work. He didn't know anyone else who could derive pleasure from learning how septic tanks were drained, but he could.

The man poked the ground behind the workshop with a pointed cast iron pole to locate the septic tank. Once he found it, he shoveled away the sod to expose the lid. Jim moved closer and watched.

The man removed the lid, un-reeled a long hose from the truck, and dropped its nozzle into the tank. He started up a pump on the truck and drained the tank. Then he replaced the tank's lid, sealed it, and put the sod in place.

He wrote an invoice and handed it to Jim.

Jim asked him, "How often does a septic tank get drained?"

"It depends on the size of the tank and how many folks are using it.

For a family of four and a tank this size, about every five to seven years ought to do it."

"How do you know when to do it?"

"Most folks just wait until the drain backs up. Others do it when they think it might be about due. How many people live here?"

"One."

"Well, figure fifteen years."

Jim had no idea how he'd use this new knowledge, but, as with everything he learned, he stored it away for future reference.

On Wednesday, Jim slept in. He'd need to be alert that night when he went into the Pine Hill offices. He stopped at Gloria's Diner for a take-out sandwich and went to the workshop. He took the project's components from the cabinet to the workbench and finished the construction details. That afternoon, he built a silencer to thread onto the sawed-off barrel.

He practiced the transformation from what looked like a common briefcase to a functioning rifle with a silencer and back again. The complete transformation in either direction took about thirty seconds. With practice he would shave seconds off both procedures. When he finished, he put everything away, cleaned up and secured the workshop, and left for the safe house in Maryland.

Jim fixed supper on the hot plate and ate slowly. Then he laid out his clothes on the bed, all black to blend into the shadows, and a tube of blackface greasepaint.

He set the alarm clock for midnight, settled in a chair, and read a book to pass the time. When the alarm went off, it startled him. He put his book down and called Mac.

"Hi, Mac. I'm going in soon. It shouldn't take long. You should be here in about an hour."

"You bet, kid. Remember, if anything goes wrong, get the hell out of there. The next job is way more important than this one."

Jim changed and packed his tools. He drove to Pine Hill. The parking lot was empty, but he parked on the street within an easy sprint from the side door.

He blackened his face with greasepaint, put on the gloves, grabbed his tool case, snuck across the lawn to the side door, and entered the building.

His first stop would be Sarah's office. He picked the lock, went in, and locked the door from the inside. He shined his penlight around the office. There were no documents on the desk or table. He opened the file cabinet. The folders for drafts and working papers were there, but no final copy.

He picked the lock on Sarah's desk, and searched the drawers. Nothing.

His mind raced. Surely Sarah had a copy of the proposal. Unless she took it home, it should be here. Jim wasn't sure where, though. Perhaps Maggie had a copy. He went out past the conference room and into Maggie's office. He picked the lock and went in.

Just after he got into Maggie's office, headlights pierced the darkness and came into the parking lot. Could it be Martin again? He went to the window. It wasn't Martin. Brent's car and then Maggie's drove in.

They walked to the back door, close to one another with their heads together.

It fell into place. Brent and Maggie were married to other people. Hotels cost money. The conference room had a couch. The team worked long hours, and her husband and his wife had become accustomed to them getting home late.

The elevator started its noisy ascent, audible even through closed doors. He wouldn't have time to get to his own office this time. It was locked and farther away than it had been when Martin made his late-night visit.

He had to hand it to Brent. He was nailing the finest fox in the building. Well, the second finest, anyway.

The elevator stopped, and its door opened. Two sets of footsteps sounded in the corridor coming his way. This could be trouble. If he had to disable Brent and escape, he couldn't complete the assignment. Plus he'd have to deal with Maggie. If it came to that, the greasepaint might let him get away without being identified, but the mission wouldn't be completed.

The footsteps stopped outside her office. Jim wedged himself into a corner at the back of the room. He heard the jingle of Maggie's keys and then Maggie's voice. "I was sure I locked this when I left." Her door opened, and Maggie came in. Jim hugged the wall and prayed that she wouldn't turn on the lights. Brent's silhouette was visible just outside the door. She came in, went to her desk, unlocked it, and took something out, which Jim assumed was the key to the conference room. Brent came in behind her and put his arms around her waist. Jim could see the two of them in the dim light from the hallway, but they apparently hadn't seen him. She leaned her head back against Brent's shoulder and moaned as he kissed her neck and cheeks and as his hands roamed across the front of her body.

Jim didn't move a muscle or make a peep. He wondered whether Brent intended to do her right there on the desk in the dark. Jim had no choice but to watch the show in silence. Eventually, he feared, they'd turn the lights on, and he'd be caught. He couldn't hide in the shadows forever.

Brent turned her around and pushed her against the desk. He pulled her skirt up and began fumbling with her panties. She reached down and touched him and stroked him through his trousers. Jim began to get aroused just watching.

"Not here," she said in a whisper. She pulled away and led him by the hand out the door. He followed like a puppy dog and closed the door behind them.

Jim breathed a sigh of relief. He needed to get out of there as soon as he could. He remembered what Mac had said:

The next job is way more important than this one.

Even so, he had a lot of time and effort invested in this mission, and he wanted to pull it off if possible.

A door opened and closed next to Maggie's office. That would be the conference room. This was bad. They could be in there a long time.

He needed to find the document, expose the film, develop it, and turn it over to Mac. If it was here in Maggie's office, he could slip out to the men's room while they were occupied, but what if Brent had to take a piss? And what if they were in the hallway when he came out of the men's room?

Jim sat in a chair and wracked his brain. He had to clear them out of there. The sounds of their lovemaking pushed through the walls, the unmistakable crunch of a leather couch keeping time, and Maggie was a moaner.

Swell. I have to stay here and listen to that.

Then he had an idea. It was a long shot, but if it didn't work, nothing would. He left Maggie's office and crept silently down the hall to the elevator. He pushed the down button, and the door opened. He watched the conference room door and went into the elevator and pushed the button for the first floor. Then, before the door slid shut, he came out into the hall and hid around a corner. The elevator made its noisy descent. After it was on its way, he came out and pushed the down button to recall it once it got to the first floor. He'd repeat the procedure until the noise flushed them out.

He didn't have long to wait.

The muffled sounds of the love-making stopped only to be followed by the sounds of the lovers dressing in a hurry. Then the conference room door opened just a crack, and they peeked out. He ducked back into his hiding position. Hasty footsteps clattered down the hall. They ran down the stairs. Jim went to a window overlooking the parking lot. Seconds later Maggie came out. She looked around frantically, jumped in her car, and sped away. Soon Brent came to the door and looked around. He peeled rubber getting out.

Jim had to laugh. What would Brent and Maggie say to each other in the morning? Would they ask around carefully to see who had come in late? Would they show up early to see if they'd left a mess? Pecker tracks on a leather couch could raise eyebrows and get folks talking.

A search of Maggie's office turned up nothing. He searched Jennie's office and came up empty-handed. Frustrated, he went back to Sarah's office for another look. And there he saw what he had missed the first time around. A wide, rectangular briefcase stood on the floor in the shadows beside her bookcase. It had a four-number combination lock with small wheels to dial in the numbers. It would be easy to crack. He put pressure on the latch while he turned each dial until it stopped. When all three dials had stopped, the latch popped open.

Sarah's copy of the proposal was in the case. He took it out, put it on the table, and opened it flat. The cost proposal was a removable appendix with seven pages. He took it and his camera into the men's room, turned on the overhead light, and took his pictures. He returned the document to Sarah's office and put everything back the way he'd found it. His watch said two-thirty.

Jim left the building by the side door, slipped across the lawn to his car, and drove to the safe house. Mac's car was in the parking lot. He went up to the apartment where he found Mac waiting inside.

"How'd it go, kid? What took so long? I went through a pack of Camels."

"I'll tell you after I develop the film."

He took the developing chemicals, tank and handbag, and the film cartridge down the hall and into the bathroom. A while later he returned with a film strip. He took a magnifying glass from the desk, held the strip up to a desk lamp, and examined the images.

"Perfect. In focus, clear, and sharp."

He hung the film up to dry.

"So what took so long?" Mac said.

As he wiped the greasepaint from his face, Jim told Mac first about not being able to find the document then about the lovers in the conference room.

Mac laughed at the story. "Fast thinking on your part. You could still be in there depending on that guy's staying power."

When the film was dry, Jim trimmed the excess from the strip, put the strip in an envelope, and handed it to Mac.

"Get some sleep, kid. I'm off to make this delivery at first light of day."

"That's good. I'm glad it's over, and I'm ready for the next one."

Mac stopped on his way to the door. "Oh, by the way, kid, I almost forgot. That pal of yours who took a bullet left his estate to you."

"His what?"

"This is all he owned." Mac handed Jim the pack of playing cards. "I figured you might like to have it as a souvenir, him being your only friend and all."

"Thanks, Mac." Jim took the cards and put them on the table.

"And I have these." Mac handed him a thick envelope. "These are aliases. Just in case. For later."

Mac left, and Jim removed the cards from the box and found all that was left of his only friend's life hidden in a small, grimy package. A dollar bill, a driver's license, a draft card, and a social security card. He hoped he'd do better when his time came. He hoped too that Jamey Barrett had found peace at last.

The envelope contained passports and driver's licenses, three each with different names and addresses. Aliases.

Chapter 34

The next assignment would be a hit, and Jim wanted to finish the briefcase rifle if only to take his mind off his lingering doubts about becoming a paid assassin. He kept telling himself if the money was there, the doubts would vanish. He hoped he was right.

On Monday, Jim went to the workshop where Jerry sat on the stool at his workbench, the pieces of a disassembled rifle laid out in front of him.

"I took the day off to catch up on some work," Jerry said.

"Glad you're here. I have to sight-in my invention. Where can I do that?"

"You want a firing range?"

"No, a pasture. Private. Near woods and away from civilization." Every year with Pop, they had always used a range to sight in rifles for hunting season. Jim wanted someplace private so no one would see the sniper's weapon.

Jerry gave him directions to a field behind an abandoned farmhouse and near a patch of woods about twenty miles south. "Hunters use the field to sight in their rifles. Shouldn't be anybody there this time of year."

Jim opened the cabinet and removed the rig in its briefcase configuration. Jerry asked, "Your invention?"

"It's in the case," Jim said.

"Not very big."

"That's the idea. See you later."

Jim stopped at the hardware store for ammunition and targets and at the grocery store for cantaloupes. He followed Jerry's directions to the field, parked next to the old farmhouse, and walked down the hill.

He placed a cantaloupe on a stump and took the briefcase to the edge of the woods. He assembled and loaded the rifle and stood next to a tree. He aimed at the cantaloupe, released the safety, and squeezed the trigger. The cantaloupe exploded.

The silencer worked well. Instead of a loud retort, the rifle made a dull thud. The shot wasn't silent but it would suppress the retort in the ambient noise of an airport or a busy street, perhaps with a crowd of noisy people nearby.

Too many test firings would tear up the silencer, so he removed it and put it aside. Then he did some target shooting, adjusting the scope as he went along.

He was walking to his shooting position after putting up a fresh cantaloupe when a man stepped out of the woods.

"Good afternoon, sir. Are cantaloupes in season now?" The man laughed at his own joke and walked toward Jim. He wore a tan uniform, a Smokey Bear hat, and a pistol on his hip.

"I've been watching you for a while from back there." He gestured toward the patch of woods behind Jim's stand. "What are you doing?"

As the man drew nearer, Jim could see a badge on his chest and the insignia of a game warden on a shoulder patch. A name tag under the badge said:

Deputy Donald Price

"I'm sighting in this weapon."

"Do you have a hunting license?"

"No, I'm not a hunter. I'm testing this configuration."

"What is it?"

"An invention of mine."

"It's a peculiar setup. It sounded like you have a rifle in that case. Would you open it please?"

Jim opened the lid to the briefcase and let Price look in.

"A sawed-off Savage," Price said. "What's that fitting on the barrel?"

"For the barrel extension. Haven't made it yet." The silencer was leaning against a nearby tree. Jim hoped the deputy didn't notice it.

"I think unregistered sawed-off rifles are illegal," Price said.

"Could be," Jim said. "But where my client does his shooting, laws are not a concern."

Price looked up at Jim. "Where's that?"

Jim looked from side to side. "Can you keep a secret? This is classified stuff. It's for the feds. Normally I couldn't discuss it, but you obviously have a need to know."

Jim was playing up to the guy's ego.

"Yes, sir, I can keep a secret."

"It's a project for the intelligence boys. They're going to take a shot at Castro. Hard to get near if you're carrying a weapon. I pitched my idea to them, and they asked me to build a prototype. I'm testing it so I can give them a live demonstration."

"Impressive. What's your name?"

"Bill Dawson." That was one of the aliases Mac had given him. "Deputy Price, if details about this invention get out, the government will cancel the project. It would alert Castro's security forces to look for guys with briefcases. I have a lot riding on this invention. So do the boys at—" He paused and looked around as if to ensure nobody was listening. "—Langley."

Price's eyebrows went up. He whistled. "I understand, Mr. Dawson. Mum's the word."

Yeah, right. You'll be at the Moose Lodge tonight bragging to your beer-drinking buddies about being in on a CIA assassination plot.

They shook hands, and Price turned and walked into the woods.

Evening was approaching and Jim was hungry.

He packed everything and returned to his car, pleased with his progress. His doubts notwithstanding, the first step in becoming an assassin was well underway. There was more to do.

While he drove, he considered what an assassin goes through. What's it like to have a man in your crosshairs, your finger on the trigger, killing on your mind? Jim didn't know. Mac knew. He'd said you get used to it with time and experience. Jim wasn't sure he wanted to get used to it, to have it become a routine part of who he was and what he did. He wasn't sure. He had time to become sure, though. He'd have to, one way or the other.

Chapter 35

On Tuesday morning, Jim called the bank in Zurich. Abercrombie had deposited his seventeen-five. Jim had them transfer thirteen-five to Mac's account, then he went to breakfast.

When he got home, the scrambler's green light blinked at him. Jim called back.

"Mac, the payment is in, and I paid back the advance plus your commission."

"Thanks. That hit is ready to go. I want you to give this a lot of thought. It pays well, but it's risky. You can do it, but it's a big one. A major political figure. You can make fifty grand. Maybe more."

"Wow! That's a healthy payday." His doubts began to melt away already. Of course, it might depend on the target.

"The client wants to be called Fish. Tomorrow morning is good for him. How about you?"

"I'll be here. But one question. You don't want to know the target. But right after a major player gets bumped, you get big money. I think you'll make the connection."

"It works that way sometimes. Remember, you have to impress the client. If he thinks we can't do it, he might go to the guy who turned down the job, and raise the ante."

Jim was curious. "Who is this guy?"

"His name is Murphy. He's a cold sumbitch. He'd whack his own mama if the money was there. And he's good. He ever gets on your ass, you're a goner."

"I'll keep that in mind."

"Make sure the client knows you can deliver. I'll try to keep Murphy busy and out of the loop for a while. See you later."

Jim decided from now on he would record all calls to or from Mac and clients. He patched his tape recorder to the scrambler.

On Wednesday, the phone rang and the scrambler blinked red. Jim pressed the record button, turned on the scrambler and answered the phone.

"Is this Shadow?" a voice said.

"Who's calling?"

"Fish."

"Shadow here, Fish. How can I help you?"

"How much do you know?"

"Mac said it's a high profile political assassination. Heavily guarded."

"Right. I need to know you can handle this. It will be the biggest thing you ever did. Give me some background. What hits have you done?"

That question came as a surprise. "You've got to be kidding."

"Okay, let me put it another way. Have you done any high-profile hits I might know about?"

"Same answer. Forget the job interview. Mac gave me the assignment. That should be enough. Let's talk details."

"I need to know if you want the job."

"I need to know what the job is. Quit dancing. Who do you want hit?"

"Understand if I tell you, Shadow, and you decide not to accept, I'd better not read in the Post about plans being hatched to hit the target. If that happens, you'd be the next target. And Mac. And I know people who can do it."

"If you're talking about Murphy, we know him too, and he doesn't scare us. Well, not a lot, anyway." Jim chuckled. "But I didn't take this call so you could lecture me about honor among assassins. Either tell me who the target is, or hang up and take your chances with Murphy."

Fish paused. Then he said, "The president."

Jim drew a breath. The target now had a name and a face. Until now he hadn't had to deal with that. He shoved his doubts into the background and continued the negotiation. "That is a big one. What's your schedule? When do you need it done?"

"Soon. He's making noises about decisions that will put us under. We need him out of the way. But there are conditions."

"Like what?"

"This is non-negotiable. There can be no dead or wounded bystanders. Absolutely none. Our associates in business and government will understand and tolerate the necessity of taking this extreme action. Many of them will profit. Some of them will approve. And a couple of them are silent partners. But if the hit takes out family, friends, innocent bystanders, that's not acceptable. We aren't animals, just businessmen. We don't want to be known as the cold bastards that killed John-John even among ourselves. So, get this straight, Shadow. There will be no extra bodies piled up. Now, what is this going to cost us?"

"What's your budget?"

"Twenty grand. Payable upon delivery."

"Get serious. I make more than that stealing documents. If you want the man's dental records, we can talk. But his death certificate costs more."

"How much do you need?"

"I'll get back to you. It's bigger than I thought. I'll call you later today, about three."

"Okay, Shadow. Three o'clock."

They hung up. Fish's voice was vaguely familiar, but Jim didn't remember from where.

He called Mac. "Mac, we need to bend the rules. This is big. You'll know the target right after the hit, so you might as well know now. You might want to pass on this one. I also can't figure what the price should be. I need help."

"I already know the target. You have a problem doing it? Like you're a fucking Democrat or something?"

"No. I can do it. How'd you find out?"

"Murphy told me. He turned it down and recommended us."

"How much do I charge? Fish has silent partners. What do you think it's worth to them?"

"Millions. We're talking the military-industrial complex here."

"You know, Mac, Kennedy intended to shut down the Company. Is this a sanction?"

"Well, the Company might be one of those silent partners, but I doubt it. Whoever it is, you can be sure they can come up with some cash. Charge a half million bucks. That's pennies compared to what they stand to lose if the Pentagon pulls the plug."

"Wow! I didn't think it could go that high. Could it push him over the top and send him back to Murphy?"

Mac laughed. "Murphy turned the job down, remember? The FBI knows him, and they'll be looking at him. And if the Company learned he was doing a rogue op like this, they'd put a sanction on him. He doesn't want to leave the country. He likes it here."

"Okay, Mac. I don't have that problem what with being dead and all. They don't know me. I'm supposed to call Fish at three o'clock. Stand by to patch me through."

Jim hung up and stared at the scrambler. He didn't like not knowing who the client was. It limited his options if something went sour. He'd have to find out.

He put the tools and cables he needed into a small toolbox. The scrambler and his tape recorder went into a knapsack, and he changed into a khaki shirt and pants like a telephone repairman would wear, darkened his complexion with makeup, and donned a dark blue baseball cap. From a distance not even Mac would recognize him.

He drove to Mac's apartment house, timing it to be there fifteen minutes before Fish expected his call. He parked alongside the building where there were no windows and took a back entrance into the basement.

A naked bulb hung from an electrical cord in the center of the room and bathed the unfinished basement in a stark white flood of light. He located the telephone junction box and opened it. Each terminal was labeled with a telephone number and an apartment number. He found Mac's two phone numbers.

Jim hooked his equipment into the phone box. He dialed Mac's incoming number. Mac answered right away. "Mac here."

"I'm ready to be patched through."

"Okay, kid. Turn on your scrambler."

Jim flipped the switch on the scrambler and pressed Record. Mac dialed the client's number, the line on the other end picked up, and a woman's voice answered.

Mac said, "Extension one-ten, please."

The operator put his call through, and a man's voice said, "Montague, here."

"Sam, it's Mac."

So Fish was Sam Montague, the asshole Miami station chief. Small world. Apparently Fish hadn't recognized Jim's voice when they spoke earlier. That was no surprise. During that op, Montague had been a big shot, Jim was just a lowly tech, they had never actually conversed, and it was more than two years ago.

Jim picked up the handset. After a few seconds a voice said, "Shadow? This is Fish."

"I have your price. Two million. Half in advance."

"Are you fucking kidding me? Two million? No way!" Fish seemed upset.

Jim went straight to the point. "Look. You know and I know that no one else can do this job. Even Murphy didn't want it. We also know how much you stand to lose if the job doesn't get done. Take it or leave it."

Fish waited and then spoke more quietly, "I have to talk to my partners. It isn't easy coming up with that kind of money. I'll call you tomorrow morning."

"I'll expect your call at ten."

Jim disconnected and called Mac.

"Mac, Fish choked on the price. He's going to mull it over and call tomorrow. Should I come down?"

"No. That's what he's hoping for. Don't negotiate. They can afford it. He'll come around. My guess is he'll call Murphy to get him to change his mind. That won't happen. Murphy is at the airport as we speak. He's going to Singapore. Talk to you later."

Jim disconnected everything and packed it in.

The next day Jim made sure he was back from breakfast before ten. Fish's call came in on time, and Jim turned on the scrambler and tape recorder. Fish kicked off the discussion.

"Okay, Shadow, first thing is about paying half in advance. We can't do that."

Jim came right back. "Not negotiable. I have risks and expenses. Things can go wrong, things that might cost a lot of money. Like legal fees. Without an advance I'd have nothing. So, there's no choice. I must have a fifty percent advance, nonrefundable."

"How do we know you won't just take the money and split?"

"Mac is how. You called him because you trust him. If I don't deliver, he loses his fee and his reputation. He'd come after me. Nobody wants Mac after them. You know that better than I do."

"What if the mission fails? What happens to the money?"

"It won't fail. I want it to succeed. So does Mac. You have not only me, but all of Mac's resources working for you. That's an awesome package. We might have a couple false starts, but we'll get him."

"When can we expect the job to be done?"

"All I can tell you is when it will start. When I see the advance deposited in my account, I start work. When the time and place are right, I'll do the hit. So, what's it going to be?"

Fish waited a while before answering. "We've got to do it. You're robbing us blind, but we have no choice. My partners know I need two million to solve our biggest problem, and they aren't happy, but they don't know what the solution involves. As far as they know, it's a bribe. I wish it was that simple."

"Then they shouldn't balk at the price. How much do they think it takes to bribe a Kennedy?"

"Okay, since it's a deal, start now. I'll make the first payment today. Same bank Mac uses, I assume. Give me your account information, I'll do the transfer while it's still business hours in Zurich. You'll get it right away. I keep a slush fund at that bank."

Jim read off his public account number, and they said their good-byes. He figured with the time zone difference, he'd have the money in his account sometime the next day.

Jim called Mac and told him, "The deal is on. Payment expected to-morrow. I'd like your help and advice with this one. Perhaps we can get together?"

"Sure. That same diner near your digs for lunch. By the way, kid, if you got your price, that's the biggest-paying assignment I've booked since I got into this racket."

Jim laughed to himself. *Wait until he finds out.*

The next morning, Jim called the bank in Switzerland. One million dollars had been deposited. He transferred two hundred thousand to Mac's account, then he went to Gloria's to wait for Mac. He had breakfast and stayed all morning. He sat at a table in the back, drinking coffee, reading the paper, and jotting down ideas, questions, and issues for their meeting.

Jim was excited. He was planning a major assassination and collaborating with one of the best, with dire international consequences and a seven figure payoff, and it got his adrenalin pumping. This was the big time, what he'd waited for. He couldn't believe his doubts had subsided so readily. Nothing like two million bucks to trump a guy's conscience. He didn't know whether the doubts would resurface, but he'd deal with that when it happened.

Mac walked in at two o'clock, looked around to see that no one else was there, and came to Jim's table. He ran his hands under the table.

Then he broke into a big grin and said, "Jesus Christ, kid. There's two hundred big ones in my account. Not only do you double the price I give you, but you get paid in advance. How the hell did you manage that?"

"That's half payment. The rest is due when the job's done."

"Holy shit! You got him to go for—" Mac looked around and said in a whisper, "—two mil?"

"Simple logic. What does he stand to lose if the hit doesn't go down? And to gain if it does?"

"Christ, kid, I ought to take you out of the field and let you be my negotiator. Nice going. Shit. We can both retire." Mac clapped his hands together and grinned.

The waitress came over, and they ordered lunch.

When she was gone, Mac said, "What kind of help do you need, kid? What can I do? I won't go with you on the hit. Forget that. Not for twenty percent."

"You want to go? I'll split the fee down the middle."

Mac smiled. "Nice gesture, kid, You'd take a smaller taste just to have old Mac riding shotgun." Mac seemed proud of that. "But no can do. I appreciate the generosity, but I'm too old for the field. Now, what do you need?"

A couple came in the front door and sat at a table on the other side of the room. Jim looked at them for a moment and lowered his voice. "Just general guidelines on how to get started and how to proceed. How you'd do it."

Mac waited when the waitress came out to take orders from the couple across the room. Then he talked to Jim about how to track the target, how to keep a low profile, and how to handle the hit itself. Jim made notes of everything.

"How come they don't teach this stuff at the Farm?" Jim asked.

"They do, kid. You weren't enrolled in that particular course of study. The Company might hire a mechanic from time to time, but they don't make one out of whole cloth. If you don't bring that skill with you to the Farm, you don't leave with it."

Jim looked at him with one eyebrow raised.

"At least that's the official version," Mac said with a grin.

The waitress came by with lunch. Mac took a sip of coffee while he waited for her to leave and then took a big bite from his sandwich. He talked while he chewed and gave Jim tips on travel, how to steal a car, and such.

Except that Mac said, "We don't steal a car. We borrow it."

"What do you mean?"

"Well, we never intend to keep it." Mac took several bites of his sandwich. "So what's this you were telling me about a sniper rifle?"

"We can go to my workshop after we eat. I'll show it to you."

They finished their meal and left for the workshop in Jim's car. Jerry wasn't there. Mac looked around. "Let's watch what we say in here, kid. I haven't had time to check it out."

Jim took the briefcase out of the cabinet. "Watch this," he said. "Nothing up my sleeves."

He held the briefcase by the handle and then went into action. A few seconds later the briefcase sported a tube metal stock in the back and a silencer in the front. He held it up to his face, pointed it, and said, "Bang." Then he reversed the procedure, and he was holding what looked like a typical briefcase.

Mac seemed impressed. "When you get it finished, I'd like to have Snuffy look it over. This is the kind of shit he's good at. Maybe we can sell it to the Company. They'd pay plenty for something like that."

"What? You need money?" Jim asked.

"Oh, yeah, I forgot. We're rich. Even so, I'd like to have a few made for future jobs. I don't plan on retiring."

"So, about your associates. I've met the teenager. Tell me about Snuffy."

Mac looked concerned. "Let's go outside."

They went out, and Mac walked well away from the building.

"Snuffy is the teenager's father. He was in the Company as a consultant, and we did shit together. He's one of the best. He stepped on a landmine in Vietnam and got put out of action. If you want something electronic, mechanical, chemical, explosive, he's the guy to see. He's a hell of a safe cracker and can open any lock you hand him. He also makes all my documents. Passports, drivers' licenses, like that. Good forger."

"Sounds like Superman."

"In a wheelchair. You'd like him. His wife is a night nurse at the hospital. She doesn't make shit there, but she handles my books, finances, and all that, and I pay her what I can. She's good at it, and I'm not, so that works out."

Jim drove Mac to Gloria's then went to his apartment. Almost everything was set for his first important assignment, the assassination of a world leader. Now all he had to do was plan the hit and carry it out.

Chapter 36

Sarah Weston had reason to be happy. An official Navy memorandum had arrived by special delivery. Her company had won the bid for the NAVAMS contract. She would assemble a team in about two weeks, and she wanted Jim Dodson on her team. She also wanted him around.

Sarah had been careful with her attraction to Jim. Throughout the proposal effort she had mostly kept those feelings on hold and tried to maintain a distance. She had not wanted to compromise the work. Too much was at stake.

She had acted on that attraction only once and had no regrets. After all, he got her off twice. That didn't happen often. She couldn't even do that to herself.

Sarah had a nice house, beautiful children, and two above average incomes. But her husband Hank bored her, and he traveled a lot. They had a comfortable married relationship, but, still a young woman, she wanted more excitement than home and hearth provided.

Jim hadn't been Sarah's first extra-marital lover. The other times were brief and she had chosen them for their safety. She was drawn to men who were happily married and wanted to maintain the status quo but who were open for a little something on the side. Her fling with Brent had been typical. They had wound up on the conference room couch one night after an evening session on a different project. Afterward Brent had made overtures to her for subsequent liaisons, but Sarah had put him off. A nice enough guy and good-looking, but a mistake nontheless. Office romances were not a good idea, and after once, he didn't interest her all that much. Most men didn't.

But Jim was different somehow. Mysterious. Dangerous, almost. She wanted to call him, but he'd never given her his phone number, and it wasn't on his résumé.

The next day, Sarah called Rod Bales.

"Rod, I need another favor."

"Name it."

"You remember that fellow I had you find out about? Jim Dodson?"

"I remember him. The kid with the questionable identity."

"That's him. Do you still have your notes from the investigation? I need his address."

"Sure. But how about that false identity issue?"

"He explained that. To my satisfaction, at least. Your people can investigate it if he comes on board. In the meantime I just want to offer him a job." *A blow job, that is.*

"You sure?" he said.

"Yes. You think you can find out how to get in touch with him?"

"Sure, honey. Give me a few days. I'll see what I can learn. Shouldn't take more than a couple of phone calls or three. But I think you're making a mistake."

She agreed, but she didn't say so. She hoped it would be worth it.

Sarah's phone was ringing when she walked into her office first thing in the morning.

"Sarah, it's Rod. I have the information you want."

She went to her desk and picked up a pad and pencil. "What did you learn?"

"A James Dodson Jr. got a Virginia driver's license earlier this year. And he bought and registered a car. He lives in Virginia. He has an unlisted phone number, but I managed to get it."

"He got his license earlier this year? Is that significant?"

"Maybe, maybe not. He didn't have a previous license. That's unusual for someone his age."

She took notes on everything he said. "It does seem suspicious, doesn't it? Is this the kind of thing a security investigation would clear up?"

"Well, we'd sure ask him to explain it. He said he's from Tazewell. That's the boondocks. Maybe he never bothered getting a license until he moved to the big city."

"Maybe because he was raised in some kind of cult. That's what he told me."

"Did you check his professional references?"

"Yes. They checked out."

Rod said, "If you want, I can look deeper. I'm straining my budget, though."

"Maybe later. I'll let you know. I appreciate your help. Can you give me Jim's address and phone number?"

Rod gave her the information and told her to be careful. It was clear he didn't like how this whole thing was playing out. He showed concern that Sarah would risk hiring someone with an uncertain background. But she hoped he trusted her judgment.

She wanted another romp in the rack with that kid. And the more she thought about it, the more she wanted it.

Chapter 37

The heat of early September had given way to October's cool temperatures and the changing of the leaves. Jim wished he could take time off, visit the Blue Ridge mountains and enjoy their brilliant splashes of fall color. But he had an assignment now, one that took precedence over everything else, one that would occupy his time until the mission was completed.

This morning he was having breakfast at Gloria's and scanning the newspapers for reports of Kennedy's travels. A man sat by himself across the room, and whenever Jim looked up, the man was staring at him and then quickly looked away. Jim didn't know who he was. He wasn't close enough for Jim to make out the man's features, so Jim returned to his newspaper. When he next looked up, the man was talking to the waitress. The next time, the man was gone.

Two mornings later at Gloria's, the man was there. He stared at Jim from a table across the room. Jim took a closer look and recognized Brad Lester from CIA.

Lester was a fellow in his mid-thirties whom Jim had known casually at the Agency. Lester had always seemed impressed with himself being a CIA employee and had often expressed a desire to transfer to the Company into covert ops. Perhaps he'd made it.

Why was CIA watching Jim? What would Mac do? If Lester was not following Jim for the Company, then he was stalking Jim on his own and might blab it all over the Agency. Everyone there thought Harold Sands was dead. Lester could stir up the shit and blow Jim's cover.

He pretended he didn't notice Lester, waited for him to leave, and followed him to the parking lot. Lester opened his car door, and Jim came up behind him and put a heavy hand on Lester's shoulder. He inserted his other arm between Lester's arm and body and twisted to pin Lester's arm behind him so any pressure Lester exerted to pull loose would only make it hurt more.

"Don't look around," Jim said in a calm, quiet voice.

"Wha—"

"Look straight ahead and listen up. You know what deep cover is? Do you?"

"Yes." Lester continued to struggle but without much energy.

"Good. Now know this. If I find you stalking me again, if I hear you've been running your mouth about me, I will classify you as a national security liability to be eliminated. Do you understand that?"

"Who in the hell do you think you are?" said Lester. He squirmed to free himself from Jim's hold.

Jim tightened his grip. "I know who I am. And this is what I can do." Jim increased the pressure on Lester's arm until he cried out with pain. "Now. Back off or you're dead."

Jim released him, turned, and walked back into Gloria's. He could see Lester's reflection in the glass door as the frightened fellow gripped his arm and fumbled with his car keys.

Jim learned from this incident that even though he'd been in a tense adversarial situation, the rage didn't surface. No danger threatened him because he had total control of the situation. No danger equals control. That was good to know.

In the meantime, he still had Lester to worry about. There was no telling how he might use the knowledge that Harold Sands was still alive. Maybe he would heed Jim's warning and drop it. But Jim couldn't be sure of that. Yet another complication.

* * *

Jim spent the next several weeks getting ready for the assignment. He read the papers to follow Kennedy's movements and practiced with his briefcase rifle, now constructed and working.

One afternoon Jim was at the town center to shop for supplies. He went into the hardware store and saw a suspicious figure. A man in a hooded parka had followed him from the parking lot and was standing beside the doorway and not shopping. He was watching Jim. The hood shaded his face, and he was too far away for Jim to see what he looked like. It wasn't Lester. The man was too short and too stocky

Jim paid for his merchandise and turned, and the man was not there. This reminded Jim of Paulo in Zurich. He left the hardware store and walked down the sidewalk. The man sat in a car outside the grocery store. He stared directly at Jim. Jim ducked past the pedestrians, went into the store, and proceeded at a quick pace to the delivery area in the back. He jumped off the ramp and ran around to the front. Hooded Parka's car was there but he was not. He was probably looking for Jim in the store.

Jim ran to his car and left in a hurry. He drove around for a while to make sure no one followed him. Then he went home and called Mac.

"Mac, you have someone following me again?"

"No, kid, why?"

"I got a tail. You think the Company is on me?"

"I'll check and see what I can find out. In the meantime, keep your eyes peeled. No telling who it is or what it's about."

Two nights later, Jim was asleep in his apartment. He awoke to a noise coming from the direction of his living room. The only light was a glow from the kitchen, an electric clock on his stove. The noise continued, a scratching noise. Jim recognized the sound. Someone was picking his lock.

He had no weapon. His pistol was in the glove compartment of his car. Dumb.

The living room door opened, and a ray of light came in from a street light in the parking lot and reflected off the far wall. The light was interrupted, apparently blocked by someone coming through the door and into his apartment.

Jim rolled quietly off the left side of the bed and onto the floor, where he waited, crouched, ready to spring. He was scared but ready. He didn't know how efficient his opponent would be. Whoever he was, if the Company had sent him, he would definitely have more experience than Jim.

The silhouette of a man loomed in the doorway into the bedroom. He was wearing a hooded parka just like the man in the shopping center, but Jim still couldn't make out his features. He held a long thin object in his right hand, tiptoed to the end of the bed, and raised the object over him. A baseball bat.

As the bat came hurling downward toward the empty bed, Jim jumped forward and tackled the assassin. They reeled backward against the dresser. The mirror fell off the wall and hit Jim on the head. He was stunned, but he could hear Hooded Parka running out of the bedroom and toward the front door. Jim pulled himself up and fumbled through the dark, chasing the intruder to the door, only a few steps behind but not close enough to grab him. The door opened wide, and Hooded Parka darted out onto the landing. By the time Jim reached the door, the intruder had vaulted over the railing to the parking lot a story below. He pulled himself up to his feet and jumped into his car. Tires screeched and the car spun around and sped away into the darkness.

Jim was breathing hard, and he dialed the phone.

"Mac, you know that tail I told you about?"

Mac's sleepy voice responded. "What tail?" The Zippo snapped shut after Mac lit up.

"The one I thought might be a Company mechanic."

"What about him?" Mac asked.

"He visited me tonight. With a baseball bat. Scared the shit out of me."

"Ball bat? You sure?"

"Got it right here," Jim said.

"Trying to improve his batting average, I guess. What happened?"

"We got into it, and he took off."

"I'll get to the bottom of it, kid. Allison is checking on it now." Mac yawned. "But couldn't it have waited until morning?"

"Sorry, Mac. Go back to sleep."

"Keep your eyes open, kid. No telling when you'll get another visit."

Jim sat and was disappointed in himself. He shouldn't have left his gun in his car. He shouldn't have let the assassin escape. If he would have subdued him, maybe he could have found out who sent him and why. He had surprised the killer in the bedroom, had the advantage, and the guy escaped anyway.

Chapter 38

November brought cooler days, cold nights, and the falling of leaves. Dottie considered herself lucky to have a window office. She must have impressed Mr. Allison when he told her about Harold's having been shot, because not long afterward, he had reassigned her to be his administrative assistant, a transfer that included a promotion, a window office, and a position in the Company.

Dottie always loved this time of year as the holidays approached. Her enjoyment of the season was diminished, however, by the uncertainty of where Harold was and what he was doing. She worked hard at her new job, but she also spent a good bit of her time thinking about him.

Now a rumor was all over headquarters that someone had seen Harold alive and well. Dottie had tried to learn more, but no one knew.

A tap on her door broke her train of thought. Brad Lester stood in her doorway. Brad had asked her out several times even before the news of Harold's supposed death. She put him off, though. She didn't like him that much, and she wasn't ready to make the break since she believed Harold was still alive. She did not, however, tell anyone what she thought, what she had told Mac.

"Got a minute?"

"Sure, Brad. What's up?"

He sat on the edge of her desk. "You know that fellow you used to date? The one that got shot breaking into a house?"

"You mean Harold? What about him?"

"The reports of his death are exaggerated."

"I've heard the rumors. But nobody seems to know who saw him."

"I saw him."

Dottie's heart skipped a beat. "You did? Where?"

"A diner in Woodbridge. Gloria's."

"Are you sure?"

"Yes. I asked the waitress if she knew him. She didn't know his name, but she said he has breakfast there at least once a week. Then he approached me. He said he was under deep cover. He got a little rough with me, but I took care of him."

"What do you mean?" Dottie couldn't imagine a wimp like Brad Lester taking care of anyone, much less Harold.

"You don't push Brad Lester around and get away with it. He'll regret it."

Dottie wasn't interested in Brad's posturing. She wanted to know about Harold. "What day of the week does he go there?" she asked.

"The waitress said she never knew when to expect him. She said he stays to himself and reads the paper. Sometimes he's with an older guy, but mostly by himself."

She wondered whether the older guy was Mac.

"Well, he might be under cover. I haven't seen him since March. We stopped seeing each other then. But thanks for telling me."

"You're welcome. So, how about taking me up on my offer to go out?"

"Brad, I'm flattered, I really am. But I'm not ready to start seeing anyone just now, and I think dating co-workers is a bad idea anyway."

"Well, let me know if the rules change," he said and left her office.

Dottie was excited. For the first time since Harold had broken up with her, she felt almost happy. This news confirmed what she had suspected all long. Harold was alive, not only alive, but in the area nearby, somewhere to be found, and she intended to find him.

Jim hadn't seen anything of his assassin since the night they tussled in the apartment. He still didn't know who sent the guy and why he, Jim, was marked for a hit. Mac hadn't let him know whether he'd been able to find out who was responsible and whether it could be called off.

If the guy was a mechanic, he probably wouldn't try at the apartment again. He'd know Jim would be ready for him, which he was. But he'd try again. Mac had said so.

After the incident with Brad Lester, he had avoided Gloria's in the mornings, but he did get a carryout lunch there sometimes, and he had supper there from time to time. One evening he left Gloria's at closing time and walked toward his car. A moving shadow cast by a street light onto the parking lot surface caught his eye. He froze and watched. A man stepped out from behind a van. Jim was unprepared. His gun was in the glove compartment like before. The man smiled and walked toward him.

"Hello, Sandman."

Jim recognized a guy he'd known at the Farm, one of the older former military snipers. Was this one of Mac's watchdogs, sent to keep an eye on Jim like Paulo in Zurich? He doubted it. Something didn't feel right. Jim was in trouble. He should never have put himself in such a vulnerable position. He had no weapon. His heart pounded, and he turned from side to side in search of a defense, anything he could pick up and throw at the guy, anything he could hide behind. But there was nothing, and Jim felt the cold chill of raw, unbridled fear for the first time in a long time.

The man pulled his hand out of his coat pocket revealing a pistol with a silencer. Jim desperately looked to either side for something to jump behind, a way to shield himself. But he stood in the open with the assassin less than twenty feet away. This was it. The man raised the pistol and pointed it at Jim's head. Jim braced himself for the fatal shot. Then he heard the sound of a silenced shot. *Phoot.*

The assassin's jaw dropped. He stood for a few seconds then fell to the pavement, a dark red stain on the back of the parka. Jim looked around for the source of the shot. A voice called from across the parking lot.

"Hey kid. Is it all clear?"

"Mac. What are you doing here?"

"Keeping an eye on you."

Mac came from behind a distant parked car, walked to the body, and kicked it over to see the assassin's face.

This was the first time Jim had seen someone shot to death. It troubled him, particularly that Mac had done it on his behalf and that, but for a second or two, it would have been him face down on the pavement.

He wondered how long it took to get used to this.

Mac turned to walk away. "They put a sanction on you, kid. Bert Allison got back to me. He hadn't known about it, but he checked it out. I guess you pissed somebody off."

"You think?" Jim looked at the body.

"This guy was a mechanic. Allison will have the sanction lifted, but keep your eyes open for the next couple of days. Let's go get a burger. Across the river. We can stop on the bridge so I can ditch this piece. You're buying."

They walked toward Jim's car. Mac took his pocket knife out and notched his pistol's grip.

"Why do you do that, Mac?" Jim asked. "You're going to ditch it."

"Habit. The gun ever comes back on me, I'll know there's a body on it."

"But you're going to deep-six it."

"Somebody could fish it out."

"What do you do if you stab somebody?"

"I don't use knives. They give me the willies. Besides, there's no ballistics with a knife."

On Sunday, November 17th, Sarah drove to Dulles Airport. Hank was flying home from a conference, his plane would arrive at eleven, and Sarah was there to pick him up. She parked and went into the terminal, found the gate for her husband's flight, and sat to wait.

Then she saw him.

Jim stood in line about halfway down the terminal building. He wore a leather jacket and blue jeans, carried a briefcase, and wore a backpack.

Sarah walked, almost ran, toward the gateway. Jim entered the mobile lounge, and the doors closed. She ran up and could see his profile through the glass. He didn't look her way, and the mobile lounge pulled away from the gate.

Sarah read the destination, Melbourne, Florida. She wondered how long he would be gone.

She walked to the other gate to meet Hank. He came out of the mobile lounge, and they went downstairs to pick up his suitcase. Then they went out to the car. He was tired and asked her to drive.

"Sure. I'm going to drive around the parking lot," she said. "I need to check on something."

She drove up and down the lanes of the parking lot until she found Jim's car. It had been parked every day at Pine Hill, so she recognized it. She wrote down where the parking space was and Jim's license plate number.

"What are you doing," Hank asked.

"It's about work, and it's related to that intelligence contract. Don't ask."

Hank leaned his head back on the headrest and closed his eyes.

Sarah pulled over at a phone booth, checked her address book, and called the home number of George, a young man who worked in the mail room.

"George, this is Sarah Weston."

"Yes, Mrs. Weston. How can I help you?"

"You live near Dulles Airport, don't you?"

"Yes ma'am. About two miles. Why?"

"I have a job for you. A personal matter and between us, understand? I don't want to hear about this in the office scuttlebutt."

"Yes, ma'am."

"Okay. Here's what you do. Each morning and each evening, go into the airport parking lot. On weekends, take a ride over there. You're looking for a specific car in a specific parking space. A Ford sedan. Recent model. I want to know when that car is no longer there."

Sarah read off the car's license plate number and told him where to find it.

The Constellation touched down at Melbourne Airport at two-fifteen in the afternoon. Jim was traveling under one of Mac's aliases so the name Jim Dodson would not be listed on the passenger manifest.

Kennedy would be in Cape Canaveral the next day to view a launch. That might provide the opportunity Jim needed.

As he walked to the parking lot, he considered the problem Sarah presented. She had been at Dulles airport, and he hoped it had been a coincidence, but he doubted it.

He waited for a car to borrow, and after about ten minutes, a light green Chevrolet station wagon drove in. A businessman got out, took a suitcase and briefcase from the back, and headed for the terminal. Jim followed him and watched him check in. The man walked to a gate for a flight to St. Louis and sat in the lounge area. This guy would be gone for a while. Jim would borrow his car.

Jim returned to the Chevy, took the car door blade from his back-pack, and unlocked the door. Once inside, he hot-wired the ignition, and the engine started.

He took out his map and located Patrick Air Force Base, the closest military base to Cape Canaveral with a runway and service facilities suffi-cient for Air Force One. It was possible that the president's airplane would land at the Cape Canaveral Skid Strip, in which case Jim figured he'd find no opportunity here. He had to assume they'd use Patrick AFB.

He found his way to Highway A1A and drove north until he was abeam the gate into Patrick. He studied the route. If they used a motor-cade, it would come out here.

The route continued north for fifteen miles to the entrance to Cape Canaveral Air Force Station. The motorcade would follow this route. He observed the terrain and buildings along the route. Other than for the small towns of Cocoa Beach and Cape Canaveral he found few places where the president could smile and wave at his fans.

Jim couldn't find a likely sniper's stand on this route, which proceeded up a narrow barrier island with the ocean to the east and the Banana River on the west. The only escape route would use the road itself down that narrow peninsula. They would have roadblocks in place before the last echo of the fatal shot faded.

There was no way to make the hit from within the perimeters of the base. He'd need credentials, which he didn't have, and there'd be Secret Service agents and MPs with guns to deal with. Every exit route, every potential escape route went through an armed guard checkpoint.

Nothing about this trip showed promise. He headed west to Tampa, arriving early in the evening. According to the newspapers, Kennedy would appear there the next day. Jim drove to the hotel where Kennedy was scheduled to speak at a luncheon and checked in.

He left the hotel and drove the route to MacDill Air Force Base where Air Force One would be landing, then to the National Guard Armory, another of Kennedy's planned stops. Jim knew better than to consider a hit at the Armory. He could hear Mac now:

Only an idiot assassinates someone in the building where they keep the guns.

He found no likely sites on the route itself, so he returned to the hotel and asked a bellboy where Kennedy would be speaking. The lad pointed out a large banquet room on the first floor. The room was unlocked and empty.

Jim went inside and found doors at the back of the room for staff to carry food in and out. A line of service carts stood against the wall. He located a closet where waiters and busboys kept their uniforms, borrowed a jacket and tie and one of the carts, and took them to his room.

Tomorrow he would be a busboy at the luncheon reception for President Kennedy. A busboy with a gun.

That evening, cops started to show up. He walked to a nearby cocktail lounge to kill time and returned late at night. The lobby was abandoned. He found the service stairway and walked up to his floor.

Jim arose early on Monday, packed, and took his luggage down to his car. He parked the car next to the loading dock.

When time drew near for the president to arrive, Jim went to his room, wheeled the cart to the elevator and went downstairs. The luncheon had started. A cop stood alongside the potted palm Jim had planned to use as a blind. Other cops and agents were positioned around the room where they could watch everyone and everything.

He looked at his watch. Kennedy was still speaking at the Armory.

This wouldn't work. The venue was crawling with cops and agents. Jim didn't wait around. He took the briefcase from the cart and walked to the loading dock. The cop stationed there stopped him.

"Where are you going, sir?"

Jim almost jumped out of his skin. He thought fast. "The boss told me to move my car to make way for the motorcade."

"Go ahead."

Jim headed for the airport. Kennedy would be going to Dallas in a few days. Jim booked a seat on the next flight, leaving late that afternoon. He used his second alias for this trip. Maybe Dallas would provide a more hospitable location for an assassin.

The 707 pulled up to the gate at Dallas Love Field at eight p.m. Jim retrieved his luggage, bought a newspaper, and took a taxicab to a motel. He checked in and went to his room. He scanned the newspaper. It mentioned Kennedy's visit but gave no details.

On Tuesday, Jim slept in without a wake-up call. He showered and dressed, walked to the hotel lobby, bought a newspaper, and went into the diner.

As he ate breakfast, he scanned the newspaper and found an article about the Kennedy visit, scheduled for that Friday. It reported the motorcade route from Love Field to the Trade Mart where Kennedy was to speak. The route took the long way around to give the citizens of Dallas a close look at their president.

After breakfast, Jim returned to the lobby and asked for a street map of Dallas. He sat in his room and traced the motorcade's route. About ten miles.

He took a cab to the airport where he watched the parking lot. Eventually an unsuspecting traveler left him a new Dodge to borrow.

He drove the motorcade route using his map as a guide. He took his time and looked at roadside sites for potential sniper's stands. He stopped at several locations, walked around, and made notes, going into buildings to check out windows and roofs that had a clear view of the street.

The last place he stopped was a small park at the southwest edge of Dallas. He put the car in a lot behind the park and walked to an area with a well-tended lawn that sloped down toward the street.

The park offered several potential sites. The motorcade would pass under a railroad overpass on its way to the freeway. A sniper could hide there. A seven-story brick building on the corner of Houston and Elm had potential perches on the roof and from the windows. The picket fence at the west end of the park offered good cover facing the motorcade as it proceeded toward him, which would give him a head-on shot.

One by one he eliminated each potential stand. Workers would occupy the seven-story building and would notice a stranger coming and going. On the overpass he'd be too close to the cops and too far from his getaway car. The picket fence was the best choice of the three, with good cover and close proximity to the parking lot, but by the time the motorcade was within range, too many people and cameras would be pointed in his direction.

He walked through a pergola and to the right and stood behind a concrete wall, which separated the parking lot and the lawn. The wall's height could support a mount for his rifle. This perch was close to the parking lot and the street where Kennedy's motorcade would pass.

He was satisfied. This location would do fine. A sign identified it as Dealey Plaza. He walked around the neighborhood and used his street map to familiarize himself with buildings and roads and to select an escape route.

Jim spent most of Wednesday in his room practicing the assembly and disassembly of the briefcase rifle.

That evening he decided to go out. If he was to enjoy any Dallas night life, tonight was it. Tomorrow he'd have to rest.

He had dinner at the hotel restaurant, returned to his room and dressed for an evening on the town. He walked to the lobby and asked the desk clerk for directions to where he could find some entertainment.

He drove to Commerce Street and looked for something crowded and noisy where no one would notice him or want to chat. The street had three burlesque houses. It might be fun to watch pretty women take their clothes off. He chose the Carousel Club, located on the second story of an office building. The entranceway displayed posters advertising the beauty of the dancers.

He climbed the stairs and went inside. The room was about half full, mostly young men who drank beer, talked to one another, and kept watch on the stage, waiting for the show to start. A combo set up alongside the stage and tuned up, and the master of ceremonies tested the sound system.

"One, two, three, four, one, two, three, four."

Jim picked a table against a side wall about half way from the stage. A waitress came over, and he ordered a bottle of beer.

The MC left the stage, and the musicians went to the bar. More guests came in and took seats around him. A young man about Jim's age sat alone at a ringside table. Jim noticed him because he and Jim were the only patrons sitting alone. He wondered what brings a young man out to a strip show by himself. He smiled at the thought. That's what he was doing.

When the room was almost full, the house lights went down, and the musicians returned to the bandstand. The room quieted down, and the patrons watched with anticipation. The band played, and a spotlight flooded the center of the stage. The master of ceremonies came from behind the curtain and delivered a line of patter to welcome the crowd to the Carousel. He announced the first act, and a pretty woman of about thirty came onstage in a long gown. This was what the crowd had been waiting for, and they cheered her on. She danced erotically to the band's bump-and-grind rhythms. She danced and stripped, and the audience whistled and cheered when each garment came off until she wore only a G-string, pasties, and high heels. A few more turns around the stage brought her act to its conclusion, and she took her bows and ran off-stage. The crowd went nuts.

The MC returned to center stage and did about five minutes of comedy, after which he announced the second exotic dancer.

When that dancer completed her act, the show continued with more comedy, a couple of selections by the band, and two more dancers.

Sometime during the evening, the young man down front left his table. Jim hadn't seen him leave and didn't see him again that night.

At midnight, Jim paid his tab and went out and down the stairs to the street. He walked around for a while to clear his head. He took the street map from his pocket and studied it. He was less than a mile from Dealey Plaza and only a block south of Main Street, part of the motorcade's route. He walked to Dealey Plaza, which was deserted. A few street lights along Elm Street bathed the plaza and its empty pergola, pillars, and pedestals in a misty haze.

Jim took in a breath of cool night air and considered what he planned to do in less than two days. His actions would change history. No need to think about that now. He returned to the motel and went to bed.

Jim woke up early on Thursday. As he lay there, he ran over what might happen tomorrow. He didn't worry too much about getting caught, missing the target, equipment failure, his escape, or any of the other things an assassin ought to be thinking about. Only that when the time came, he might not have the guts to pull the trigger. He'd have to wait and see.

Unable to fall asleep again, he got up and went to breakfast.

He didn't know much about the president, so he hailed a cab and went to the library. Not much had been written in books about John Kennedy. No complete biography had been published. From articles in periodicals and from a book about JFK's wartime experiences, Jim learned the president had served in the Navy during World War II, had commanded a PT boat and was something of a war hero.

Jim read about Kennedy's terms in the House and the Senate. There were no prominent pieces of legislation, no major issues at his forefront, nothing to define him as a statesman, nothing in Jim's view that would exempt him from an assassination. Jim wasn't sure whether he wanted to read enough to convince him to abandon the mission or continue with it.

On the eve of the assassination, after months of preparation and an enormous down payment from the client with that much more payable upon delivery, Jim was still not sure he would or even could go through with it. Tomorrow would tell.

Chapter 39

On Friday, Jim was up early after a night of uneasy sleep. He dressed in slacks and a sports jacket. A light rain was falling, forecast to stop before noon.

He prepared the briefcase weapon, loading it and making sure all the parts worked. He packed his things, took his luggage to the car, went to the lobby, and checked out.

He had breakfast and called Mac.

"Today," was all Jim said.

"Good luck, kid," was Mac's only response.

He arrived at Dealey Plaza at nine and parked in a space close to the concrete wall with the car aimed out for a quick exit.

The presidential motorcade would depart Love Field at about noon, putting it at Dealey Plaza sometime around half past. He didn't want to be noticed hanging around. Someone might recall seeing a young man just waiting there, standing in the rain.

He walked toward the district where the strip clubs and hotels were. It looked different in daylight. He went into a hotel, sat at the counter in the coffee shop, drank coffee, and read the newspaper. After a while he left, went to another restaurant, and did the same. He killed time this way until eleven-thirty. Then he walked back.

People lined the sidewalks. Jim stood among them. Less than an hour to go. Someone had a portable radio playing. A newscast reported the president and first lady's arrival at Love Field and the motorcade's departure.

The rain stopped. Jim checked his watch to estimate the motorcade's position. When it was about ten minutes away, he walked to his car and retrieved the briefcase. Then he walked to the concrete wall, stood there, and waited.

Time drew near. It had warmed up, unusual for November. A man with a movie camera had climbed onto the concrete wall at the west end of the pergola. A woman stood behind the man and held on to him to steady his footing.

Jim's own image could show up in snapshots and home movies. There were a lot of cameras out, but he stood in the shade, and the cameras pointed his way would be across the street. He would be little more than a shadow in those amateur pictures. He smiled at the irony.

Two men stood behind the picket fence at the position he would have used. He wondered why they were there instead of down front with the others.

At almost half past twelve, cheers rose from the spectators on Main Street.

Now it starts.

Two police escort motorcycles made the turn onto Houston Street followed by the first automobile in the motorcade, an open black Lincoln limousine with a flag fluttering on each front fender. Jim's pulse quickened. He could feel it in his chest. He could almost hear it. It was like the rage but with complete control.

Jim strained to see which passenger was the president. The motorcycle escort made its left turn onto Elm. A woman in a pink pillbox hat sat in the limousine's left rear seat. That would be the first lady. Kennedy was probably on her other side. A man and woman were in the seats in front of the Kennedys. As they drew closer, Jim saw the president to the right of the first lady waving to the crowd. The target was in sight. Jim's mouth went dry, and his breathing quickened.

A black convertible followed the limousine. Several men in dark suits stood in the open car and scanned the spectators. Secret Service. Would they see him?

Jim's eyes swept the crowd. Everyone was looking at the limousine.

No one was looking his way. Carefully and methodically he went into action. He released the pivoting stock from the bottom of the case, swiveled it, and snapped it into place. The silencer dropped into his left hand. He guided it into place and threaded it onto the barrel.

What am I doing?

He moved with automatic, programmed reflexes that ignored his thoughts, which were independent of his actions and clouded by doubt.

He kept the briefcase assembly below the top of the wall so no one would see it. There was no one behind him in the parking lot. Everyone had moved down to the curb, straining for a look at President and Mrs. Kennedy.

As the limousine completed its turn onto Elm, Jim could see Kennedy clearly now. The motorcade moved toward him. When the limousine was almost abeam his position, Jim went down on one knee and rested the briefcase rifle on the wall, his right hand in firing position. He released the safety and placed his forefinger on the trigger.

He had practiced these movements many times. There was no way he would not go through with it. But was it wrong? Was it so wrong that all his rationalizations and justifications couldn't make up for the despicable deed he was about to do?

Keep thinking about the money.

He pressed his eye to an aperture in the briefcase above the stock and sighted through the scope at Kennedy's profile. As the car moved, Jim rotated the rifle on a horizontal axis. Any time now. He tightened his squeeze on the trigger.

Then he hesitated. Not like he had with the buck as a teenage hunter. Not out of a reluctance to kill. It wasn't that. He didn't freeze as such. He couldn't shoot yet. His aim traced a line perpendicular to the passing limousine, and from this position the bullet would penetrate Kennedy's skull from his right side, pass through his brain, exit his left side, and kill Jacqueline Kennedy.

An innocent bystander. Not an option. Against the rules. His and the client's. Not negotiable. As the target moved forward, Jim rotated the rifle to the right until the angle of the shot defined a trajectory that would miss everyone else in the car. It seemed forever, but it had been only a second or two.

Without warning the unmistakable crack of rifle fire came from his left and above. The horror that followed was visible through the scope. Kennedy's hands went to his face, fists clenched, elbows raised. He leaned forward and to the left. The first lady put her arms around him. Another shot rang out, and seconds later Kennedy's head jerked violently and exploded into a bloody red mist. Then the third shot came.

Somebody else had shot Kennedy and blown his brains out.

Jim couldn't tell where the shots originated. The sounds came from his upper left, but echoes can trick you about the origins of sounds.

Kennedy's head had snapped back. But that could have been a muscle reaction to the trauma of a gunshot wound to the brain. It could have come from anywhere. Jim pulled his face from the weapon and scanned the scene, right to left. There were no other shooters in sight.

That other shooter could be anywhere, which meant Jim could be caught in the crossfire.

His reactions now were quick and deliberate. He pulled the rifle down from the wall and, as he'd practiced a thousand times, unthreaded the silencer and shoved it into its compartment. He rotated the stock into place below the silencer. With a live round still in the chamber, he set the safety.

Then, holding the briefcase by its handle, he looked up at the plaza. Many spectators had hit the ground and cringed there, looking around, terrified. Others ran in all directions, some toward the picket fence, but none toward him. Some people screamed, many cried.

The motorcade sped up and disappeared under the underpass. Cops on foot walked in all directions through the plaza looking for whatever they could find, most with their pistols drawn.

Jim walked to his car, tossed the briefcase onto the front seat and got in. He looked at Dealey Plaza. A policeman stood next to the picket fence with his pistol drawn as if he expected the assassin to still be there. The two men who had been behind the fence were gone.

Once again his instincts had been right. If he'd chosen the fence, those men would have been too close, and he might not have had time to select another position.

A car pulled out ahead of him with two men in the front seat. He could see only the backs of their heads. He pulled out behind them. When the car reached the street, it sped away. Jim drove out of the parking lot and away from Dealey Plaza.

Having been beaten to the punch by another shooter, Jim didn't think he needed to cover his trail, but he decided to stay with his original escape plan anyway. Someone might want to trace his movements someday. A fragmented trail is as good as no trail at all.

As he drove, he reviewed what he'd seen and heard that day. Who was the other shooter? Did Mac send backup without telling him? Did Fish send in another assassin? Did Murphy change his mind? Or was it an altogether different contract and a coincidence that the other assassin chose the same day and the same location?

Jim hoped coincidence accounted for it and that it would work to his advantage. He would collect his million dollar payoff, and with no blood on his hands, his conscience, if that was even a factor, was clear.

He left the city and headed south. He felt a wave of relief that he had not killed the president, but he knew now that he would have. His mind had been clouded with doubt while his body executed the well-programmed actions.

Then, after the fact, he would have had to deal with the moral consequences of the killing. He knew himself. He couldn't live with that kind of guilt. He would have rationalized his actions to clear his conscience.

But it wasn't necessary. Another hunter had shot first and killed the buck.

He turned on the radio and twisted the dial. The assassination was all over the news. Jim searched for anything that made sense but found only confusion and speculation. Kennedy had been taken to Parkland Hospital, and reporters had no information about his condition.

Jim had seen Kennedy's head blown apart. Kennedy's condition was dead. Within the hour the radio confirmed Jim's diagnosis.

He kept the radio on for the two and a half hours it took to drive to

Killeen, the first leg of his escape route. News broadcasts reported that the assassin had been caught and was in police custody. Apparently the man had also shot a police officer on the street as he tried to make his escape.

They identified the assassin as Lee Harvey Oswald. Apparently he'd shot Kennedy from a window on the northwest corner of Elm and Houston, one of the locations Jim had considered for a firing position.

Instincts again. Jim's choice turned out to be the better one. The other guy was caught. Jim got away.

Jim pulled in at the small Killeen airport, parked his car, and wiped it down. Then he took his luggage and walked to the line of private airplanes tied down along the runway. He found a Cessna 150 tied where it couldn't be seen from the office. It was in good condition, and no weeds grew around its tires, suggesting it had been flown recently. Everyone in the office would be glued to the television and would not notice an airplane departing with someone other than its owner at the controls.

He tossed his luggage in the passenger seat and made a hasty pre-flight walk-around. He opened the cowling and, with his side cutters, clipped the wires connecting the magnetos to the ignition switch, essentially hot-wiring the airplane.

He untied the little Cessna and hand-propped it. The engine came to life. He pulled the wheel chocks and climbed into the left seat.

Winds were light and variable. He taxied to the active runway, performed a fast run-up procedure, pushed in the throttle, and the airplane rolled forward. A gentle pull on the control wheel, and the little craft was airborne. At four hundred feet, he left the pattern and banked to a southeast course, the second leg of his escape.

Unlike the last time he stole an airplane, this time he brought charts. Live and learn. He unfolded the sectional chart and plotted a course to Austin.

The flight went without incident. Weather was good, and there wasn't much traffic. Ten miles out of Austin he called the tower, using a phony tail number just in case. He landed and taxied to the general aviation ramp. He wiped the plane down, took his things, and walked to the main terminal building.

Leg two of his escape plan was complete.

He bought a ticket to Chicago, the third leg of his plan. As he awaited its departure, he sat in a bar and had a stiff drink. This flight used the last of his three aliases. He'd use Jamey Barrett's name to fly home from Chicago, the final leg of his escape.

The TV played nothing but news of the assassination. It showed film of Lee Harvey Oswald in police custody. Jim examined Oswald as the cops escorted him into the jail. Reporters yelled questions at Oswald who denied everything. Jim was almost sure he'd seen that face.

But it had been dark in the nightclub with only stage lighting to illuminate the face of the lone man who sat at ringside. And he'd seen the man only in profile. Jim wasn't certain they were the same man. But, if they were not, like Harold Sands and Jamey Barrett, they could be brothers.

It was past supper time, and Mac had kept close to the TV all day. The kid had said today was to be the day, and so it was. He hoped the kid had left the scene without being caught. Mac followed reports of a cop who was shot on the streets of Dallas and of the capture and arrest of someone named Oswald, their main suspect in the assassination.

Who is this Oswald guy?

He flipped channels and watched news accounts. The telephone interrupted him with the red light blinking.

"What's up, Sam?"

"Jesus Christ, Mac, what kind of organization are you running?"

"What's bothering you, Sam?" Mac carried the phone around the room while he paced.

"Your fucking guy not only gets caught, he kills a cop in the process. A cop, for chrissake. Not to mention putting a slug in the Governor. That's not what I contracted for. I specifically told him, no innocent bystanders."

Mac needed to cool Montague down. "Relax, Sam. This shit happens. Can't be helped. He got the job done."

"And he'll do hard time for it too. Probably get the chair. You better hope he doesn't rat you out. And you better not rat me out, Mac. I'm getting real nervous about all this."

"Slow down, Sam. There's no connection to you. You got your money's worth."

"About that. I don't figure I owe this Shadow asshole the rest of the fee. Not the way he fucked it up."

Mac sat again. "Now hold on, Sam. You do not weasel out of your obligation just because a few things didn't go how you wanted. The objective was achieved. We expect full payment."

"I don't see it that way. Your guy put us at risk."

"How do you figure that? He doesn't even know who you are."

"But you do." Montague was almost whining.

Mac's voice went cold. "And I expect you to keep that in mind when you think about who you're fucking with."

"Are you threatening me, Mac?"

"If you have to ask, I must not be doing it right." Mac's voice grew quieter. He spoke slowly now and with deliberation. "Let me be perfectly clear, Sam. If you don't pay what you owe, you pay in another way. And there won't be an open casket."

Montague's voice whined. "Jesus, Mac. We're supposed to be friends, for chrissake. We were in the field together. We've done business. You had dinner at my house. With my wife and kids. What's this shit all about?"

Mac ignored the plea. "Make the payment as agreed. In full. Otherwise, be looking over your shoulder for the rest of your miserable fucking life. Which won't be long."

Mac hung up.

Sam Montague sat at his desk, trembling and frightened but also burning mad. Everything had fallen apart. Shadow, aka Oswald, was in jail. He couldn't hurt anybody, couldn't reach Sam. Mac was the problem, a real threat, the direct link. He needed to solve that problem and fast. He dialed the phone.

A whiskey baritone answered, "Yeah?"

"It's Sam Montague."

"Hi, Sam. Got the TV on? Looks like you got your wish."

"I got something else needs doing."

"Somebody?"

"Yes."

"High profile?"

"No. But it won't be easy. And I need it soon. Real soon. Tonight if possible. Tomorrow at the latest."

"You know my fee. Double it for not easy and soon. Half in advance. Cash."

"I'm in my office. Get over here right away."

Mac kept the TV going, smoked, drank beer, and flipped channels. Millie sat next to him on the sofa, his ratty old robe wrapped around her and her legs stretched out with her bare feet resting on a threadbare hassock. He was in boxer shorts and an undershirt as he moved from the sofa to the TV set and back. She looked around her for what seemed to be the tenth time at the disarray and clutter.

"When's the last time you straightened up in here?" she asked.

"I don't know. When did I move in?"

"This Dallas business is a mess," she said. "Do you think it was our people?"

"Your people, not mine. I don't think so."

She slipped off the sofa onto the floor, curled her legs under her in front of him, and rested her elbows on his lap with her chin in her hands.

"You up for another one?" she asked.

"Time will tell," he said. "I'm not as good as I once was, but I'm as good once as I ever was."

"We already used up once. And you didn't take your eyes off the TV the whole time." She laughed.

"Well, see what you can do. No guarantees."

She gave it a try, but the result wasn't promising. Then the phone rang.

Saved by the bell.

"Hi, Mac," Jim said. "I'm in Chicago. I'll be home about five this morning."

"Well, I'm kind of in the middle of somebody."

Jim laughed. "Sorry to break up the party. You want to wait until tomorrow?"

"No. Won't take me that long." Mac was glad to hear from the kid, glad to be spared the task of trying to perform again, and he had questions. "Okay kid. I've been watching the news. Who's this guy Oswald?"

Millie pulled back and looked up at Mac.

"I was going to ask you about him," Jim said.

"Not one of mine. So we don't know him?"

"I don't."

"Good. I talked to Fish. He's making noises about the money. Doesn't want to pay. Something about innocent bystanders."

"Did you change his mind?"

Mac laughed at Jim's coded wording. "I hope so. We'll know more next week. I need a detailed report of the mission. We need to get together right away."

"Okay. How about at the workshop?"

"Perfect. I'll see you there as soon as you get in."

Mac hung up, and Millie kept staring at him.

"Did you have something to do with Dallas?" she asked.

"No. You saw the news. That guy Oswald did it. That's what I was asking the kid. We don't neither of us know him."

"Well," she said and reached for her dress and shoes. "I better get going. We can do this another time."

"I hope so. Mind if I don't walk you to your car? I don't want to miss any of this." He nodded toward the television set.

"I can take care of myself," she said and pulled the dress on over her head. He believed her. The thump when she dropped her purse on the table had told him that.

She leaned over and kissed him goodnight.

"Sorry I couldn't get it going again," he said.

"Me too."

"But we'll always have Paris."

They both laughed.

About five minutes after she left, Mac's phone rang.

"It's me," Millie said.

"What?"

"There's a guy sitting in an old Chrysler in the lot across the street. I can't see him, but he's watching your place."

"Thanks, Millie."

"You want help?" she asked.

"No. I'll keep an eye out."

At four-thirty a.m., Mac dressed, stuck a revolver in his jacket pocket, and walked to his car. The Chrysler was still there. He pulled out of the parking lot and turned south. The Chrysler followed and fell in two cars behind him. One headlight was dimmer than the other, so Mac could keep an eye on it even when it followed from some distance back. When Mac turned onto the freeway, he gunned it and sped away, hoping to shake the tail. But when he took the exit to where Jim lived, he spotted the car again, about a quarter mile behind him. This guy was good. No way Mac was going to lose him.

As he drove to Jim's workshop, the Chrysler stayed back. Mac turned into the driveway and parked on the gravel. When he got out of his car, headlights from the road shone through the trees. The headlights stopped moving and went dark. Mac slipped into the shadows and waited. Nothing happened.

A sign on the workshop door said:

Closed. Hunting Season. Back in December.

He picked the lock, went in, and made a quick scan of the building. He slid the floor lamp closer to the door, turned it on, and aimed its light at the doorway like a spotlight. The wood stove was loaded with wood and tinder, so he struck a match and tossed it in, all the while watching the door. Then he sat in the rocking chair, took the revolver out of his pocket, and waited.

After about five minutes, the doorknob turned. The door opened and revealed the outline of a tall, thin man.

"Hey, Murphy," Mac said, "What brings you out so late at night?"

Chapter 40

At almost daybreak Jim turned onto the street that led to the workshop. He drove to the driveway and stopped short. Mac's car was there. The door to the workshop was ajar, and a light was on inside. That was odd. Mac wouldn't leave a door open. He didn't want to alert whoever was in the workshop, so he parked on the street behind a beat-up Chrysler and got out, quietly closing the car door. He'd seen the Chrysler before, but he wasn't sure where.

He crept up to the workshop door and looked in. A man stood across the room at Jerry's workbench, his back to the door and in the shadows, dialing the telephone. The man said, "It's done. When can I pick up the balance?"

The man wore a maroon T-shirt, jeans, and boots. A jacket hung over the stool next to Jim's workbench. A pistol was on the workbench just out of the man's reach, a single-shot twenty-two caliber target gun fitted with a silencer.

The man turned around and faced Jim but stayed in the shadows. He stuck a joint in his mouth, scraped a match on the workbench, and lit the joint. His face came into view in the glow of the flame.

Jim opened the door and stepped inside. The man froze. Then when he saw Jim, he relaxed, drew in some smoke and said, "Sandman? What the fuck are you doing here?"

"Hello, Spider. I was just about to ask the same question."

"Spider was my Farm name. Out here I'm Murphy. Want a hit?" He held out the joint.

Jim shook his head. "Didn't know you were Murphy. Out here I'm Jim. So what's going on?"

Jim kept his eye on Murphy and the pistol.

Murphy said, "Over there," and he gestured toward the middle of the room.

A figure sat in the rocking chair in the shadows. With the light from the fire in the stove, Jim recognized Mac slumped down. Jim walked over. Blood seeped from a small hole in Mac's jacket at the center of his chest. Mac's eyes were glazed. His breathing was shallow. A Camel cigarette butt smoldered on the concrete floor next to the rocking chair.

"Christ, Murphy. Who shot Mac?"

Murphy leaned against the workbench and folded his arms. "A contract. I followed him here. Welcomed me with open arms. I had the advantage. He sat in the rocking chair, lit a smoke, and I shot him."

"But Jesus, Murphy, he's still alive."

Murphy took another hit on the joint. "He's bleeding out."

"Why wasn't he suspicious? Nobody knew about this place. Why would he just let you walk in here?"

"Come on, man, it's Mac. You don't follow Mac without him knowing it. He was in here waiting for me. Saw it was me, dropped his guard and put his piece away."

"But Mac? Why would you take a contract on your friend, for chrissake?"

"Pay was good. The client owed Mac money. Business is business. What are you doing here?"

Jim's eyes darted around the room looking for something he could use. He looked at Mac. Time was running out. If he didn't tend to Mac soon, he'd bleed to death. Jim needed an edge.

"I just got in from Dallas and was meeting Mac here."

"Dallas? They sent you on that? I thought the cops got the guy that did it."

"It's complicated. But I was there."

"I can't believe they sent you. You're Monty's Shadow? No offense, Shadow, but you're green. You never bumped anybody."

"What about that guy in the parking lot near the Farm?"

Jim looked for an opening. He had to take Murphy out soon. Mac was looking pale.

Murphy laughed. "What? Bullshit. You didn't kill that guy. It was a setup. One of my guys. He went in the tank so you'd think your stupid Sandman Snap, or whatever, works. Why do you think nobody ever heard about the kill? He took a dive." He laughed again. "The oldest trick in the book."

"I heard his neck snap."

Mac groaned. Something had to happen soon.

"You heard him break a stick of wood in his pocket. A setup. We practiced it."

Jim watched for an advantage, an opportunity. The conversation was a blind to keep Murphy off guard. Jim held the rage at bay while he talked, stalling for an edge.

"Murphy, let's make a deal. If Mac dies, I don't want Montague knowing. I need him to think Mac is still alive. He owes big money."

"Too late. I already told him."

"I heard. But Mac's still alive. Has to stay that way. Tell him you got the wrong guy, or only wounded him, or something."

Murphy's gaze darted around the room. Apparently he was looking for an advantage as well.

"No can do, Junior. I accepted his money."

Jim was scared. He was clearly out of his league. Murphy was the best.

"I can pay you a lot more to back out and help me get Mac to a doctor."

Murphy stood up straight. "I have a reputation. Montague knows people."

Jim's rage continued to build. It burned from behind his eyes. Something had to happen soon.

"We don't have to do this. We'd make a hell of a team."

"Fuck you and your team."

Murphy sprang at him and hit him across the jaw with the edge of his hand. Jim fell, caught Murphy's legs with his feet, and knocked Murphy against the workbench. Jim was surprised at how easy that was.

Jim had an age advantage, and the rage had taken full control now, but Murphy was bigger and had more experience. Murphy bent over, put his shoulder into Jim's midsection, and lifted him into the air. Then he slammed him down on the concrete floor. Jim rolled and came up. They faced one another, circling, each looking for an entry, waiting for an advantage. Then before Jim saw it coming, Murphy fell backward, caught himself on one hand, and drop-kicked Jim in the face. Jim rolled with it, and when Murphy fell back from the kick, Jim kicked him in the groin. Murphy fell to the side, and Jim chopped him on the nape of his neck. Murphy dropped face down on the floor. He was stunned.

Jim kneeled down with one knee in the small of Murphy's back and his other foot on the floor. Kill or be killed. He reached around and grabbed Murphy's chin with one hand and placed his other forearm across the side of Murphy's neck. Then he made a sharp sideways pull. This time he heard the sounds of real vertebrae breaking apart. Not a simulation, no trick, no piece of wood in a pocket. Murphy's head turned toward Jim, his eyes opened wide, and he silently mouthed his last words, "Shit. It worked."

Jim paused to catch his breath. He looked at what he'd done. This was real. He'd killed a man. He set out to do it, and he did it. Never mind that Murphy was a piece of shit, that he'd tried to kill Mac, maybe succeeded, and that he was trying to kill Jim; he was, up until seconds ago, a living, breathing person. No more. He would never think another thought, have a desire, know pleasure or remorse. It was over for him, for now and for eternity, and Jim was the reason.

He snapped out of it and went into action, rushing to the chair. Mac was still breathing, his eyes open. He looked at Jim and tried to speak but couldn't. Jim picked him up, carried him to the door, kicked it open, and carried him out to his car. He put Mac in the back seat, covered him with his jacket, got in, and sped out.

As he drove, he talked to Mac. "Hang in there, Mac, it won't be long. Stay with us." There weren't many traffic lights on his route, but he ran the few that were red. Twenty minutes later, he skidded onto the emergency ramp at the hospital, squealed to a stop, and killed the engine. He ran out of the car and into the ER's entranceway.

"I have a shooting victim in my car! Shot in the chest!"

Two orderlies grabbed a gurney and ran out to the car. They wheeled Mac into the lobby, past Jim and through a large pair of double doors. The receptionist called him to her desk.

"Who are you, sir?"

"Bill Dawson."

"Can I see some ID?"

Jim took the counterfeit license from his wallet and showed it to her.

"How did he get shot?" the receptionist asked.

"I think it was an accident. I didn't see it happen."

A nurse came out from the doors where they had taken Mac. She said to Jim, "Can you come over here so we can talk?"

"Is Mac dead?"

"No, he's critical but stable. Come on over here."

Jim followed her to a sofa in the waiting room.

"May I please see that driver's license?"

Jim handed it to her.

She examined the license and asked, "Who are you?"

"Bill Dawson."

"No, who are you really?"

"Ma'am?"

The nurse held up the driver's license and smiled. "This is Snuffy's work. I'd know it anywhere."

"Who are you?"

"Barb. Snuffy's my husband."

Jim sat back and looked at her. "Yes," he said. "I think we almost met once. You drove Mac home."

"More than once. Who are you?"

"Jim."

"Thought so. The kid. What happened?"

"Somebody shot Mac. I got to him before he bled out and brought him here. How is he?"

"Hanging in there. He's tough. But if I were you, I'd get out of here. We have to report gunshot wounds to the police."

"Okay. Call me if anything changes."

"I will. When you can, come to our place so we can talk about this. Same building as Mac. Number three."

Jim left the hospital and drove to the workshop. He sat at the bench and looked at Murphy's body. He'd have to move fast. Rigor would start soon, and the body would be hard to manage.

He went outside and took the wheelbarrow from against the wall. He brought it in and hoisted the body into it.

An iron bar and a shovel were in a corner where Jerry kept garden tools, and Jim took them behind the workshop and poked around until the bar hit the septic tank with a clunk. He shoveled the sod off the tank and used the bar as a lever to remove the lid.

He returned to the workshop and picked up Murphy's jacket. Murphy's car keys and an envelope filled with cash were in the pockets. He locked the envelope and Murphy's gun in his storage cabinet.

He wheeled Murphy toward the door and outside, took the rig around back, grappled Murphy off the wheelbarrow, and lowered the body into the septic tank, feet first. Murphy sank into the shallow sludge and to the bottom. His lifeless face was the last part of him visible as it poked up out of the sewage.

Doesn't he look like himself?

He drove to the hardware store and bought several bags of quicklime. He returned to the grave site, poured the quicklime into the tank, and replaced the lid. Then he drove Murphy's old Chrysler into the driveway and parked it out of sight of the road. He'd ditch it when there was more time.

Exhausted, he drove to his apartment and went straight to bed.

Chapter 41

At noon on Sunday, Jim headed north to Snuffy and Barb's place. He looked forward to meeting Snuffy. He arrived shortly after twelve-thirty, and knocked at apartment three. Barb opened the door and invited him in. Snuffy sat in a wheelchair in the living room eating lunch from a tray and watching television.

"Hello, Jim. We finally meet."

The apartment was small with shabby furniture and a lot of clutter. Various types of tools, machines, and electronic equipment were strewn on the dinette and coffee tables, Snuffy's makeshift workshop, no doubt. A television set in the corner had the news on.

"How's Mac?" Jim asked Barb.

"He'll make it. But they don't know whether he'll walk again."

"Lot of that going around," Snuffy said.

"What's happening on the news?" Jim asked.

"Somebody shot Oswald," Snuffy said.

"What? Just now?"

"A little while ago. In the police station. I'm telling you. The shit's about to hit the fan. Who shot Mac?"

"Murphy."

Snuffy just looked at Jim. He had a cold look in his eyes. "Where's Murphy now?"

"Dead."

"Did Mac do it?"

"No."

Snuffy nodded. "Why'd he shoot Mac?"

"Our client owes us. Mac leaned on him, so he called Murphy."

"Who's the client?"

"Sam Montague. You know him?"

"Yes," said Snuffy. "A mealy-mouthed toad. Mac liked him, but I never did. A real politician at the Company. Shake your hand then stab you in the back. Does he know about Murphy?"

"No," Jim said. "He thinks Murphy got the job done."

"Perfect. Mac can call him. Monty will shit." Snuffy laughed.

"From the hospital?" Barb said.

"Why not? You'll need the master scrambler, Jim. It's in Mac's place. We have keys."

Jim went upstairs. Mac's apartment had the same layout as Snuffy's but more of a mess. Books and papers everywhere, file cabinets with drawers half open, dishes in the sink, ashtrays piled high, and several loaded pistols scattered around the room. The master scrambler was on Mac's desk. Jim disconnected it and was about to leave when something caught his eye. A sealed envelope was sticking up in a letter holder and was stamped "DECEASED" in large red letters.

The envelope was addressed to someone named Valerie Sands.

He took the envelope from the holder and held it for a moment. Then he put it in his pocket and took it and the scrambler downstairs.

The TV was still on. A doctor at the hospital in Dallas pronounced Oswald dead. The police had a nightclub owner in custody. The nightclub was the Carousel in Dallas.

"This Ruby guy one of ours?" Snuffy asked.

"No. I don't know where he came from. But I was in that nightclub."

"How about Oswald? He with us?"

"Don't know him either."

"Christ, Jim, how'd you get all that help from people you don't even know?"

* * *

Jim turned on his television early on Monday. His telephone rang several times throughout the morning, but he ignored it. There was no one he wanted to talk to. After the second time, he called Snuffy.

"You folks trying to call me?"

"No. Barb's at work, and I'm watching the news."

"Okay. I'll check in every now and then. I'm not answering the phone."

"Get some rest, Jim. You've had a busy week."

After the phone rang a couple more times, Jim disconnected it.

Coverage of the funeral followed Kennedy's casket on a horse-drawn caisson from the Capitol rotunda to St. Matthew's Cathedral and after the service to Arlington National Cemetery. A processional that included Mrs. Kennedy, family members, and heads of state and royalty from everywhere walked behind the caisson. An estimated one million people lined the streets along the course of the processional.

Jim was struck by the level of emotion the president's death had evoked. TV cameras panned the spectators, many of whom were crying openly. The sight of a grieving widow walking bravely behind her husband's casket brought home the personal significance of this event.

Jim pondered his own participation in the assassination conspiracy, and he wondered how, seeing this outpouring of grief, he would feel now if he had pulled the trigger as he had planned.

If he had shot the buck—

But the analogy stops there. A buck has no wife and children to grieve him, no adoring public to mourn his senseless loss. The death of a buck provides bounty for the hunter's table. All this loss provided was money in a Swiss bank account for Jim, wealth and success for a few mobsters, politicos, and corporate moguls, and uncertainty and apprehension for a world left shocked and paralyzed with grief.

Nothing in his experience could match it. He vaguely remembered FDR's passing, but he had no memory of the aftermath. There had been no television coverage in 1945 to impress upon the mind of a four-year-old boy the significance of the death of a president.

But the image that moved Jim more than any other was of the little boy known and loved by the public as John-John, who on his third birth-day bravely faced his father's casket and saluted. With no father of his own to remember, Jim didn't think such an emotionally-charged event could penetrate the reclusive and protective wall he had built so many years ago. But it did.

If Jim was to ever question the value of his presence on this earth, now was the time. As he reflected on the course of his life leading to November 22, 1963, he knew that, given the chance, he would have pulled that trigger.

And, as he viewed the immediate effects and considered the long-term consequences of the act, he knew doing it would have been wrong.

Chapter 42

Mac was resting with his eyes half closed when he felt a presence in the room. He was barely awake when he knew someone was there, and he didn't come fully out of it until the visitor leaned over and kissed him on his forehead. He opened his eyes.

"Millie," he said. "What brings you out?"

"Snuffy called. Said Murphy did this. And that your protégé took care of him. Why was Murphy on you?"

"That was his Chrysler the night you called. He had a contract on me. Monty owes us money and doesn't want to pay."

"Montague? You doing business with that asshole?"

"Big payday. Or so he promised. He reneged and sent Murphy."

"Bastard. You want him taken? He might come after you again. I wouldn't like that." She reached over and touched his arm.

"I'd rather wait until I collect. After that I don't give a shit what happens to him."

"Tell you what, Mac. I'll give him a call. He might listen to me."

"Wait a day or two," Mac said. "We're going to scare shit out of him. He thinks I'm dead."

She laughed, gave him another kiss, and said goodbye just as Barb came in with a medicine tray. They nodded hellos to each other, and Millie left.

Jim packed the master scrambler in his knapsack and headed out, picking up his mail from his letterbox. Among the few items was a letter from

Sarah. He wondered how she had found his address. A new identity change was looking more and more likely. He tore it open and read it on the way to his car:

> *Jim, I've been trying to reach you. You aren't answering your phone. Please call me ASAP. It's about the project and some work for you.*

He folded the letter, tossed it in his car, and headed up the highway toward the hospital.

About a half hour later, he walked into Mac's room.

"How's the old man doing?" he asked Barb.

"Hell of a recovery," she said. "He's a tough old bird. But cantankerous. The old fart complains about everything."

"Can he get out of bed?"

"With a wheelchair and somebody to push him around."

Mac's half-eaten lunch was in front of him. He just glared at the tray, but his face lit up when he saw Jim.

"Hey, kid. Welcome to the chamber of horrors. Want some hospital food? It cures what ails you. By killing you."

Barb mumbled something as she took the tray away.

"Barb," Jim said, "can we take Mac somewhere private where there's a telephone?"

"The head nurse's office. I already asked if we could use it."

They helped Mac into a wheelchair and wheeled him down the hallway to the office. He made wheelchair jokes along the way.

Once they were in the office, Barb locked the door. Jim took the scrambler out of the knapsack and connected it to the phone.

"Tell me something kid. How'd you find out it was Montague?"

"I recognized his voice from Miami in '61. I taped all our phone calls."

Mac tossed his hands up. "I might have known. So much for the Chinese wall."

Jim dialed Montague's office number, handed the receiver to Mac, and put his headphones on.

"Monty, it's Mac. We have to talk. Turn on the box."

"Mac? What the fuck? I thought—"

"You thought I was pushing up daisies. Wrong. Turn on the box. Now."

After a click, "Mac, believe me, it was only business. You scared me with all that talk about bumping me off. But Murphy said you were dead."

"Murphy was mistaken. He's off the job."

"Son of a bitch. You can't trust anyone anymore."

Jim covered his mouth to stifle a laugh.

"Okay," Mac said. "Only business. I understand that. But now we've got to talk more business. You need to make that deposit in Shadow's account. You need to do that real soon."

"Come on, Mac, Shadow's dead. That guy Ruby shot him."

"That wasn't Shadow, Sam. You need to make that payment."

"You expect me to believe that? You send a guy to shoot the president, he gets himself shot, and now you say it was somebody else? Bullshit."

Montague's words seemed assertive, but the shaking in his voice gave him away. He was scared.

"There's somebody here who wants to talk to you." Mac handed the telephone to Jim.

"Hi, Fish. Shadow here."

"What?" Montague's voice trembled. "First Mac, now you. Doesn't anybody stay dead?"

"The president stays dead," Jim said and handed the phone to Mac.

"Sam, if you don't pay up, two things are going to happen. First, you won't be around much longer. Second, the world will know about your conspiracy. Your company goes down the tubes, your friends are investigated, and your widow and kids go on welfare. Shadow taped all your conversations. Do you think the Warren Commission might want to hear the tapes?"

"Jesus Christ! No! You got me over a barrel, Mac. This is blackmail. Not to mention unethical. I have to get the money together. I'll need a week. I can't promise."

"I can," Mac said. "If you haven't paid by next Friday, stay indoors with the shades drawn. You'll have not only me on your ass, but the guy who took out the leader of the fucking free world, and Millie. She wants a piece of you too."

"Millie? Christ, Mac! What's Millie got to do with this?"

"Millie looks out for my interests. She's already pissed that you put a contract on me. She's not as forgiving as I am. So take your pick, Monty. Pay up or, well, you know."

Mac hung up. He looked exhausted just from the phone call.

"He'll pay. Barb, can you get me to bed?"

She went ahead to make sure his bed was ready. As Jim wheeled him back to his room, he asked, "Mac, how did Murphy get the drop on you that night? I didn't think anyone could sneak up on you like that."

"I knew somebody was following me, but I didn't know who. Too dark. When it turned out to be Murphy, I figured he was there to claim his finder's fee for Dallas. I dropped my guard, and boom."

"That doesn't make sense, Mac. If that's what he wanted, why wouldn't he just knock on your door?"

"Maybe he knew I had company."

Chapter 43

One afternoon in early December, Jim came in from visiting Mac. His phone was ringing. He hadn't answered it since he'd come home from Dallas, but he was sure Sarah was trying to reach him. Sooner or later he'd have to deal with her, so he answered.

"Jim. It's Sarah."

He was right. She was stalking him. "Hello, Sarah. What's up?" He tried to sound congenial, but he was sure he sounded distant.

"I tried to come see you a couple of times but didn't catch you in. Did you get my letter?"

"Yes. How'd you know where I live?"

"Friends in high places. You forgot to leave your number with me."

"Slipped my mind, I guess."

"I forgive you," Sarah said. "But guess what? We won the contract."

"I'm not surprised," Jim said. "It was a good proposal."

"My guy at Navy said our competitor underbid us, but our technical proposal was far and away the better one."

"That's great." He considered the irony. He'd given the client the numbers he needed, and then he'd helped the target write a winning proposal. He wondered whether conflicts of interests entered into the espionage business.

"We can use you on the project," Sarah said.

"I'm not available, Sarah. I told you about the other assignment. It's been extended. Maybe in a few months."

"Well then," she said, "would you like to get together again off the clock?"

"Maybe later. I've got a lot going now. I'll call you." He said good-bye and hung up. He hoped she'd get off his ass, but he doubted it.

Sarah knew a brush-off when she heard one, and she wasn't used to it and didn't like it. She was frustrated. It had been more than two weeks since George had reported Jim's car was not at Dulles, and now that she had finally reached him, he didn't want to see her. This was going to take harsher measures. She called Rod Bales.

"Rod, you have friends in the FBI, right?"

"What do you need, honey?"

"This wouldn't be for me. But I have information they might want. It has to do with the Kennedy assassination."

"Really? What've you got?"

She had his attention. "Remember the young fellow that seemed to be working with a fake identity?" she said. "Jim Dodson?"

"Yes."

"He's gone from the project now, but on the Sunday before Kennedy was killed, I saw him board a plane going to Florida."

"And?"

"He returned the the day after the assassination."

"How do you know that?"

Sarah didn't want to tell him she had sent George to watch Jim's car. "I just know," she said.

"But what difference does that make? Kennedy was killed in Texas."

"Kennedy went to Florida the day after Jim did."

"Interesting. But Sarah, they got the shooter. The case ought to be closed."

"I know, Rod, but folks are saying there might have been more than one assassin. I just think it's curious that a man with a questionable background follows the president around and comes home right after he's assassinated."

"That's suspicious, all right. I'll pass it on. They might want to talk to your young friend."

Sarah hung up the phone and sat back. If she couldn't get him on her terms, at least he'd have to deal with the FBI. She wasn't sure how screwing up his life that way would make him want her again, but she didn't know what else to do.

The next morning Jim pulled into the lot at Gloria's diner. As he usually did on the rare mornings when he ate there, he scanned the parking lot looking for Brad Lester's car. This time he spotted Dottie's car instead. He started to drive away, but decided against it. If she'd tracked him this far, next she'd find where he lived, then who knows what else? Sarah had used her Navy contacts to find him, and Dottie had the resources of CIA to fall back on. He'd have to face her if only to find out what she and others might know about him. Not to mention he really wanted to see her.

He braced himself for the confrontation. He'd almost rather have to deal with Lester again than face a pissed-off Dottie. She sat at a table next to the far wall, drinking coffee and looking at him. She wasn't smiling.

Jim's heart did a somersault. He walked to the table, made a stern face, and said, "First things first. My name is Jim. Forget you ever knew me by any other name. If you call me anything else, I'm out of here, and you never see me again. Agreed?"

"Agreed, uh, Jim. Can't I just call you honey, like I used to?"

"No. Now what brings you here?" Jim spoke as if he was angry when all the time he was more than glad just to be sitting next to her.

"There's rumors all over the Agency. You were seen here."

Apparently Lester hadn't heeded Jim's warning.

"Didn't you get my letter. Don't you understand the meaning of deep cover?"

"If you want to be in deep cover, Jim, you shouldn't eat breakfast where Agency people go. Brad Lester spotted you and told me. Apparently you come in here a lot. That's something else you shouldn't do. I don't know much about covert ops, but I know that much."

Jim sat back. Dottie sure could go straight to the point. He had to agree with her.

Dottie said, "I've been here every morning waiting for you."

"Why, Dottie? You could be putting me at risk."

"They said you were dead, Harold." She started to cry.

"It's Jim. I know they said that. That was someone else. So stop crying."

She didn't stop crying but said between sobs, "I saw him at the morgue. I knew it wasn't you. Then I got your letter."

"Bad timing on my part. I didn't know about the dead guy when I sent it."

"They said he had your fingerprints. How'd that happen? Is the Agency in on this?"

"Don't ask. You already know more than you should."

"Are you working with your friend Mac?"

Jim looked around the room. "Jesus, Dottie! Don't say stuff like that."

Dottie took a tissue from her purse and blew her nose. "I'm sorry, honey. But I have to know what's next, what to do. Is there any reason I should wait for you? Do you have another girlfriend?"

"No, of course not." He looked at her face. More tears. He looked down at the bend of her knees, her ankles, her small hands, and he remembered how much he liked just looking at her. Everything about her was perfect. His gaze scanned the rest of her. Everything was as he remembered. Except for the tears and the red nose. Old feelings rushed in and hit him hard. He took out a handkerchief and wiped the tears from her cheek. He touched her hair.

He knew better, but he said, "When do you have to be at work?"

"I took the week off. I've been looking for you, coming here in the morning, driving around town, looking for your car, going in the stores, everywhere."

This would be a mistake. "You want to come home with me for a while?"

"Yes."

"Then you can go back to work. Maybe we can get together from time to time. So I won't have to see you cry again."

"You won't have to see it if I'm not allowed to see you."

"But I'll remember it."

"And you won't see it if I am allowed to see you too. Either way you don't have to see me cry." She smiled. Her eyes were still red and her cheeks wet. He wiped them some more.

Jim stood. "Let's get out of here."

"Don't you want breakfast first?"

"No. I'll eat a banana or something."

"Do you have one for me? I didn't have breakfast, either."

He took her by the hand. She got up from her chair, and they stood looking at each other. She smiled that pretty smile that always got to him and said, "I'm so glad you're not circumcised."

"What?"

"It's how I knew you weren't dead. The dead man was circumcised. It was one of the happiest moments of my life."

He laughed.

"What's funny?" she asked.

"How many women can say the happiest moment in their life was when they looked at a dead guy's dick?"

They both laughed. This was how it used to be. This was right. He stopped at the counter and paid for her coffee. Then they left together.

They lay close together afterward for a long time. Then Dottie said, "Okay. Now listen. If this is going to work out, you'll have to meet my folks. You've only been putting it off for five years."

He smiled. "You won't tell them I'm the same guy that's been avoiding them all these years, would you?"

"No. That was Harold, the rat. Daddy would never have let him in the house after the way he dumped me. Then, when you, I mean he, supposedly got killed, Daddy seemed relieved, as dreadful as that sounds. So, what do you think?"

"We'll see, Dottie. Let's take it one step at a time." Pressure. First Sarah and now Dottie. How does a guy get any work done? He wondered how Mac had made it all these years without being tied down. He'd ask him some day.

Mac lay in bed watching television when two men in plain clothes came in.

"Hi, Andy," Mac said. "How's tricks?"

"Mac," the big fellow said. "This is a surprise. Meet my partner, Special Agent Lincoln."

"Good morning, sir," Lincoln said. "You two know each other?"

"Yes," Andy Franks said. "We go way back. Special Agent Lincoln, since I know the witness, you handle the interview."

"Right," Lincoln said. "Sir, we have questions about why you're here. Some kind of accident?"

"That's what they tell me. But I don't remember anything after Friday night. I stayed up watching TV. All that shit about Kennedy. The next thing I know, I'm in here with a hole in my middle." He shifted in his bed. "Turn that thing off so we can talk, and help me crank this bed up." Mac pointed to the side of the bed, and Lincoln cranked it.

"The fellow who brought you in said it was an accident," Lincoln said. "We'd like to talk to him. Do you know where he is now?"

"No. I don't even know who he is."

"His name is William Dawson. Do you know him?"

Mac recognized one of the aliases he'd given Jim. "No."

"He showed admissions a Virginia driver's license, but we can't match the name to anyone who fits his description. Do you have any idea why someone would shoot you?"

"Didn't you say it was an accident?" He pulled at his pillow to give himself a better headrest.

"Have you had trouble with anyone?"

"No." Mac could lie with the best of them.

"Owe anyone a lot of money, or anyone owe you some?"

Only about a million bucks.

"No."

"An angry husband or boyfriend after you?"

"I wish. I could use a little excitement."

Franks smiled. Lincoln continued his questions. "Sir, do you know where you got shot?"

"Right here in the chest."

"No, sir. I mean, in what geographic location.

"Not a clue."

"And the bullet is still in you."

"Right up against the old backbone. They'll cut it out when I'm up to it. Might not walk again."

"We're sorry to hear that. We'll need that bullet when they get it out."

"It ain't going anywhere. Look guys, I'm getting tired. You're welcome to come another time."

"That won't be necessary. We'll write this up as an accident with an unknown shooter. Let us know if you hear from the guy who brought you in. We still want to question him."

Franks said, "Amos, I'll meet you outside at the car. I want to get caught up. Won't take long."

Lincoln left, and Franks sat on the edge of the bed. "So, Mac, what's this shit all about?"

"Beats me, Andy. Why is the FBI interested in small-time shooting accidents?"

"Warren Commission. We're looking into anything that happened in the time frame around Dallas. You were shot the day after Kennedy. Just routine. When I saw you, I thought maybe we were onto something. I didn't let on to Lincoln because I wanted to see what you had to say. So, who really shot you?"

"I don't know, Andy. Maybe an old enemy settling a score. Are you going to tell your partner who I am?"

"No. I don't see any connection. I won't find one, will I?"

"No. I retired. So, how've you been? Still chasing cheerleaders?"

After Franks left, Mac pulled himself out of the bed and into his wheelchair, wheeled himself out to the lobby, and called Jim.

"Hey, kid, the FBI was here."

"Really? How'd it go."

"Piece of cake. Why don't you drop by?"

About an hour later, Jim came walking into Mac's room. Mac was patting down his bed looking for bugs when Jim came in.

"I can't get out to check the rest of the room," he said.

Jim did the search. "Nothing here."

"Good, What'd you do with Murphy's piece?"

"In the river. And I notched it for you."

"Won't be the same, kid. I have my own style of notching. How about Montague? Did he pay up?"

"Paid in full. Your share is in your account."

"Man, that's great," Mac said. "Millie must have called him."

"Who is this Millie, anyway?"

"Millicent Messick, kid. Your guidance counselor."

Jim's eyes widened. "Miss Messick? What's she got to do with it?"

"I guess you didn't know. Millie was the best mechanic we had in Europe. Next to me, of course. A legend in the Company. Targets never saw her coming. Little wisp of a woman comes doddering down the street, wearing a shawl, carrying a shopping bag and a cat, next thing you know, the worms got you."

"Damn. Mousey Messick. We used to laugh at her. And she leaned on Montague?"

"She said she would. If Monty thought Millie had a contract on him, he'd shit his pants and move to Antarctica." Mac laughed. "You don't want to piss her off."

"Your retirement party. Now it makes sense. You've seen her lately?"

Mac smiled a big smile to himself. "She's called every day and visited a couple times."

"I can't get over this. How come she's a high school recruiter?"

"She wanted out of the cold and the field. It gets to you after a while. So they transferred her here. I figure if she ever gets bored with the Company, I'll hire her. Or marry her."

* * *

Jim needed to change identities again. Mac had said so, and dropping the Dodson persona might put Sarah out of his life along with whatever Navy spooks she might set on him.

He needed a new name, car, residence, everything, like before, except this time he already had an identity to assume. No stomping though graveyards, reading obituaries, and altering government files. This identity was a custom fit, wrapped up in a tidy package, and ready to be assumed.

He sat at the desk in his apartment, opened the greasy deck of playing cards, and removed Jamey's drivers license, social security card, and draft card. He put them in his wallet.

He went to the DMV and signed his car over to James Barrett and to the bank to change accounts. He moved out of his apartment and checked into a ratty little motel.

The switch to Jim Barrett had been an easy change. He knew Jamey's background inside-out, bore a close resemblance to Jamey, and, since Jamey was a nickname for James, he had the same first name.

And with no more effort than that, Jim Dodson became Jim Barrett.

Jim visited Mac to tell him and Barb about his new identity. Afterward he pulled out of the hospital parking lot, and a dark blue sedan with two men in it pulled off the curb across the street and fell in behind him. He made a couple of turns and pulled in at a gas station. The blue sedan parked across the street and waited while the attendant filled Jim's tank. He drove to his new home at the motel, and the tail stayed on him.

What's this shit? Who's following me? And why?

The sedan parked across the street from his motel. As usual, he did a quick scan of the small room looking for signs of an intruder. He couldn't just put tape on the door because the maid came in every day.

This time he found a tap on his phone. Someone had installed a small transmitter inside the phone's case. He recognized it as the kind they used at the Company. He removed the bug's battery and drained its charge with a paper clip. Then he put the dead battery in the transmitter. They wouldn't know he'd busted them, they'd just think they had a dead battery.

He went outside, across the street, and to the Chevy. It had federal government plates. The occupants looked surprised to see him approaching. He walked up and tapped on the driver's side window, and the driver rolled the window down.

Jim leaned on the window frame and said, "I'll be in the rest of the night. You guys might as well get your Christmas shopping done." He laughed, and the guy rolled the window up, started the car and sped away.

He still didn't know who they were.

Now Jim felt like he had to tell Dottie everything. If she was going to be part of his life, he had to trust her with his secrets and give her the chance to back out of their relationship if it would be too much for her. He drove to her apartment.

They sat together on the sofa. He told her about Pine Hill, Dallas, and Mac's injury. He left out his one-night-stand with Sarah, the sanction the Company had on him, and his elimination of Murphy.

She sat quietly through the whole story. Then she said, "Honey, were you really going to shoot the president? Could you have done that?"

"I had doubts throughout the whole thing. I guess we'll never know."

He walked to the living room window and looked out across the parking lot at the office buildings on the other side of the highway. He looked at the lights and wondered who each one of them represented. He wondered how the assassination had changed them.

"One problem," he said. "To keep seeing you, I risk running into your Agency friends, ones who knew me. I don't know what to do about that."

"Can I help?"

"First, convince Brad Lester that I'm under deep cover, and he should stay out of it."

"You could shoot him," Dottie said with a grin.

"Don't joke about that. I might have to do it. Anyway, your employment is a complication. Someday I'd like us to get married if you're willing, but we can't as long as you work for the Company. They check up on spouses pretty close. I don't need that just now."

"Well, that's the closest thing to a marriage proposal I ever got. I guess it will have to do."

Chapter 44

On Christmas Eve Jim drove south heading home from a visit to Mac. A state police cruiser fell in behind him two cars back. It stayed on his tail for a while. Whenever he turned, it turned.

He went through a light just before it changed to red. The cruiser had to stop behind the cars that separated them. He threw the Ford into second gear and floored it. The engine roared, and the car leapt forward and sped down the highway. The cruiser's flashing red lights came on, but before it could pass the cars, Jim had gone over a hill and around a curve out of sight of the cops. He turned into a small residential section and threaded his way through the streets and among the houses until he came to the main road where he pulled into a gas station and parked behind the building. The cruiser drove slowly past his position with the cops looking all around. He waited a minute until they were gone and pulled onto the road heading north.

Almost immediately another cruiser pulled out behind him and turned on its flashers. Jim pulled off onto the shoulder. Two policemen climbed out of the cruiser, walked over, and stood on either side of his car, hands resting on their pistols. Jim rolled down his window.

"Sir, may I see your driver's license and registration?"

Jim took out his wallet and handed the documents to the cop, who examined them and returned them to him.

"Mr. Barrett, step out of the car and turn around with your hands on the roof." The policeman patted him down. For once Jim was glad his piece was in the glove compartment.

"You'll have to come with us," the cop said.

Jim didn't protest. He had always liked uniformed policemen and treated them with respect. "Am I under arrest?"

"No, sir. Not yet. Our instructions are to bring you in."

"Where are you taking me?"

"The police barracks down the road. You can follow us."

Jim pulled out behind the cruiser, and the other cruiser fell in behind him. They weren't giving him room to take off again. They drove to the police station, went inside, and the cops took him to an interview room and left him.

A wooden table and three chairs sat at the center of the room. and a large two-way mirror on the far wall faced the table. He sat in one of the chairs.

Two guys in plain clothes came in and closed the door. They were the two guys who'd been tailing him. The first man said, "I'm Special Agent Franks, FBI. This is Special Agent Lincoln."

They sat across the table. "Let's get started," Franks said. "Mr. Barrett, where were you the week of seventeen November?"

"That was over a month ago. I don't remember."

"Did you take a flight to Florida on Sunday, seventeen November?"

Sarah Weston was behind this, of that he was sure.

"Why would you think I did that?" Jim was careful not to lie to them. He was sure it was against the law to make false statements to the FBI. He would just offer vague answers or answer with questions.

"Because you were seen at the airport boarding the airplane."

"Maybe whoever thinks they saw me is mistaken."

Franks said, "Did you return to Dulles from Chicago in the early morning on Saturday, twenty-three November?"

"Does someone think they saw me then too?"

Franks leaned forward and glowered at Jim. "No, asshole, your name is on the passenger manifest, at least the name you're using now. Now answer the fucking question."

"Easy, Andy," Lincoln said. "Cool down. I'm sorry, Jim. My partner has a bit of a temper. You've probably worked with guys like that."

"I work alone," Jim said. "You ought to try it."

Franks stood, walked to the mirror, and looked in the glass with his back to them. Lincoln went on. "Here's what we've got so far. You were seen boarding a flight to Melbourne, Florida on the seventeenth. That identification is solid. The person who saw you knows you well. Except as Jim Dodson, not Jim Barrett. That flight was the day before President Kennedy went there."

Franks turned, put his hands on the table, and said, "And there's more, lots more. The day you went to Florida, someone stole a car from the airport parking lot in Melbourne. That car turned up in Tampa. Guess who was speaking in Tampa after he spoke at Cape Canaveral."

Jim just looked around.

Franks paced the room, circling the table. "It gets better. Another car was stolen from the Dallas airport the week the president was assassinated. That car was found a few days later in Killeen, Texas. An airplane was stolen in Killeen and was found in Austin." He stopped and looked directly at Jim. "I believe you have a pilot's license?"

"No license," Jim said. That was true, at least as far as Jim Barrett was concerned.

Franks turned the chair around and sat. "So far we have you in Melbourne, Tampa, Dallas, and Austin. There are flights from Austin to Chicago. We found no record of you taking one, but you came home from Chicago that night. Are we establishing a pattern here?"

Jim just looked from one to the other.

Lincoln said, "Jim, what we're here about is this." He leaned back, gazed at the ceiling, and twiddled his thumbs. "Did you have anything to do with the assassination of President Kennedy?"

"Me? Last I heard, the cops caught the guy that killed Kennedy." Jim was worried. These questions were hitting too close.

"That doesn't mean he acted alone," Lincoln said.

"Can't help you with any of that. Too bad you can't ask Oswald." Jim didn't know how far he could push these guys before it got ugly.

"Okay, next item," Franks said. "That item being, who the fuck are you? There are too many inconsistencies. We've already got you identified as Jim Dodson. But your driver's license says James Barrett. Which is it?"

"I'd go with the license, if I were you."

"Jim Barrett, who you claim to be, grew up in the same house in which Harold Sands, a former CIA operative, was shot and killed during a break-in. Coincidentally, that house is now owned by special agent Lincoln here, and he shot the burglar. And I was the investigating agent for that shooting."

"You got a score card?" Jim said. "I'm having trouble keeping up."

"Jim," Lincoln said, "do you know Harold Sands?"

"I heard about the shooting." Jim looked past them over their heads, thinking about his friend. "You know, they said he had a gun. He never liked guns. He was a gentle guy. You don't suppose somebody dropped it on him, do you? I mean, like, after killing him and all that to cover their ass?"

Neither man spoke. Lincoln's left eye started to twitch.

Franks said, "Enough of that. Are you aware that neighbors told the cops there used to be a kid named Harold who hung out with Jamey Barrett and that they looked like brothers?"

"That would be us."

"You know, of course, Harold Sands had a pilot's license."

"Yes, I believe he did."

"And could have stolen that airplane in Killeen."

"No. You'd already shot him. How does a dead guy steal an airplane? Besides, I never knew him to steal anything."

"We have too many coincidences here, Jim," Lincoln said. "Like the car. Harold Sands sold his car to Jim Dodson who sold it to Jim Barrett. It's the car you're driving now."

They waited for Jim to respond. He just sat and looked at them, wishing he'd listened to Mac about the car.

Franks said. "According to the records, Harold Sands was an honor student. But they let Jamey Barrett graduate just to get rid of him. Then there were arrests for drunk and disorderly and vagrancy."

"Well, some people change."

"People don't get smarter, sonny. If you're the mentally deficient James Barrett who barely made it out of high school, how come you're so fucking smart in here? How is it Jim Dodson was smart enough to write a winning proposal for a software company? Answer that."

"Maybe you should ask Jim Dodson."

"I'm asking him, asshole. But guess what. We can't find any high school records for Jim Dodson. Not in Tazewell where you said you were from, not anywhere else."

"I lived in Agent Lincoln's house before it was his. Since then, I've lived different places."

"And, what's more," Franks said, "Jim Dodson never registered for the draft."

"Want to see my draft card?"

"The newspapers where Jim Dodson was born have no record of the accident that killed his parents and no obituaries. Missing pages. Even at the Library of Congress, for chrissake. How convenient. Jim Dodson doesn't exist. Except right here in this room."

"Interestingly," Lincoln said, "We got a call from a deputy game warden in Virginia. He encountered a young man sighting in an assassin's rifle in Stafford a while back. The young man fit your description. The assassin's rifle was a 30-30 built into a briefcase. The deputy called us because he thought it might have something to do with Dallas."

"I read Kennedy was shot with a 6.5 millimeter."

"That doesn't mean there wasn't somebody else there," Franks said.

Lincoln referred to his notes. "The guy with the briefcase was named Bill Dawson, the same name of a guy who brought a gunshot victim to the hospital the day after the assassination."

"What did he say?"

"He was gone before anyone got there. We haven't found him. But we did spot you coming and going to and from that same hospital several times since then."

Franks leaned over, pushed his face inches away from Jim's and said, "Guess what? Jim Dawson is the name on a passenger manifest on eighteen November from Tampa to Dallas. The day after you flew to Melbourne.”

“There's even more,” Lincoln said. “When we looked for records of Jim Dodson in Pennsylvania, we weren't first. It seems a young man beat us to it several months back. A young man whose description matches yours.”

“You guys must have a hell of a budget for an investigation this comprehensive.”

“We're on the Warren Commission's dole, bozo,” Franks said. “So we have all the fucking budget we need. Which means we ain't going to let up on your ass anytime soon. So why don't you save us all a lot of time and tell us what you know about the mysterious Jim Dodson?”

“Sorry. I don't know any Jim Dodson.”

“You bought a fucking car from him. How can you say you don't know him?”

“Oh, was that Jim Dodson? That's been a while.”

Franks slammed his hands on the table and turned away again.

“Jim,” Lincoln said, “This is getting us nowhere. Clearly you don't intend to cooperate. Would you be willing to sit for a polygraph?”

Jim smiled to himself. “Sure. Why not? When?”

“Day after tomorrow? Nine o'clock? FBI headquarters.”

“It's a date,” Jim said.

“Okay, Jim,” Lincoln said. “We won't keep you any longer. You have a friend in the next room who wants to talk to you. Wait here.”

They left, and after less than a minute, the door opened and Bert Allison came in.

“Hello, Bert. I haven't seen you since you had me burned. Been here long?”

“Hello, uh, it's Jim now, isn't it? Let's get out of here.”

They left the police station and drove south, Jim following behind Bert's car. They stopped at a diner, went in, took a booth, and ordered lunch. Bert opened the conversation.

“Okay, Jim. So, what have you been doing?”

“Odd jobs.” Bert didn't need to know about his association with Mac.

The waiter took their lunch order. Bert waited for him to leave. "We believed you were dead," Bert said. "Mac confirmed it. Then one of our people saw you somewhere and blabbed it all over headquarters. Then the FBI called. They said they were going to pick you up and interrogate you for the Warren Commission. I asked to observe."

"Who'd they say they were interrogating?"

"All three of you. Confusing, don't you agree?" Allison laughed.

"Did you tell them I'm Harold Sands?"

"As far as we're concerned, Harold Sands is dead, and will stay that way."

"How so?"

"Because you cannot be a former Company operative, and he was. A lot of people are trying to tie the Company to the assassination. This episode, if it ever got out, would add fuel to that theory."

Jim wasn't sure where this would lead. "Why are you helping me, Bert? Why not just burn me again and throw me to the sharks?"

"I need to shield you. If all this shit got into the Warren Commission report, imagine the embarrassment for the Agency. Books will be written. Your picture and our name would be in all the newspapers. We don't need that."

The answer made sense. Jim was beginning to believe there might be something here for him. "What would you like me to do?"

"Come see me at headquarters day after tomorrow. There's something I want to discuss, but not here. Get through this polygraph test, and come over when you're done with it. Let's rehabilitate the rogue."

Lunch arrived, and while they ate, Jim picked up where they had left off. "If by 'rehabilitate' you mean what I think, there's something you should know."

"What's that?"

"I worked as Jim Dodson for a woman named Sarah Weston at Pine Hill Software. She's been stalking me, and she's the one that set the FBI on me."

"Couldn't keep it in your pants, could you?" Bert grinned.

"She had some Navy spooks check up on me, and they pretty much blew my cover."

"Okay. I'll take care of that." He scribbled notes on a notepad. "Sarah Weston. Pine Hill Software. Consider it a closed issue."

Jim spent Christmas alone. Dottie had gone to her parents and would return the next day. He watched TV, had a peanut butter and jelly sandwich for Christmas dinner, and went to bed early.

At nine a.m. on Thursday, Jim stood at the reception desk at FBI Headquarters and asked for Special Agent Lincoln. An assistant came and led him to a room where a polygraph machine was set up, ready for the test. The examiner sat next to the machine.

Jim's main concern with Polly was the control test. He wanted the machine to correctly indicate whether he was lying or telling the truth during the control test.

He sat in the hot seat, and the examiner wired him up and asked the control questions.

When the examiner asked a control question and Jim intended to lie, he increased his rate of breathing, tightened his leg muscles and his diaphragm and thought about things that would ramp up his heart rate. Thinking about Sarah Weston under the covers worked. Other times he thought about Murphy, the Sandman Snap, and what was now being called the "grassy knoll."

Then they proceeded with the real test. Jim relaxed and answered all the examiner's questions, some truthfully, others not.

Two hours later, when the test was over, the examiner took a minute to summarize the results on a form. He tore off the graph paper, folded it, and put it, the results, and a list of the questions into a file folder. Then he led Jim to Special Agent Lincoln's office and gave the file to Lincoln. Jim sat and waited to be told his fate. Lincoln took several minutes to read the file. Then he began. "I don't expect you to comment on anything I'm about to say, Jim, but here it is anyway. We are one hundred percent certain you were involved in what happened in Dallas."

This news didn't surprise Jim, but he wished it had been different.

Lincoln continued. "We don't know the extent of your involvement, but we know you were there. However, it's all circumstantial. We've taken a lot less than this to a grand jury."

"How'd I do on the test?"

"You passed it, but I'm not sure how. Right now, only one thing is keeping you out of a holding cell."

"What's that?"

"The powers that be want this assassination put to bed. Oswald all alone. No conspiracies. Just a nut-case loser with a mail order rifle who got off a couple of lucky shots. I don't believe it and neither do my colleagues, and I doubt the country will, either. So, Mr. Sands, Dodson, Barrett, or whatever your name is, was, or will be, that and that alone is what's letting you walk out of here today."

Jim was relieved.

"But know this," Lincoln said. "You're on our radar. Anything happens, and we'll be looking at you. Closely. One of the proverbial 'usual suspects.' So my advice to you, Jim, is to get yourself another line of work, and stay away from the people and places where the bad shit happens."

"Duly noted," Jim said.

"And another thing. Don't get it into your head that you'll write a book and become rich and famous. Such a book, along with the circumstantial evidence we have in your file, would be enough to put you away for a long, long time."

With Amos Lincoln's parting words echoing in his mind, Jim drove away from Washington, D.C. across the 14th Street Bridge and up the GW Parkway heading for Langley. He hadn't been at CIA Headquarters for over a year, but not much had changed. He called Bert's office for someone to escort him. They sent Dottie.

"Are you working for Bert, now?"

"That's classified," she said with that giggle. "You don't have a need to know."

They went to Bert's office where Dottie dropped him off and returned to her own office.

"Moving up in the world?" Jim asked, looking around the nice office.

"Division chief now," Bert said. "How'd the test go?"

"Passed it."

"I'll get straight to the point, Jim. I want you to come to work for me."

Jim was surprised at the offer. "In the Company? As a field agent?"

"For the Company. As a consultant. We can't bring you in through normal employee channels. I don't think Jamey Barrett could get a security clearance."

"You can always give me a lie detector test."

"Very funny. Jim, we don't care if you were in Dealey Plaza, on the freeway overpass, or on the roof of the schoolbook depository. We don't even care if you were driving the goddamn limo. We do know if you were involved somehow, you weren't doing it for us, and that's all that matters. We don't give a big rat's ass about who wanted Kennedy hit or who did it. That's for the Secret Service and FBI and Warren Commission to sort out. It's not our problem. Unless one of our people was involved, which simply cannot be."

Jim didn't know whether to believe him, but it didn't matter.

"So, what do you think, Jim? Come back to work?"

"I'll consider it."

Bert got up and closed the door. "I have a few things that might interest you. We're going to beef up our adviser program in Vietnam. You can take whatever assignments you want. When you're not in the field, you can work here in the computer lab doing research."

"I can do that without a clearance?"

"It can be arranged."

That surprised Jim. Bert definitely had clout. "Okay, I'm not Harold Sands anymore, but what about the guy who spotted me on the outside?"

"After you rousted him, he went to management and said you'd gone rogue. They put a sanction on you. The first mechanic they gave the sanction to was found dead in a parking lot, and nobody wanted the sanction after that. They all know Mac is your rabbi, and Christ, Jim, who wants to go up against Mac?"

Jim smiled at that.

"When I learned about the sanction, I had it lifted. But if I'd thought you were involved in a rogue assassination, I'd have let the sanction stand and called in somebody like Murphy."

"Thanks for the reprieve, Bert. What about Lester?"

"He's history. He broke a prime rule when he blew your cover. And by the way, you won't be troubled again by your lady stalker. Admiral Taylor is taking care of it."

"Wow! I'm impressed."

"Think about my offer and give me a call. It's time for you to come in from the cold."

Sarah Weston concentrated on a set of manpower estimates for the next project. She found that when she focused on work, she thought less and less about Jim. Except when she didn't. The telephone brought her out of her reverie.

"Sarah, it's Rod."

"Hi, Rod, what's up?"

"A bit of a situation here, doll."

Whenever there was a "bit of a situation," it wasn't good news. "What?" she asked.

"Word came down from Taylor about your friend Jim Dodson."

Sarah was taken aback. Rear Admiral Rufus Taylor was the Director of Naval Intelligence. She couldn't guess what the connection was.

"About Jim?"

"McCone called Rufus and asked a favor. Whoever in Naval Intelligence is tracking one Jim Dodson is to cease and desist. That means me."

John McCone was Director of Central Intelligence. This was getting serious.

Rod continued. "The DCI also requested we ensure that a lady named Sarah Weston, whoever she is, quits stalking said Jim Dodson."

She reacted to that. "Stalking? What's that supposed to mean?"

"I don't know, sugar. I don't know about your relationship with the elusive Mr. Dodson, but whatever it is or was, it has to stop."

That set her off. "You don't say. Well, if there is any such relationship, and I'm not saying there is, what goddamn business is that of the brass?"

"Hey, don't shoot the messenger. I'm just passing on an unofficial, unwritten directive. Up to you. But if it isn't complied with, Pine Hill Software's future in Naval Intelligence is in the dumpster. No big follow-on project, and the NAVAMS project will be canceled without notice. Do whatever is best for you, but understand there can be consequences."

She regained her composure. "Okay. I understand. Who do you suppose Jim really is?"

"I don't know. But he has a long reach. When the directors start talking to one another, something big is behind it."

"Consider your directive complied with." She meant it, but she wasn't happy about it.

"I was hoping you'd see it that way. And you aren't to discuss this with anyone. Now, when will I see you again?"

She paused a moment. Rod was a good-looking guy, married, and safe. He had made his interest in Sarah known ever since they met at a high school soccer game.

"I don't know, Rod. Soccer season isn't until the spring."

"I was thinking something less with the kids and just you and me."

This could work out. He could do great things for her company if she did great things for him.

Why the hell not?

"Sounds interesting Rod. Would you like to meet me for a drink later tonight? We can discuss the new project without all these interruptions."

"That would be nice. Do you have a spot in mind?"

"How about Cholly's? Say about seven-thirty?"

"I'll see you there."

She hung up the phone and leaned back.

The hell with Jim Dodson. It's his loss.

* * *

Dottie escorted Jim to the lobby. He'd enjoyed their lunch together in the Agency cafeteria. It had brought back pleasant memories. They walked out across the CIA logo on the shiny tile floor past the security guard and out the main entrance. The winter air was cold, and they pulled their overcoats around them.

As they walked, he said, "Bert offered me a job. I'd be working here. And taking field assignments."

"Dangerous?"

"No. Intelligence analysis. Computer programming. That kind of stuff." He didn't think she was fooled by his evasive answer.

"Will you be an employee?"

"No. A consultant. Off the books."

"Oh." She looked away from him, clearly disappointed. He understood what she must be thinking. If he was an employee, nothing would prevent them from getting married.

They sat on a bench next to a sidewalk. Jim said, "I want you to read something and tell me whether I should know what it says."

He gave her the Valerie Sands envelope. She opened it and unfolded and read the letter. Tears came to her eyes as she read. Jim looked out across the parking lot and pretended not to notice.

When she finished reading, she said, "You need to know what this says. Are you sure you don't want to read it?"

"Just tell me."

"Valerie Sands was your mother."

"I guessed as much. What else does it say?"

"Here," she said "You read it," She gave him the letter, and he read:

June, 1961

Dear Valerie,

I guess you thought you'd never hear from me again. Earlier this year, I met a young man named Harold Sands. One look at his face and his last name, and I knew he had to be yours. I called in some favors and traced his background, and it led to you.

Harold turned into a fine young man. He has your looks and Len's brains. He does not know I knew his father.

Mac's name was scrawled at the bottom with a phone number. Jim looked at Dottie, took a deep breath, and stared out across the parking lot. After a moment, he put his face in his hands and rocked back and forth. Dottie pulled him to her and held him close for a while.

When she released him, he sat up, handed her the letter, and said, "All my life I never cared who my parents were. They didn't want me, so I didn't want to know who they were, where they were. And now that I know just this small fragment about my mother, I want to know more. And about him too. How else can I know who I am?"

A half hour later, Jim parked in front of the hospital, went in and down the corridor to Mac's room where Mac was sitting up in bed reading a magazine. The television was on, the volume turned low.

"Hi, kid. You know what? Can't smoke in here. I'd kill for a Camel. What's up?"

"Can I turn this off?"

Mac nodded, and Jim turned off the set. He sat in a chair across from the bed. Mac put his magazine on his lap and waited.

"Bert Allison offered me a job as a consultant," Jim said.

"No shit. Are you going to take it?"

"I think so. I had to make sure Dottie was okay with it." Jim had stopped caring whether Mac approved of him making decisions based on what his girlfriend wanted.

"Take it. You won't regret it. Allison's division comes up with interesting duty. Just don't step on any landmines. How'd you reconnect with him?"

"The FBI. They grabbed me to ask about Dallas. That boss lady from where I was a mole set them on me."

"See, kid? I told you to be a bum fuck."

Jim smiled, remembering Mac's advice. "Live and learn. One of the FBI guys named Lincoln is the guy who shot Jamey. Not a bad guy after I got past that. The other one is a real prick named Franks. They said they talked to you about getting shot."

"Andy Franks." Mac shifted in his bed. "I told you about him. The guy that likes cheerleaders."

They both laughed. Jim said, "What's Snuffy going to do with you laid up?"

"Well, kid, we got all this money now. I plan to get a bigger place and move Snuffy and Barb and Danny in with me. I'll need a full-time nurse, and she's the ticket. Snuffy and I can retire, smoke cigars, drink beer, and have wheelchair races."

Jim pulled his chair closer to the bed. He couldn't put it off it any longer. "Mac, tell me about Valerie Sands."

Mac paused for a moment and looked first at Jim, then at the ceiling. "Jesus H. Christ, kid. How'd you find out about her?"

"I found the letter you wrote to her."

"You know, kid, reading other people's mail is a federal offense. I could have you sent up for a long time. Who else read it?"

"Dottie."

"Fine bunch of spies we are. Can't keep a little secret like that."

"Seriously, Mac, I want to know,"

Mac put his hands up, palms out as if to surrender. He raised one eyebrow and pulled his mouth to the left into a mock half grin. His magazine slid off his lap and fluttered to the floor.

"Well, I guess the letter tells it all. Valerie Sands was your mother. I shipped out in '39, which is the last time I saw her. I guess you were in the chute by then, but she didn't tell anybody. When I read your file, I made the connection, last name, age, your picture. Then when I met you, I knew who you were right off. Kid, you're the living image of your mother. A fine-looking tomato, I might add, but don't let it go to your head. I pulled a few strings and got your files to find her. I wrote her and it came back marked 'deceased,' and that's all there is to that."

"Why didn't you ever tell me, Mac?"

"She was dead. What would be the point?"

"No, I mean that you knew my father."

Mac seemed reluctant to discuss it. Then he said, "We worked together. It would have led to a lot of questions, kid. Like now."

"Is that why you became my handler after the Farm?"

"It's in your genes, kid. The acorn doesn't fall far from the tree. Remember I told you about another guy who was really good at this shit but was dead?"

"Yes."

"That was your old man."

Jim was moved by this news. He felt a connection with the father he'd never known. The tears came just as they had when he and Dottie read the letter. He forced them back.

"What happened between him and my mother?"

"She divorced him when he didn't come back. I don't think he ever knew about you."

"Where did he die?"

"Germany in '52. On your birthday, if you can figure that. Caught a bullet during an op in Frankfurt."

"How do you know it was my birthday?" Jim remembered his twelfth birthday, the day they sent him from an orphanage to a reform school.

"I remembered it was Friday the thirteenth. Then when I read your file, I noticed the coincidence."

"Does anyone else know about him?"

"Allison was our handler. But I don't think I ever mentioned it. And it's a common last name, and he ain't bright enough to make the connection. I don't think he knew your mother, either. But Snuffy knows. He was with us when your old man bought it."

Jim moved closer. "You were there when my father was killed?"

"Me and Snuffy."

"Was Allison there?"

Mac laughed. "You kidding? He was probably home in bed drinking hot chocolate. Management. Paper pusher. Didn't do the field. He never saw the noisy end of a piece in his life. If he'd have been there he'd have been hiding under a honey wagon shitting his knickers."

Jim continued to dig. "Did Snuffy know my mother?"

"Yes. Barb and Valerie were close."

"What about the guy who killed my father? What happened to him?"

"I'll put it this way, kid. The guy who did it came to regret it."

Jim could imagine the kind of payback Mac would have delivered.

"Can Snuffy add anything?" Jim asked.

"I doubt it. We don't talk about our departed colleagues. Matter of policy. And bad luck."

"What was my father like?"

"Smart. Always with the jokes. He liked the ladies too, and they liked him. Quick with his hands and good with firearms. He spoke about a dozen languages too."

"What was his name?"

Mac paused a while. He looked into Jim's eyes. Then he said, "I guess I can tell you. Leonard Sands. One of the best. The books were closed on him because of the deep-cover nature of the op. He was in the cold. And that's all I can say."

As Jim stood to leave, Mac turned and fluffed up his pillow. Then he said, "I dropped my magazine. Would you get it for me? And turn the TV on. You wouldn't happen to have a cigar on you, would you?"

Epilogue

In the months and years following the assassination of President Kennedy, an international mystery unfolded with factions divided over what took place on November 22, 1963, in Dealey Plaza, Dallas, Texas.

The Warren Commission released its report ten months afterward, concluding that a lone assassin, Lee Harvey Oswald, fired three shots from a sixth-story window in the Texas School Book Depository, fatally wounding the president.

Conspiracy theories emerged following publication of the report. Books and television documentaries examined the evidence in careful detail. They addressed Oswald's associations prior to the assassination, described perceived inconsistencies and contradictions in the official time line between the shooting and Oswald's capture, and speculated on the role of Jack Ruby, who, the conspiracy theorists believed, had been dispatched by other conspirators to silence Oswald.

Most citizens believed there was a conspiracy, but they never agreed on which of the suspected groups of conspirators was responsible. The only consensus was that Oswald did not act alone. Otherwise, there would have been no conspiracies about which to theorize.

Jim followed the Kennedy assassination reports, documentaries, and conspiracy theories over the years. He read all the books, studied the testimonies of witnesses to the assassination and its aftermath, and inspected snapshots and film clips. While everyone else looked to the picket fence, the overpass, the grassy knoll, the School Book Depository, he concentrated on the concrete wall that reached from the pergola toward Houston Street. In all the photos, Jim found no indication anyone was behind the wall. And nowhere in his memory did anything conclusively indicate that other assassins were in Dealey Plaza that day. He never ruled it out, however, and wondered about the two men behind the picket fence. But nowhere in the photographic evidence was there anything showing someone with a rifle.

Not even a shadow.

About the Author

Al Stevens is a retired author of computer books. For fifteen years he was a senior contributing editor and columnist for Dr. Dobb's Journal, a leading magazine for computer programmers. He lives with his wife Judy and a menagerie of cats on Florida's Space Coast where he writes by day and plays piano, string bass, and saxophone by night.

Also by Al Stevens

On the Street Where You Die (Stanley Bentworth #1)
A Dead Ringer (Stanley Bentworth #2)
Confessions of a Cat Burglar (free book, referenced in A Dead Ringer)
Clueless: The Pantyhose Slasher Cases (Stanley Bentworth #3)
Off the Wall Stories
Golden Eagle's Final Flight (with Ron Skipper)
Ventriloquism: Art, Craft, Profession
Politically Incorrect Scripts for Comedy Ventriloquists
Welcome to Programming
Teach Yourself C++ 7th Edition

...and many other computer programming and usage books.

http://www.alstevens.com

Amazon Author Page:
http://www.amazon.com/-/e/B001K8M1SA

www.ingramcontent.com/pod-product-compliance
Lightning Source LLC
Chambersburg PA
CBHW071127170626
46809CB00002B/524

* 9 7 8 0 9 8 8 6 6 2 3 0 8 *